SMOOTH IRISH SEDUCTION

Weldon Brothers Series: Book Two

USA Today Bestselling Author

JENNIFER SAINTS

Published by Novels Alive Publishing, LLC

Copyright Information

Copyright © 2011 by Jenni Leigh Grizzle
First published 2009 by Jenni Leigh Grizzle
All rights reserved.

ISBN: 978-0-9824863-8-2

More Titles by Jennifer St. Giles

Trevelyan Series Writing as Jennifer St. Giles
Mistress of Trevelyan

His Dark Desires

Killdaren Series Writing as Jennifer St. Giles
Midnight Secrets

Darkest Dreams

Silken Shadows

Shadowmen Series Writing as Jennifer St. Giles
Touch A Dark Wolf

Lure of the Wolf

Kiss of Darkness

Bride of the Wolf

Silent Warrior Series Writing as J.L. Saint
Collateral Damage

Tactical Deception

Weldon Series Writing as Jennifer Saints

Wild Irish Ride

Smooth Irish Seduction

Hard Irish Luck

Frankly, My Dear Series as Jennifer Saints

Cocktail Cove

Upcoming Releases

Hot Irish Lass (Weldon Brothers - Book 4)

Down Easy Street (Frankly, My Dear - Book 2)

Fly Me to the Moon (Frankly, My Dear - Book 3)

Find Jennifer Online:

www.jenniferstgiles.com

http://twitter.com/jenniferstgiles

https://www.facebook.com/jenniferstgiles

Dedication

I dedicate this book to all of those who devote their lives toward the rescue and healing of others. Thank you for all that you do to reach out to the hurting hearts, bodies, and souls of your brothers and sisters in this vast world of pain.

Acknowledgments

There are an eternity of stories to tell and thousands of ways to tell them, some simple, some complex, some soothing, some adrenaline pumping and I love writing them all. I love story and I love romance, the weaving of two hearts together to create a fabric of love that will help protect from the world and its painful realities. Love heals and I know one day my heart too will heal.

First, I want to thank readers everywhere, for without you the world of a writer would be a very lonely place. I hope you enjoy *Smooth Irish Seduction* where love shapes and heals the hearts of Nan Miller and Jackson Weldon.

Secondly, I want to thank all of the hardworking people who put their hearts and time to make *Smooth Irish Seduction* possible. Annette Batista! Kudos to your amazing talent and golden heart. Thank you for being my friend, for loving my stories, and for believing in me despite the odds. Dayna, my friend and collaborator in many projects that we hope will help and heal women around the world, thank you for staying the course when it cost you so very much, and for having the fortitude to make things happen when they should. Much love and thanks for always being there. To my sister Tracy Clark, whose love and spirit have given me so much throughout my life. You've been there through the thick and thin and have always given me your heart and your belief. Love you! To PJ Ausdenmore, thank you for loving Smooth Irish and for your quick help! You are a heroine.

"Eventually you will come to understand that love heals everything, and love is all there is."

Gary Zukav, author

CHAPTER ONE

Nan Miller smiled back at the baby blues staring her way and winked. "So, hot stuff, how about a date?"

"You'll have to take a number," Dr. Schwartz said then laughed. "Candy and Sarah have already asked."

"Just my luck. I'll probably have to stand in line behind every single woman in Savannah, Georgia, once word of his arrival gets out." Nan shook her head and lovingly brushed the infant boy's tiny fist with her gloved hand, feeling a knot of tender emotions squeeze her heart.

Someday, after she had her career established, she hoped to be holding her own child. So many people didn't know how blessed they were to have family—a mother, a father, a sister, or brother, just someone to belong with in this vast universe.

Provided that Mr. Right made an appearance, she thought. Nan already knew she was better off alone than being with a Mr. Wrong. Her mother had made that mistake.

You're going to have to wipe Mr. Wrong from your mind to find Mr. Right, the conscience angel on her shoulder whispered.

Nan winced. So far every plan she had for doing just that had failed. Lately, a lobotomy wasn't out of the question.

"He is beautiful, isn't he? But then I'm a little biased," said the new mother, who managed to look completely glowing despite her exhaustion. But even she didn't compare to her husband. The proud father looked as if he would either keel over from the stress of labor or burst with joy at the end product-his son. The mothers always faired better than the fathers during labor.

"All bias aside, he's gorgeous," Nan assured the woman. "He'll be a real heart stopper." Of that, Nan had no doubt. The infant's blue eyes and shock of black hair reminded her too much of a grown up version she was trying—without much success—to forget. Every morning, she woke and cursed the day she'd met Jackson Weldon. And every night she…

No! Absolutely not. She was not going to think about *him*.

Stifling her errant thoughts, she focused on finishing the tasks before her as she readied the baby to go to the newborn nursery while Dr. Schwartz talked with the baby's mother.

At twenty-nine, Nan was farther down the road from the nowhere place she'd spent years flipping burgers, but she was not far enough for comfort. Not yet. A sense of incompleteness worried at her despite her nursing degree. She needed more. If she could manage to be awarded Memorial Hospital's continuing education scholarship this year, that more would be a lot easier to grasp onto. Besides, a new plan just might help her strike Mr. Wrong from her mind.

Is that what you want?

Of course! Nan shoved the conscience angel off her shoulder. A new plan for her life is just what she needed. The board would choose a deserving employee at the end of this year and Nan planned to be the best candidate.

Having whipped her thoughts into shape, she read over the notes that would go to the nursery with the baby, checking to make sure the details of the difficult delivery were accurately recorded and the doctor's orders were clear.

Her shift had ended two hours ago, but when her patients reached the final stages of labor, Nan always stayed to see her patient through. During that delicate time, having the same nurse eased the laboring mother's anxiety, especially if there were complications.

Candy, a fellow obstetric nurse, returned to the delivery room which was made to look like a cozy bedroom in a house complete with blue ruffled curtains and homespun quilts.

"I'll finish up here. Head Nurse Litton wants you to go home before you end up on a stretcher." Candy lowered her voice so that only Nan could hear. "You work too hard. How you can do double shifts without a complaint is beyond me." The working conditions at Memorial Hospital were not ideal and many of the nurses felt the pressure of having to juggle too many patients with minimal help.

Nan bit her lip as a tinge of guilt heated her cheeks. She wasn't as noble as Candy made her sound, at least, not since Jackson invaded Nan's dreams. Now she not only worked diligently to reach her goals, but she also worked with exhaustion in mind. Too tired plus too tired equaled zero dreams, which meant no Jackson invasions...

Nan blinked, realizing Candy had spoken to her. "I'm sorry. What did you say?"

Taking the baby's chart, Candy shooed Nan toward the door. "You better go home before you fall down. I said that major hunk Dr. Swanson came by the nurses' station earlier asking for you and you didn't even react."

"Me?" Nan blinked with surprise.

"Yes, you. Don't look so innocent. I saw him eating lunch with you yesterday."

"That's only because the lunch room was full and he was kind enough to invite me to his table when I walked by."

"Uh, huh," Candy said with a bright gleam in her eyes that said she wasn't about to be fooled. "Out of all the people passing his table, he just happened to invite you to sit."

"Yes," Nan said. She was far too pragmatic to see Dr. Swanson's invitation as anything but a simple kindness on his part. Brad Swanson was the most renowned neurosurgeon in the Southeast, a medical giant. If Nan had had an "A-list" for Mr. Right, Dr. Swanson's dedication and determination would put him at the top of it.

Sure Candy was making too much of Dr. Swanson's visit, Nan said goodbye to the new mother and baby and left the delivery room. Dr. Schwartz followed her out.

"Nan, congratulations on receiving the Lois Emerson Merit Award again. You deserved to be honored twice in a row."

"Thank you, Dr. Schwartz. I was completely surprised. Once was wonderful. Twice left me speechless." The award was given to honor excellence in nursing care. To Nan it meant she was one step closer to being chosen for the scholarship. That Dr. Schwartz recommended Nan, doubled the honor. Nan greatly admired the woman who balanced a career and a family.

"You've earned it. And I'll be putting my recommendation in for you next year as well. This delivery might not have had as happy an ending, if you hadn't have had the instinct to call me when you did."

"I'm only thankful that both mother and baby are all right."

"Thanks to you. Go home and get some rest."

"You, too."

"No such luck. I left my husband with six five-year-old girls coming over for my daughter's birthday party that should have started an hour ago. Even though he's a flexible kind of guy and completely supportive of my career, I'm sure he's snatched himself bald by now. So I'd better hurry."

Nan laughed as Dr. Schwartz hustled away. Careers didn't necessarily make for a smooth family life. Nan made a mental note to add flexible to her Mr. Right list.

In the nurses' station, Nan keyed a few quick notes into the computer and then logged off for the day. She settled back in her chair and breathed a sigh of relief that was short lived. When her gaze focused on the clock, she suddenly remembered that she was supposed to be at her friend Alexi's house for a potluck BBQ. In ten minutes. She was too tired to rush and too tired to go, which was just as well. Since Alexi was Jackson's sister-in-law, odds were he'd be at the BBQ and she didn't need any more fuel to fodder her nightly fantasies of him.

She hadn't seen him in months, but she could clearly picture every nuance of his bad boy persona. He was the devil who promised heaven in his every move, but offered nothing for the future. She'd grown up under a futureless cloud and she wasn't ever going back there.

Digging her cell phone out of her purse, Nan dialed Alexi's number, braced to face the riot act Alexi was sure to deliver.

"I've got your number, Sugar."

There was no mistaking the deep sensual voice. Nan's heart jumped and an oh-so-hot, sweat broke all over her body. Her voice, caught sideways in her windpipe, squeaked. "Jackson?"

"My name on your lips is a good start. Please Jackson is even better. Ever had phone sex, Nan?"

Air flew from her lungs. An army of hormones attacked her sensibilities and everything else she had too. Liquid fire, pooled, flowed, and stroked.

Oh, my! A quick glance around the nurses' station told her no one had even noticed her. She should disconnect; pretend she hadn't even called. That would be the smart thing...

Instead she griped her cell phone tighter, swiveled her chair to face the wall, and shut her eyes. His voice did things for which she was starved. A moment she told herself. Just a moment to relay her message to Alexi. Then she'd hang up.

"Afraid sugar?" Like smooth Irish cream, his voice glided and curled into a warm knot right where his deep tones stroked the most.

"No." Since she'd forgotten to breathe, she sounded wispy instead of practical.

"Is that a no to sex via a live wire, or no to the fear."

"Both," she gasped, planning to ask to speak to Alexi just as soon as she caught her breath.

"Virgin ears. Mmm, that means I'll be your first. Can't you feel me? I'm right up against you. Feel the heat? My hands on you... my mouth. I can still taste your honeysuckle lips. I keep wondering if the rest of you is as sweet. Do you wonder too, Nan? Wonder how all that explosive attraction would play out between us if we let it loose? Remember the kiss outside the bar against the wall that day? We almost made love right then and there."

Nan gulped for air, she was drowning. Drowning in him again. She popped her eyes open, hoping that the images he evoked would evaporate. They didn't.

"No," she said desperately. "No, I don't remember. I don't wonder. Tell Alexi I can't make it tonight. We're all wrong for each other Jackson, sorry." Nan cut off the call before she heard anything else to tempt her otherwise. She stared at the wall, stunned by how much her need for him had grown since she'd stopped seeing him.

"Nan?" A firm finger tapped her on the shoulder. "Anything wrong?"

She swung her chair around. "Dr. Swanson?" she said, trying to blink his golden blonde image into focus, but a blue-eyed raven-haired devil kept imposing himself onto her retina.

He waved his hand in front of her face. "The one and only, but please, call me Brad. You look tired."

"I am a little," she said, blinking again. This time her vision blessedly cleared and she latched onto Brad's GQ, Armani draped bod with both eyes like he was the last lifeboat before the flood. She gave him her brightest smile. "What can I do for you?"

His eyes widened. "You should smile like that more often. It's quite breath taking."

Nan's jaw loosened with surprise at the personal compliment.

Brad shook his head as if bouncing out of a trance. "Ahem, well, I stopped by to ask you if you'd like to be my date for the charity banquet next Saturday. It's not normally my sort of thing, but I thought if you'd like, we could, uh, go together."

Had Mr. Famous Neurosurgeon just asked her out on a date in the middle of a colleague filled hospital? Nan shook her head to clear out the Jackson oriented cobwebs and saw Brad frown.

"Is that a no because you are working?" he asked.

"No. I mean that wasn't a no to you. That was a no to…never mind. Yes, I would like to go with you to the benefit."

"Excellent," Brad said, giving her the full force of his charismatic smile.

Nan prepared herself for a jolt of excitement, something along the lines of the lightning bolt Jackson had sent shooting through her with his "ever had phone sex" line. To her dismay, nothing happened.

She had thought she wouldn't date until she'd erased Jackson from her mind. But that was something all of her disciplined determination had failed to do—a real first for her.

"Just so you know how to dress, we'll be sitting with some of the hospital's board of directors and they tend be on the conservative side." He frowned again and then shook his head. "Sorry, I'm sure you'll be fine. I'm heading for a cup of coffee before going home. Care to join me?"

Nan wasn't sure she'd heard everything Brad had just said. Had the man actually been worried that she'd embarrass him? Perhaps, she looked more of a mess after a day's work than she thought.

"Coffee sounds good. I'll meet you in the cafeteria in about five minutes, okay?" She'd go powder her nose, tidy her unruly hair, and freshen up a bit before meeting him over coffee.

"Perfect. See you shortly then." Brad turned and left the nurses' station, his stride every bit as efficient as his manner. Nan stared hard at his broad shoulders and trim waist, doing her best to drum up a spark of the fire that even just one lick of Jackson's voice set ablaze.

Brad had asked *her*. The most professionally perfect man available had singled her out to have dinner with him, where she'd be personally introduced to some of the board members who would be choosing the recipient for the scholarship she'd applied for, and all her body could do was vibrate like a tuning fork for Jackson's sensuality? She definitely needed a lobotomy.

Over the years, she'd worked hard and played little, but she wasn't a virgin. So, why out of the few men she'd known, why did Jackson, a man she hadn't slept with, had only passionately kissed, loom so much larger than any other?

Was it the pull of the tragedy that she knew was buried beneath his "I don't care" air? Not that Jackson himself had ever spoken of it, but Nan knew from Alexi that Jackson's first wife had died a few years back.

It'd been three months since she'd last seen him, a total of seventy-one days from New Year's Eve to April Fool's Day. She knew because she'd like a fool had counted. *You dated him for less than two months. Odds are you aren't ever going to forget him.*

Not true. I can and I will, Nan told herself and the sooner she reached the coffee shop the better off she'd be.

~~*

*J*ackson let the receiver rest against his ear until it hurt. Good, he knew pain. He could deal with that. It was this damnable attraction he had for Nan Miller that didn't fit the comfortable rut he'd dug for himself.

He liked messing up her quick mind with a soft suggestion, liked watching her blue eyes go liquid and dark with desire. Hell, maybe his whole problem is he wanted her and she walked before he could have her.

Alexi had mentioned Nan might come tonight. That's why he'd come. He glanced around at the cozy, well-ordered home his sister-in-law had lovingly fashioned. Its very warmth shouted at him to get the hell out. He didn't belong there. Outside he could hear the twang of banjos as his uncles plucked out a tune or two. He could hear a few dozen yard apes running around, hear their laughter, hear his brothers Jesse, James, Jared ragging the kids and each other. Every now and then his mother, Emma, would lovingly rope in their teasing play with a firm word or two to keep everyone in line. Having raised four wild Weldon boys, she had an iron hand to go with her gold heart.

Since leaving Chicago, Jackson had done his best to lay low when it came to family. He didn't much belong any more. Didn't deserve it. Didn't want it.

"Come on out. We're putting together a game of rag football." Jesse, his brother and pregnant Alexi's husband, stuck his head in the door.

"Maybe next time." Jackson stood. "I think I'm going to head on."

Jesse's smile died. He stepped inside and slammed the door.

"How long are you going to shut us out?"

"Don't start dishing out guilt trips, bro. You've got a wife and a kid on the way. Go worry about them."

Jesse's hands fisted. Jackson could see frustration, anger, and even a hint of pain waver in his brother's eyes, but it left Jackson unmoved. Of his three brothers, Jesse had always been the closest, but not anymore. Nothing and nobody seemed to penetrate the numbness he felt. Nothing, except maybe the woman who'd just hung up on him. The same woman who'd walked out in the middle of their date. Just left him sitting in Salty's Bar all alone to ring the New Year with only a bottle of whiskey to kiss.

Jesse planted a fist against the door. "What is it with you? You want me to feel guilty because I found Alexi? And you lost…"

"Amy? No. I just want to be left the hell alone. Got that?" Jackson shouldered his way outside. He found Alexi sitting at the picnic table with his mother.

"Great BBQ," he said, grabbing a chicken leg off the platter on the table. He did it to appease his mother. He knew she'd be more apt to leave his departure unchallenged if he had food in his hand. "Nan called, Alexi. Said she wasn't going to make it tonight."

"Don't tell me she's working overtime again?"

"She didn't say."

"I'll call her tomorrow and read her the riot act." Alexi narrowed her eyes. "So, um, did you two talk a little?"

"Nope," Jackson said nipping any interrogation in the bud. Alexi had been matching him up with Nan since she married Jesse eighteen months ago. Jackson winked at his mother and kissed her cheek. "Later, sweetcakes."

She ruffled the ever-present dishtowel she held at him. "Distracting me with smooth talking isn't going to work, young man. You can leave if you want to, but don't think you aren't going to be missed. Some day you're going to have to get- never mind." Thankfully, she stopped whatever it was she'd been about to say. Anywhere that sentence could have gone wasn't something Jackson wanted to hear.

He nodded good-bye, waved off his father who was motioning him over for the rag football game, and cut around the corner of the house to his motorcycle. Soon he was eating up the road with no destination in mind, just living the moment for the moment a mile at a time.

~~*

*N*an shut her eyes and relaxed into the steamy tub, sighing as her headache eased when she sank all the way to her chin. Hot water, made silky smooth with bath oil, sluiced over her naked body. The rigors of a day's work slowly faded, and a sensual heat soaked into her bones. Jackson's voice came flooding back.

Ever had phone sex, Nan? A virgin...I'll be your first... she tingled all over. The image of a lady waiting came to her...a lady who'd waited for so long she could wait no longer...

The front door opened. She was alone, had planned it that way when she'd written the note. No one could save her; no one would stop her. Her heart sped triple time to the sound of booted feet coming her way. She knew it was him, knew he was coming to her at last. Tonight she'd know all the secrets behind his heated looks across the ballroom. Already she could see his raven hair brushing his shoulders as he walked, his stride, measured and predatory. She could feel the fire of his gaze. His dark eyes were intense and demanding. Tonight she would feel all she'd been denied in her chaste upbringing and in the years of an arranged marriage to an invalid. Tonight on the anniversary of her widowhood, she would have her first lover.

Suddenly the time for waiting had gone. Sir Jackson Weldon strode into her bedroom; the heat of his presence burned more than the gentle fire in the hearth beside her. He didn't stop until he stood over her. He didn't speak until his gaze surveyed all that the steamy bath water and candlelight revealed. His dress was casual, just a half-buttoned shirt and breeches. As if her note had caught him undressing, and he'd abandoned all to come to her.

He cocked one eyebrow. "Lady Miller, your note implied you were in dire straits and needed my immediate assistance."

She bit her lip, suddenly unsure. She'd heard whispered wild stories on how many had boldly claimed their lovers, and had dreamed for years of claiming her own. "I am," she said softly. "I am," she said again, then she stood and stepped from the bath, the water pooling upon the wooden planks at her feet. She didn't stand alone long. Without another word he swept her into his arms, his lips claiming hers, his tongue plundering, as his hands possessed. Wet, wicked with need, she braced her hands on the breadth of his shoulders as he lifted her, bringing her breasts to the heat of his tongue. He swung her around and laid her back upon the bed.

"I seem to find myself in dire straits and also need your immediate assistance," he said, his voice soft with amusement, husky with desire. He took her hand and placed it over the bulge of his arousal. Throbbing heat filled her hand.

"Oh, heavens," she said, blinking with surprise.

He grinned. "Not yet, but it will be heaven." He ripped his shirt open and buttons flew about them. His boots and trousers followed so quickly that she barely had time to see all of him before he pulled her to the edge of the bed and drove deeply into the very place she ached for him. She winced with the discomfort and the alien feel of being invaded.

He froze; his eyes widened with surprise. "A virgin?"

"No, not anymore." She grabbed his arms, wanting him. "Show me heaven."

"Heaven help me, my Lady. At this point I've no other choice." He strained as if fighting a huge battle then groaned in defeat. After a moment's hesitation as he stared down into her eyes, burning a way right to her soul, he moved out of her a little, then slid back deep inside her, more gently this time. He did this again and again until the fire inside her flared so hot she had no

choice but to meet his thrust with her own. Then his hands roamed over her, touching her everywhere, playing mercilessly with her breasts and nipples. The fire blazed hotter, and just as she thought she couldn't stand it another moment, she shuddered uncontrollably with more pleasure than imaginable. Sir Weldon's body jerked against hers the same way and then they lay still together for a while, her heart pounding thrice for every breath he panted. She opened her eyes to see him smiling at her.

"I think we'll reach heaven and go beyond, Lady Miller. I'm already dying with pleasure," he said and began to move again. Her eyes widened and her breath caught. There was more? Surely she'd die.

Water pooled at her feet and Nan shivered from the cool air caressing her heated skin. She hadn't taken time to grab a towel when she'd jumped from the tub, and she needed to get back into the hot water or dry off and dress before she took a chill, but she couldn't. Not until she'd written down every darn word of the Sir Jackson Weldon fantasy still playing in her mind.

Droplets plunked off her nose and hair, spilling onto the page, but she continued to write. By bringing the man to life on the page, maybe she could exorcise him from her mind. And once she had that battle won, maybe then she could rein her hormones back into their calm, controlled places.

As she wrote the story, she deliberately gave Sir Weldon blond hair and green eyes instead of black hair and blue eyes, a feeble attempt to direct her subconscious mind toward Brad Swanson. He was the perfect example of the kind of man she needed in her life.

She finished the last word, snapped her secret black book closed, and stuck it back under her pillow. Ever since she was a little girl, she'd written down her thoughts, her stories, her hopes. It was the secret place where she let the happily ever after dreams of a little girl who'd known nothing but heartache live. The one place where the realities of life could never invade and steal her hopes away.

Shakespeare, her cat, gave a loud meow, protesting his hunger outside of her bedroom door.

"All right, I'm coming," she called and went after a towel. As she passed, she pulled the plug on her bath. She didn't think she could take anymore of what the hot silky water had induced. She'd go feed Shakespeare and keep her mind on what was important, not what her body clamored to have.

She also ruthlessly ignored any guilt she had over telling Jackson that she had no interest in where the attraction between them could lead. She might play it out, over and over again in her foolish writing, but she'd never let him know that.

The ringing of the doorbell stopped her in her tracks. With her fantasy of Jackson fresh in her mind, every fiber of her foolish body was hoping the devil was on her doorstep.

CHAPTER TWO

*N*an's *pulse leapt with anticipation.* Mouth dry, she tiptoed up to the peephole, careful to not make any noise. Centering her eye on the viewer, she felt her stomach clench and sink with disappointment.

She opened the door to her neighbor, resigned to hear over a cup of tea the woman's account of Shakespeare's misdeeds in the neighborhood.

An hour later, Nan came to the dismal realization that she envied her cat's sex life. He was neutered, but that didn't seem to stop him from wooing every female cat in the neighborhood. Cats didn't have to live by a plan or be disciplined. They just let the good times roll and then landed on their feet.

To make matters worse, her disappointment that Jackson had *not* been on her doorstep rankled even more than her cat envy. She hated to think that there was any truth to the *absence-makes-the-heart-grow-fonder adage.* She'd already learned that the *out-of-sight-out-of-mind* thing was a joke.

By the next morning, she'd made a twenty-item list of what comprised the perfect man in a attempt to give her left brain the opportunity to show her right brain how messed up it was for fantasizing over Jackson Weldon, and felt pretty good about the exercise.

Puttering around in pajamas that had more frayed edges than an Egyptian mummy, she watered her colorful zoo of indoor plants that served as her family. She discussed with them the idea of

buying another book on gourmet cooking. She needed a
distraction and some tricky recipes just might be the ticket.

"Well, Goldie, what do you think? Shall we try Italian?" The
Golden Trumpet didn't shout back an answer, so she moved on to
her Blue African Lilies. She'd heard some old wives tale that they
brought happiness to the home that they grew in. Whether it was
true or not, Nan had bought herself some and took extra care to
keep them healthy and thriving.

She enjoyed coaxing miniature roses to bloom, drinking in the
vibrant summer colors of the gloxinia, and smelling the fresh
rosemary and basil from the planter in her kitchen window. Being
surrounded by the lush plants kept memories of her childhood at
bay.

For her mother, flowers had been a sign that good times were
ahead. But nothing she'd planted or bought had lived. Either
she'd had a black thumb or the stresses of her life had proved too
distracting to care for the plants except intermittently. To Nan,
flowers were the symbols of hope her mother could never seem to
hold on to.

The ringing of the phone pulled her back from the past.

"You stood me up last night and the only way you can make
amends is to take me to lunch and then shopping. There has to be
something out there to make a beached whale sexy."

Nan laughed at Alexi's complaint. "If you're a beached whale
then I'd hate to see what the rest of us women look like eight
months pregnant. You're a glowing Madonna and you know it."

"Tell me a thousand more times and I might hear you.
Seriously, let's hit the mall."

"Okay. Let me finish watering my jungle and I'll be by to get
you."

"Good."

Hanging up, Nan misted the rest of her plants with water, put a little spoonful of fertilizer into her button fern, and then readied herself. She pulled into the unpretentious drive of Alexi and Jesse's beachside bungalow on Tybee Island less than forty minutes after Alexi's call.

Alexi must have been sitting on go. She was out the door before Nan could exit the car. Waddling around and opening the passenger's door, her friend practically rolled into the car.

"I thank my lucky stars that you were home and not working on your day off again. I need a break from chaos."

Nan grinned. It wasn't often that Alexi became frazzled. "What is it? Still having problems with getting help at the art gallery?" Nan backed out and headed to the mall.

"No. Karin has Southern Lights running smoothly, despite Lucy's 'help.' Lucy has decided that she is going to be an artist as well as a prima ballerina."

Nan laughed, her heart warmed. Lucy, a little girl who'd spent more of her life in the hospital than out was very dear to Nan, but even dearer to Alexi. It still amazed Nan how much Alexi cared for others despite her silver spoon heritage. If Alexi hadn't taken Lucy under her wing and Jesse hadn't helped find Lucy's father, Lucy might not be alive today.

"What has me going nuts is the orchestral band that I had scheduled to play at the hospital's fundraising banquet has cancelled. I've been scrambling to find a substitute all morning and I refuse to give it another thought until tomorrow. We're going to go have fun instead. A new lingerie store called Sinfully Silky has opened, and we're both going to buy something decadent."

A lingerie store? Nan frowned at the road. To date, her worst extravagance had been to spend a day at a spa being pampered just before Alexi had almost married Mr. Wrong and escaped with Jesse in a mad dash from the altar.

"You know, Lexi. I don't think I've ever bought fancy lingerie before." It used to be that she didn't have the funds for such luxuries, but now...

"You've had your nose to the grindstone since the day we met."

"Habit I guess," Nan said, thinking back. At twenty-two, when most people were starting their careers, Nan began working her way through nursing school. She'd made a plan and had stuck to it no matter how tough, graduated by twenty-six, and in the three years she'd been working at Memorial Hospital, she'd made excellent strides in establishing a stellar career.

During that time, everything else like travel, gourmet cooking classes—instead of learning from books, and having a family had been put on hold, and it would have to stay on hold. But she could now afford a few luxuries—like silky lingerie instead of frayed cotton.

Nan pulled into a parking slot and looked up to find Alexi studying her seriously.

"I'm worried about you," she said.

"I'm fine." Nan gave Lexi a reassuring smile.

"When are you going to give yourself permission to live? Have a little fun in your life. Are you afraid to let yourself have fun? Are you afraid to let go and live?"

"I'm not afraid to live. I've battled my way up from nothing and still have more to achieve. And I do too have fun," Nan said, opening the door, hoping Alexi would abandon the conversation.

"When?" Alexi challenged, grabbing Nan's hand.

"Why, uh…I have a date to the benefit with *Mr. Perfect.*"

Alexi's eyes widened. "Who?"

"Dr. Brad Swanson."

Alexi blinked. "As in the neurosurgeon?"

"The one and only. The man's a genius. The most dedicated doctor on staff."

"Nan, I don't know the man, but I know of the man. I can already tell you're headed for trouble. His career is going to be a cold bed partner."

"Who said anything about sex?"

"If he doesn't spark that kind of interest at a distance, believe me, there's big trouble ahead."

"A date to the benefit does not a wedding make. Besides, anything serious is on hold until I get my masters."

"You know, I can't help but think your decision to continue your education is related to your break-up with Jackson. The timing is too coincidental, so much so that I almost hope you don't get the continuing education scholarship."

Nan blinked, completely shocked. Alexi had been her greatest supporter as Nan had battled to get her degree. Alexi went on before Nan found the words to respond.

"And the reason why isn't because I don't want great things for you, but because I do want great things for you. I don't think the happiness you want lies in another degree."

"Jackson has nothing to do with my decision." For some odd reason, tears pricked Nan's eyes and she blinked them quickly away. Alexi had struck something deep that Nan just didn't want to acknowledge. She forced a smile. "Ready for some wild shopping fun? I hear a number of women spell happiness M A L L."

Alexi laughed, but the worry didn't fade from her eyes. "Nope those women only use the mall as a substitute for what they really want."

Nan got the feeling that Alexi wasn't just speaking about compulsive shoppers, but about her and her decision to keep climbing the educational ladder. She was greatly relieved that Alexi let the subject drop.

With Alexi egging her on, Sinfully Silky's lingerie proved to be more temptation than Nan could resist. She bought several decadent things that included a leopard print bra and panty set that looked positively animal on her and a black lace set that was the newest thing in women's underwear. Alexi bought a couple of things that looked great despite her pregnant state, and then bought a barely there satin and lace teddy to wear when she "got" her figure back. Between them, they left the store with a mound.

"I can't believe we've bought all of this." Nan crossed her eyes at the packages piled into the rented baby stroller. As Alexi pointed out, she needed the practice in pushing a stroller and it beat lugging the bags or hiking back and forth to the parking garage by a long mall mile.

"Believe it," Alexi said then came to such a sudden stop that Nan nearly tripped over the stroller.

"You weren't kidding about the practice bit. Mark sudden stops off your strategy list." Nan laughed as she turned to see what had grabbed Alexi attention.

"This is it," Alexi said.

Nan frowned at the mannequin draped in sexy sophistication. The burgundy silk and satin ensemble glimmered with dark sable highlights.

"Lexi, I love you when I say this, but you're going to have to wait until after the baby to get that."

"Let's go in." Alexi wheeled into the store and caught the salesperson's attention. "We need that dress," she pointed to the display, "to fit her." Alexi pointed Nan's way.

Nan gasped. "No. That's way too, I don't know, *wow*, for me." She backed up.

Alex grabbed her arm. "It's not too anything for you except perfect. Perfectly elegant and perfectly sexy. Just the sort of dress you need for the fundraising banquet party. If Brad Swanson is any kind of man you're going to knock his surgical booties off."

Nan looked at the dress and shook her head again.

"Trust me," Alexi said, pulling Nan to the dressing rooms. "What can it hurt to try it on?"

"I'll look like a fraud."

"Why?"

"Because…" Nan didn't have an answer, and she hated to think it was because Alexi might have a point to what she'd said earlier about being afraid to live life. "I don't guess it will hurt to try it on." Nan followed the salesperson to the dressing room, grumbling. "How do you know there's even going to be a party? What if you can't replace the orchestra?"

"Don't worry," Alexi said then laughed. "I've got it handled."

The dress, reminiscent of vintage forties style, looked like a dream, and could be worn with or without the sleek cape. Nan felt and looked like a million in it. She bought it.

"Now we've got to go home," Nan said, walking out of the boutique. "I'm out of funds for at least the next thirty years."

"We can go now," Alexi agreed, looking entirely too pleased, as if she'd been the one to buy the killer dress. Nan frowned, wondering if she had missed something.

By the next day, she'd forgotten Alexi's pleased look, having replaced it with a frown of her own in the restroom mirror at work. Nobody told her that lingerie should come with warning labels. Labels that said *Danger—silky underwear is hazardous to your peace of mind.* Every time the body-warmed silk slid over her sensitive skin, Jackson crossed her mind. It was humiliating. She marched from the nurses break room in a huff and ran right into Head Nurse Litton.

"Nurse Miller, I was just looking for you. May I have a word with you in my office?"

"Of Course," Nan said, wincing at her supervisor's stern visage. Head Nurse Litton ran the Labor and Delivery Department like a captain ran a tight ship. Everything from her cropped hair to her short nails was as crisp and practical as her starched uniform and manner.

Heat flooded Nan's cheeks. Following the head nurse, Nan slid into the empty chair in the office sure she was about to be lectured for being distracted.

Nurse Litton frowned down at the file opened on her desk before speaking. "Seems we've run into a problem on the Nurse's Trouble Shooting Committee. Since you were working when we met last, I'm sure you're unaware that Sandy Mason had to resign as spokesperson for the group. Her husband is being relocated with his company. To sum up a long meeting, it was proposed that the nurses vote for a candidate to replace Sandy. You received the most votes and I have to agree with our co-workers, you'd be perfect for the position. We need a Nurse in touch with the staffing problems who will tactfully address issues like the antiquated way the pharmacy insists on packaging medications. Your Lois Emerson Merit Awards will go a long way in making the hospital board take our grievances seriously."

Nan swallowed the lump of surprise in her throat along with the knot of trepidation that formed. She didn't feel qualified for the position for one thing. Then, secondly, to do an effective job for the Nurse's Trouble Shooting Committee, she would have to be willing to argue with the board on behalf of her fellow nurses—an action that wouldn't necessarily endear them to her and put her in the best light as a choice for the scholarship. But, then, it was a tremendous that her fellow nurses had that much confidence in her.

She'd always been a "behind the scenes" advocate for changing the nurses work environment, which was up toward the top of the "most stressful job to have list," and got worse every year as hospitals faced rising costs with fewer funds.

"I'm flattered. I don't know any other way to say this, but I don't think I'm qualified for the position. Sandy Mason has a Masters degree in Nursing Science and Business Management. I don't."

"Sometimes it's not the college credits that count. Sometimes it's the effort and work experience that matter more. I think you'll do just fine."

Nan drew in a deep breath. "I'm going to need to think about this."

Head Nurse Litton smiled. "Take your time. And rather than giving me an answer, why don't you try next month's meeting with the hospital board on for size? If you're still uncomfortable with the position afterwards, then we can look for a replacement." Nurse Litton snapped the file closed, indicating Nan's dismissal.

The knot that had been in Nan's throat sank to her stomach and stuck. Thanking the head nurse for the honor, Nan had no choice but to leave things at this point for now. In truth, it was the perfect compromise. She could do her best to meet up to the honor the nurses had bestowed on her, and then if it wasn't the right job for her, she had a way to pass the position on.

If only it were all that simple. Twice in the next month she was going to be brought before the notice of the board. She could only pray that she made a favorable impression at the banquet, so that any negative issues she addressed at the trouble shooting meeting would balance out the board's opinion of her.

~~*

"*Hell hath no fury like a* southern storm," Nan muttered in dismay as she paced across her den to look at the lightning slashing the Saturday evening sky. Pre-banquet cocktails had started fifteen minutes ago and Brad had yet to pick her up.

She was a porcupine of sharp nerves—worry over the possibility that Brad could have crashed in the storm, anxiety over making a good impression during the dinner with the hospital board, self-conscious over her new dress, and just plain irritation at her continued preoccupation with the he who-she-would-not-name person. Not thinking his name was her newest tactic in trying to free her mind from thoughts of him. She didn't think it was working, but she was sticking with it until she came up with a new plan.

The phone rang and Nan rushed to it.

"Nan, it's Brad."

"Thank goodness. Are you all right?"

"Fine. A patient of mine ran into a few complications and I haven't felt comfortable leaving the hospital until now. Can you meet me at the yacht club?"

"Sure," Nan said, forcing herself to take a breath rather than ask Brad why he'd waited so late to call her. She could have gone to the yacht club, been on time, and missed the heaviest part of the storm raging outside.

"I'll meet you there." Brad hung up.

Nan blinked as the dial tone rang in her ear. Considering the yacht club was five minutes from the hospital and almost thirty minutes from her place, Brad was only going to be fashionably late, while she'd be miserably so. And growing later by the second. Nan hurriedly gathered her stuff and had to settle for a large green garbage bag as rain gear. Her raincoat and umbrella were in her nurses' locker at the hospital thanks to Channel Two's meteorologist and her travel umbrella was already in the car. She would definitely have to switch her loyalties to another station. The weatherman's prediction of calm and cool missed the mark by a wide country mile. The night was as steamy, wet, and wicked as a coed sauna.

The whole way there she had to creep at a snail's pace as the storm lashed and wailed. Its towering fury made her and her second-hand BMW seem very miniscule, like she was the fly and it was a King-Kong sized swatter.

The relief she felt as she pulled into the Savannah Star Yacht Club's parking lot was short lived. She wasted two minutes waiting for a valet to appear through the driving rain. When no one showed, she gave up and searched for a parking space. She found one in the last row and the far end of the parking lot.

Bolstered with a deep breath, she dashed into the thunderstorm. Her only protection from the gale force wind and driving rain were

a mini umbrella and a trash bag. She wielded them like a sword
and shield, determined to hold onto her enthusiasm for the evening.
She refused to let irritation be a third party on her first date with
Brad. After all, she fully understood duty to a patient. How many
times had she herself stayed over when she felt she was needed?
Plenty.

By the time she'd walked ten feet, a wet hand had wiped out
the sophisticated touches she'd added to her appearance. Her
burgundy silk cocktail dress lost its elegant flair and the svelte
hairstyle she'd spent an hour on went haywire. This couldn't be
happening.

Tonight she'd wanted everything to iron out without a wrinkle.
Instead a major kink developed, knotting her confidence with it.
She couldn't sit with the hospital board looking like a drowned rat.

She'd run a long way from the shy little girl who'd grown up
poor on the backside of a country road, and the storm was doing its
best to blow her back there, like Dorothy in the *Wizard of Oz*. But
unlike Dorothy, Nan knew her heart's desire would never be to
return to where she came from. Only bad memories resided there.

Hurrying toward the distant lights of the yacht club, she
ignored the niggling thought that Brad, a man brilliant enough to
make neurosurgical history, surely could have saved her the grief
of trudging through the storm of the century. Why hadn't he called
earlier?

The harder she pushed against the wind, the longer the parking
lot grew. The storm swelled around her to frightening proportions.
Her heart pounded and a tiny shiver of fear raced up her spine.
She shouldn't be out in this mess. She should have waited for the
storm to ease, no matter how late that would have made her.

Neither her umbrella nor the garbage bag staved off the dragon
bite of the lashing wind. Lightning strobe lit the sky and thunder

set her ears to ringing. Suddenly, a wind gust ferried up from behind like a freight train. It flipped her umbrella inside out, blew her dress up, and knocked her off her three-inch heels.

She fell face forward against the hood of a pick-up truck with an inelegant whoosh and lay stunned a second; the breath forced from her lungs. Rain drenched her black lace underwear, and the pooling droplets of water on the hood soaked the front of her dress.

"Mary Poppins you're not, sugar. But you'll do," a familiar and unwelcome voice drawled.

"Oh!" Mortified, Nan snapped upright just as a warm hand brushed her derrière. Jackson! Of all the rotten luck. What in the hell was he doing here?

She refused to acknowledge the pleasurable shiver tingling through her. Instead, she spun around, ready to do harm with her warped umbrella.

Having a man inadvertently see the lingerie she and Alexi had splurged on irked. Having that man be Jackson really rattled her cage. Nan refused to even think for a minute that her fantasies about Jackson played any role in her new underwear purchases.

Lightning briefly illuminated the strong curve of his stubble-rough jaw, devilish smile, and raven's wing hair whipping in the wind. Damn, the man had no right to look so sexy in the middle of hell. He stripped off his black leather jacket, pushed her umbrella aside, and leaned in close.

"You bait a nice hook, sugar."

"You. You Peeping Tom!" Her search for something sophisticated and deadly to say fizzled as ridiculous.

"Careful. You're giving me ideas for a new profession."

She didn't have a chance to reply before his leather jacket descended over her head and his strong arm encircled her.

"Tell me how sorry I am later, sugar." He plucked the inverted umbrella from her, popped it back right, and held it before them as he propelled them toward the back door of the yacht club, not the least daunted by the storm's fury. But then, Nan didn't think much got past Jackson's thick wall. She gritted her teeth, irritated. Both the timing of Jackson's appearance and the man were too welcome for her peace of mind.

She tingled from the heat of his arm about her, the feel of his lean, hard body next to her, and the tangy scent of musk and leather enveloping her.

"Here we go." He hustled her into a lit hallway.

Anxious to rid herself of his scent, she slid off his coat. Cool air assaulted, making her too aware of the heat from his body behind her, touching her, like he'd said on the phone.

Can't you feel me? I'm right up against you. Feel the heat? My hands on you... my mouth.

She shivered. The creamy watered silk walls, crown molding, and plush carpet contrasted sharply with her soggy, bedraggled state and she turned to face him, feeling like a swamp rat. He'd moved closer and her chest landed smack up against his hot, very male one.

"Where are we?" Drawing back, she teetered, dropping his coat.

"Backstage of the ballroom and just where we need to be." He grinned and settled his hands on her hips. When he spoke, his deep voice rumbled right to her core and set off a series of delicious quakes. "It's been a while, sugar. A long while. You hung up too soon last week. We didn't get to the good part."

CHAPTER THREE

*N*an *tried to stop the quakes* of desire from spreading by clenching her stomach muscles. It didn't help. Jackson let his shoulders rest on the door behind him and drew her between his jeans-clad, booted legs. She didn't have to look to know how his jeans fit or how his leather boots gleamed. Not a thing about his dark Irish looks and southern bad boy manners had changed.

"Yes, a long while," she whispered past the lump in her throat. A droplet of water ran down her cheek, dripped onto her breastbone, and slithered between her breasts. Jackson's gaze followed its path, heated, then lingered. Nan looked down. Her halter-top gown lay plastered to her body like skin, the wet silk clearly defining the rise of her breasts and nipples. Something about her dress, besides the wet, was off, but the hot missiles firing at her erogenous zones scrambled her brain cells and she couldn't figure it out.

She slammed her eyes shut. Surely, this had to be another one of her fantasies. Any minute she would wake up and find herself alone, writing in her secret black book.

"Way too long," he growled, sliding his hands from her hips to cup the fullness of her bottom. Nan opened her eyes to the pure sexual intensity in his. Nope, not a fantasy. He was as potent, and as real as it got. He wanted her and she wanted him. Not a problem.

The problem was what came after the bedroom. She wasn't about to get involved with a man going nowhere. He lived his life by whim; she lived hers by a plan. She had goals; she was going somewhere in life and he wasn't budging from the comfortable hole he'd dug.

Any second he would kiss her. Desire sizzled up her spine and overrode rational thought. One more kiss wouldn't hurt, would it?

"Or not long enough?" he said, setting her back on her feet. "I forgot you're baiting your hook for a bigger fish. Brad Swanson. Alexi mentioned you're seeing him." Tension tightened his lips, coolness edged into his eyes, and his husky voice had turned harsh.

Jackson made it sound as if she and Brad had a thing going and Nan wondered what Alexi had told him. Even if she did have a thing going with Brad, Jackson's tone was out of line. Her back stiffened as she went to set him straight. "Just because I have goals and direction doesn't mean I'm a…a hook baiter, and it doesn't give you the right to use that tone of voice, either. We aren't an item."

Now that Nan had a moment to think about it, Alexi had a hell of a lot of explaining to do. Nan didn't think it coincidence that Alexi had asked to go shopping the same day the orchestral band cancelled. Alexi had probably planned the Sinfully Silky shopping knowing that Jackson's band was going to be the substitute. And the dress Alexi had talked her into...

Jackson snatched his coat off the ground and shoved it her way. "Those black lace panties looked like bait to me, and unless you're wanting to turn my whole band on, you better keep that a while yet, because your nipples are begging to be nibbled." He stared at her breasts again.

Nan finally realized the loose silk cape to her dress was missing. She must have lost it in the storm. Instead of subtle, elegant sensuality, her wet dressed screamed I'm hot baby. Oh no! Could things get any worse?

"There's a dressing room you can use to fix yourself up, but if I were you, I'd go home and get warm. Seeing Brad can't be worth catching a cold."

"Direct me to the ladies' room, please."

"Fine." His voice vibrated with anything but fine tones.

Fine, she told herself. If Jackson wanted to think she was a bait hooker, or a hook baiter, however it was said, then it was fine with her. Just fine. She wasn't going to set him straight that this was her first date with Brad. And she wasn't going to give Jackson the satisfaction of seeing her leave the party. She'd go repair what damage she could in the bathroom and then keep her date with Brad.

After the party, she'd kill Alexi.

Jackson turned on his heel and left. Nan had to hurry to keep up with his six-four stride. So what if he was a walking wish list—dark hair, sexy eyes, and lean, have-to-touch muscles? So what if he wanted to share all of that with her? So what if he looked even more sexy than usual in jeans and a white dress shirt instead of his usual t-shirt grunge. So what if he made her insides melt. She wanted more in a man. She wanted a man going somewhere.

Jackson stopped in the narrow hallway and turned her way. She hated the thrill pumping through her blood. His glare mirrored her mixed emotions. Even though he was angry, he still wanted her.

"Listen, Jackson—"

"The ladies room is behind you. I'd better find Alexi and tell her you're safe and sound." He whipped around and walked away without looking back.

~~*

Fool. *Cursing himself, Jackson* strode away from Nan. The woman was trouble. He should be two-stepping in the opposite direction anytime she came near with her livewire sensuality. Five minutes in her company and he became so hot he could give new meaning to the concept of "southern fried."

But damn, seeing her bottoms up over the hood of his pick-up, all black lace and creamy skin got to him. Everything about her did. The fire of her hair, the way her blue eyes grew dark with passion and excitement, or cool with disapproval. Her honeysuckle scent with a touch of the exotic spicing it up incited him to drink from her sweet mouth. Unfortunately, she came with strings attached. Strings like commitment and a future—strings he didn't deserve to stroke, pluck, or strum.

Like the songs he played on the guitar, something about Nan reached inside him beyond the numbness and made him feel. Jackson missed a step. *No, not feel. It was just a sexual thing.*

She'd gotten stuck in his head somewhere between the "I do's" and the final toast at Jesse and Alexi's wedding. It might have had something to do with the fact that she'd caught the bridal bouquet and he'd made damned sure that his younger twin brothers, James and Jared, didn't catch the garter. They had no business running their hands up *her* long legs. He'd gotten the pleasure of touching her silky skin, of being up close and personal with her honeysuckle scent.

Grim, he pushed his hands into the pockets of his jeans to ease the pressure off his fly and moved back into the fray of the cocktail party. People dressed in tuxedos, glittery gowns, and exchanging superficial chatter filled the room. They were as effervescent as the champagne bubbling in the flutes they held.

Alexi spotted him immediately. He quickened his step to save her from walking through the crowded room. If it weren't for

Alexi, and her zeal to improve children's medical care at the hospital, he would have avoided this social function like the plague.

"Did you find Nan?" she asked, frowning then the blood drained from her face. "Why the serious look on your face? Something's happened to Nan, hasn't it?"

"No. She's fine. A little wet, but fine. Now relax."

"Really, you wouldn't lie to me?"

"I promise. Nan is fine. The only thing I lied about was the wet part." He smiled until he remembered just how well he could see the full contours of Nan's breasts beneath the silk of her dress. Then his smile dropped as his pulse rate rose. "She's more than just a little wet, she's drenched. I sent her to the ladies dressing room back stage to dry off, though in my opinion she should go home and have a hot bath."

"Thank you for going after her. Doctor on call or not, I can't believe Brad didn't go pick her up, not with this storm. I wanted to smack him when he showed up without Nan."

"Swanson has always been a self-absorbed, stuffed shirt."

"I didn't realize you knew him."

"In Chicago." Realizing he'd said too much, he turned to go. "Time I went backstage to finish setting up our equipment for the dance."

"Sure you and your band don't want to eat in the main room?"

"Positive. No offense, but we'd be more comfortable in the backstage lounge. Where's Jesse? I haven't seen him around."

"He's not here. The storms delayed his flight from DC."

Jackson froze, and unease crept up his spine. "You didn't drive yourself here, did you?"

"Of course. I had to be here hours ago. I missed the rain completely."

"You're eight months pregnant, Alexi, you shouldn't be driving."

"Jesse usually runs me about when he's in town, but when he's gone and I'm feeling fine, I drive myself."

Jackson shrugged. It wasn't any skin off of his back what his brother and sister-in-law did. He turned to go again, but couldn't make his feet move. "Look. Next time Jesse's not around and you need to go somewhere, call me. Hell, call James, or Jared, or anybody. Okay?"

"Well, that seems like a lot of trouble to impose—"

Jackson could already see she wasn't going to pick up the phone. He grabbed her hand. "Just promise me you won't get behind the steering wheel again until after the baby's been born. I'll drive you home tonight and you call me even if it's to fetch ice cream in the middle of the night. Okay?"

Suddenly realizing people about them were beginning to stare, Jackson eased his grip on Alexi's hand and lowered his voice. "Please."

Alexi blinked her obvious surprise, but relented. "Okay, Jack. But you're worrying over nothing. It won't be much longer before I won't even fit behind the wheel and still reach the pedals." Her smile came at odds to the questions he saw in her eyes.

He didn't want questions. This is why he avoided family. This is why he avoided people. Proximity led to involvement, something he didn't want.

"I'll check on Nan," Alexi said and left.

Jackson drew a deep breath and headed backstage. As he strode across the crowded room, the sugarcoated atmosphere swirling about him clashed with the feelings crowding in on him. He'd have to talk to Jesse. The fool didn't realize he could lose everything he held dear.

Rolling his shoulders to dispel some of the tension knotting his muscles, he focused on the mess of cold metal equipment. He preferred handling the mechanics of music to dealing with the dynamics of relationships on any level. Nan left him feeling like a rolled up hot-to-go pretzel. As many times as he told himself to forget her, she boomeranged right back into his mind.

~~*

*N*an, *bent doubled under* the hand dryer, fluffed the curtain of her damp hair. Her dress hung under the other hand-dryer receiving intermittent blasts of hot air. All she had on was her black lace lingerie topped by Jackson's jacket, which barely covered her garters. Her lack of dress in comparison to the marble, gold-leafed plushness of the dressing room made her feel decadent. Beneath the heat of the dryer, another fantasy had taken root. This time she sat on Jackson's Harley, and they were taking a wild ride, but he wasn't driving down a road. He was driving deep inside. . .

"What did you do to Jackson?" Alexi demanded. She waddled into the room like she couldn't make the last step of a long journey.

"Jackson!" Nan yelped guiltily then bit her lip, ashamed over her disappointment at seeing her friend enter. Giving her hair a last scrunch, Nan stood upright. The cool, sophisticated style she started the night with was now a jumble of bedroom-mussed hair. Nan frowned at Alexi. "I didn't do anything to him. Why?"

"The expression on his face is rivaling the storm outside. He was fine before he went to look for you." Alexi rubbed the small of her back and stretched her shoulders.

"He went out looking for me?"

"Yeah, I was worried and when I got no answer at your apartment, he volunteered to make sure you were all right."

Nan let the subject of Jackson drop, but finding out he'd ventured into the storm for her stuck in her head. Had Brad been concerned? He obviously hadn't been watching the front for her or he would have seen her drive up.

Alexi sank into the jade leather loveseat just inside the dressing room door. She slipped her feet from her pumps and tried to massage them. The girth of the child growing within made the task nearly impossible. She gave up and rolled back against the cushions, then commented on Nan's attire. "Black garters and leather. I wore mine for Jesse the other night."

"And?"

"He laughed."

"I'll kill him."

"No you won't, because I love him. Besides, he laughed because he didn't think there was anything on this God's earth I couldn't make sexy."

"He can live. That's so romantic."

Alexi grinned. "Since my sex life is fruitful, let's discuss yours."

"I'm not about to discuss my non-existent sex life. But I am going to read you the riot act while I massage your feet. That whole shopping trip and dress buying thing was a set up. You knew Jackson was going to be here tonight, didn't you?" Nan pushed the button to keep drying her dress and joined Alexi, motioning for Alexi's feet.

"Guilty," Alexi winced. "I thought it would do him good to see you looking great and out with another man. God, that feels good." Alexi moaned.

"You also made it sound as if Brad and I had a relationship."

Alexi winced. "Well maybe a little. If he thought that you were—"

"Let it go, Lex. Jackson isn't the right man for me."

"Better than Brad. If a man let me fend for myself during the storm of the century on our first date, there wouldn't be a second."

"He's dedicated to his career and his patients. I understand and admire that." Nan sighed. "Besides, what you have with Jesse doesn't happen for everyone."

"So, you've never met a man that lights your fire?" Alexi asked, tongue in cheek.

Nan narrowed her eyes. "I'm not discussing Jackson."

Alexi smiled, pleased. "Who brought up his name? Not me."

Uncomfortable with the direction of the conversation, Nan turned the spotlight on Alexi. "Your feet are swollen. Bet you haven't rested all day."

"I did rest for about an hour. My feet are always swollen these days. I suppose its part of the package." Alexi lovingly rubbed the side of her protruding stomach. "By evening junior and I are ready to call it a day."

"You need to slow down. Not do so much. Maybe we better not go to the play Wednesday night." Worried, Nan ran an assessing eye over Alexi, searching for any other signs that a complication might be rising.

"No. I'm fine, really. I'm looking forward to seeing *A Midsummer Night's Dream*. Sitting and laughing isn't going to overtire me."

"Have you told Dr. Schwartz how you're feeling?"

"A little."

"That doesn't tell me much. What was your last blood pressure?" Nan pressed her fingers against Alexi swollen ankles to determine the level of edema and checked the pulses there.

Alexi laughed. "I'm fine, really. My blood pressure was a hundred and twenty over eighty-five at my last check-up. She said some swelling at the end of the day is normal, though it wasn't as bad as this then."

"That's a higher pressure than normal for you. Any headaches, dizziness, blurred vision? Swelling in your hands?"

"Just a little, but nothing to speak of, Nurse Miller. You're sounding as worried about the baby as Jackson was a few minutes ago. You'd think I was planning to go skydiving instead of just drive myself home. Both of you are going to have me spooked."

"Maybe I'm being a little paranoid. But do me a favor. Stay off your feet a few days, call Dr. Schwartz for another check-up, cut back on your salt, and increase your protein intake."

Alexi groaned. "You do know how to knock a woman when she's down. All I've been craving lately is French fries dripping with catsup. Between you and Jackson, I'll be propped up and homebound for a whole month with nothing to console me." Alexi lowered her feet to the floor and slipped on her shoes.

Nan frowned. "This late in your pregnancy the least little fender bender could cause a major problem."

"You know how many do's and don'ts are dumped on a woman the moment she gets pregnant? I had to give up chocolate. Caffeine isn't good for the baby. Pretty soon they're probably going to tell me I have to give up sex, too. I'll go crazy. A beached whale, stuck at home, no chocolate, and no Jesse." Alexi frowned, seemingly having the weight of the world settle on her.

"Come on, it can't be all that bad. Just think. In a little over a month, you'll have it all. Jesse, a baby, and choc—uh, scratch the chocolate while breastfeeding. I've heard it gives babies gas. Call me. I'll drive you where you need to go until after the baby is born, but I won't take you to get French fries or chocolate." She hugged Alexi. "I'd better get dressed."

"No fries. I'm dying here!" Alexi wailed in mock distress. "This is pain!"

"Think about something else." Nan scooted off the couch and struck a pose. "How about this outfit for dinner with the hospital's bigwigs—"

The door burst open, and Jackson filled its frame. "What in the hell's going on? Is she having the baby?"

Nan jumped with fright at the thunder in Jackson voice. Her jaw dropped and she froze on the spot, much as she supposed a deer would pinned by the headlights of a Mack truck. Jackson looked wild and dangerous.

"I heard dying. . .pain—" His gaze fell on her and he stopped dead in his tracks, his mouth wide open mid-word. His eyes blazed to laser points as he cut a path down her body. His look sucker-punched Nan in the gut. It wasn't until her breath whooshed from her lungs and she felt the suspicious tickle of air on her left breast that she realized what he was seeing. Oh God. She snapped the jacket closed.

Jackson had already covered half the distance to her. The look in his eyes was one of a man intent on retrieving his jacket. Now.

From the sidelines of this tableau, Alexi burst into laughter, holding her baby-swollen girth. "I wouldn't have missed this for the world, but I'd better get out now."

Jackson shook his head as if coming out of a trance. "I thought. . ." Nan saw him spare Alexi a brief glance.

Alexi grinned. "You heard a pregnant woman who just realized she had to give up French fries."

Jackson frowned then grinned. "I came to tell you both they're serving dinner." He swung his gaze back to her and Nan wanted to run and hide. "You wear my jacket well."

"Doesn't she?" Alexi piped on her way to the door. "You should see what's underneath."

"I did," Jackson drawled.

Mortified, Nan hugged Jackson's coat closer and sent him and Alexi a murderous look. "Both of you shut up and get out."

Alexi laughed and disappeared out the door. Jackson followed, only he didn't leave. The door closed, shutting them intimately together. He folded his arms and leaned against the door as his bedroom blues made another slow assessment of her. She burned, wanting his electric touch like a desert thirsting for water. Yet, she denied herself and kept a disapproving frown centered on her face.

He moved her way then, coming so close that she could feel his heat. He cocked his brow at her and glanced down at her exposed cleavage before he grabbed the jacket and pulled her against his arousal. "I'll get *it* later," he said softly.

Nan mouth went dry. Still, she managed to add just the right touch of ennui to her voice. "Will you?"

Smiling, he backed away and opened the door then looked at her. "Of course. A man can't live without his jacket." Nan swore his grin housed the devil.

Minutes later, Nan dashed from the dressing room as if Satan was on her heels. He who she was again trying not to name seemed to be everywhere. She slid into her seat next to Brad Swanson at the banquet table, seeing that the salads had already been served, but no one was eating.

Several members of the upper echelon of Memorial Hospital were seated at the table and were waiting for her with disapproving frowns—the Chairman of the Board of Directors, the long dead founder's great-granddaughter, the administrator, several departmental heads, and Isabel Barra—a VIP consultant from Switzerland known in the nursing circles as Bella Barracuda. This was not good.

Cheeks flushing, Nan nodded a greeting. They watched as she unfolded her napkin and placed it on her lap. She cleared her throat. "Sorry I'm late."

Her apology seemed to set everyone in motion, but their looks of disapproval remained. Nan expelled the air she had trapped in her lungs.

"Didn't think there'd be much traffic out," Brad whispered, leaning her way.

"No traffic. Just rain, buckets of it and a wicked wind from the West." Nan rubbed her temple at the beginnings of a headache. She was a storm blown mess, while not a hair on Brad's GQ-cover-head would think to lie out of place, or a wrinkle would dare crease his tux.

So, why did her salad have more appeal at the moment?

She shouldn't have skipped lunch, she thought as she forked a delicate bite of Romaine lettuce into her mouth.

"Time got away from me at the hospital, and I couldn't pick you up. I didn't know it was raining so hard when I called. Glad you're finally here." Brad picked up the salad dressing, poured it on her salad, his own, and handed it to the man on his right.

"Looks like some of that rain got you," the man said as he took the salad dressing from Brad. She recognized him as the head of radiology. The nurses called him x-ray eyes because he always looked as if he were trying to see through their clothes.

"Just a bit," Nan managed to say past the lettuce lodged in her throat. Brad hadn't even *asked* her if she wanted salad dressing. She grabbed her water goblet.

"So, Ms. Milner, Brad says you work for us in the Labor and Delivery Department." Nan recognized Talbert Townsend, the hospital's Chairman of the Board from the huge portrait of him hanging in the hospital lobby.

"Yes I do, Mr. Townsend." The man had her name wrong. Mentally scrambling on how to set him straight, she smiled over the elegant bouquet of magnolias serving as the table's centerpiece—the crowning touch to the linen tablecloth, crystal, and gold rimmed china.

Brad, busy with his salad, hadn't noticed the error, nor had he taken the time to introduce her to everyone at the table.

"I'm not sure we've been properly introduced, Mr. Townsend. My name is Nancy Miller. But please call me Nan."

"Miller? Like the beer?"

Nan frowned. "Exactly."

"You say you're related to the brewing family? Met them in Europe a few years back." Townsend's aged, Rip Van Winkle countenance brightened at the prospect.

Nan stifled a groaned. The man needed to up his hearing aide. "No, no relation."

"Really Talbert." A woman Nan assumed to be Townsend's wife patted his hand. "Were she a relation of the Miller's, she wouldn't be a nurse in Labor and Delivery."

Her tone indicated the position would be well beneath anyone of financial prominence. Twenty years her husband's junior, she looked like an overblown Marilyn Monroe who'd stuffed her ample dimensions into a skintight sequined dress. She wore so many large diamonds that it was a wonder the weight of them hadn't snatched her nose out of the air.

"Well, whatever her relations, she does work for us." Townsend narrowed his brow in irritation at his wife then leveled his look back at Nan. "Tell me how you like working for Memorial Hospital, dear?"

The benevolent smile Townsend settled on his thin lips clearly indicated he expected her to sing praises of her wonderful employment experience at Memorial Medical Center. Trouble was she couldn't. The entire purpose of the Nurses Trouble Shooting Committee was to address the issues of under-staffing, heavy patient workloads, and problems with antiquated procedures. But none of those topics were appropriate dinner conversation. Nan cleared her throat. "I've found employment with Memorial very educational and worthwhile. Being on the Trouble Shooting Committee, I'm—"

"Nan loves it." Brad cut in. "She's dedicated to her job. Did I tell you about my research with Dr. Von Heller in Europe, Mr. Townsend?"

"No. I'd like to hear about it, boy." Townsend said.

Nan blinked. She'd been about to tell Townsend that she looked forward to the special Trouble Shooting Committee meeting the board would be attending next month. Her words stuck on the lump of surprise in her throat. What was wrong with Brad? He'd deliberately cut her off.

"Had the unique opportunity to study with Von Heller on the feasibility of expanding neurosurgical procedures beyond the peripheral to the spinal," Brad said.

Nan stepped on his toe with her heel. He looked at her in surprise. She smiled. "I seemed to have dropped my napkin. Can you reach it?"

"Of course." He slid his chair back and leaned down to retrieve the napkin she'd thrown on the floor.

"It's over there." Nan leaned down as well. "What do you think you're doing, cutting me off in mid sentence," she whispered.

"Trying to help. I heard today that you were heading up the meeting next month about the hospital's staffing problems," he whispered back. He cut his gaze back and forth from her to the tabletop. "Bringing up the issue now will only damage your cause."

"I wasn't going to. I feel twice as strong about being censored mid-sentence."

Bella Barracuda peeked under the table. "Everything all right?"

"Just fine," Nan said through gritted teeth.

Brad popped back upright and Nan followed. The circle of disapproving eyebrows rose several notches higher. Nan decided that for the sake of the evening, she'd let Brad's interruption go. Mr. Perfect was turning out to be not so perfect for her after all.

Bella Barracuda spoke first. "I do remember the summer you worked with Von Heller, Brad. You were brilliant." She sent Brad a lingering half-shuttered look. "Dr. Von Heller still comments on the progress you two made."

Brad nodded then went into a long diatribe about the experiments they'd conducted and their hopes of major nerve regeneration for the future. Nan swallowed, but couldn't ease the tightness in her throat. Her appetite dwindled and the evening went down hill from there. She smiled, showed appropriate interest, and made an intelligent comment or two on related medical topics, but on the whole the evening was a big disappointment. Most of the conversation centered on travel in Europe. She'd never been.

A stuffy hour later, she walked with Brad from the banquet room to the Magnolia Ballroom. Jackson's band played a popular song, and Jackson sang it better than the original artist had. His smoother-than-Irish-Cream voice slid like hot silk over her senses. Really not good, and the evening was just getting started.

CHAPTER FOUR

"*Would you like to dance?*" Brad asked, holding out his hand.

She put her hand in his. He had capable hands, hands that wrought miracles in people's lives. She should be thrilled to be with him. Instead, all she could think was that Brad's hands didn't have the feel to them that Jackson's callused one's did. Nan gritted her teeth and wanted to smack herself upside the head. Or smack Jackson.

The evening thus far had been a complete disaster in regards to her dress and her hopes of making a good impression on several of the hospital's board members, but that didn't mean she and Brad couldn't salvage something from it. And it was up to her to do it. She needed to focus on Brad and all of those twenty-five traits that made up Mr. Right. She followed him onto the dance floor and adjusted herself in his arms. "There's a silver lining to this rainy evening," she told him smiling. "We'll just have to find it."

Nan forced herself to relax in Brad's arms as he led her in a slow dance. Their bodies moved well enough together to the beat of the music, but Nan couldn't seem to shut her eyes and lose herself in the magic of the song. She kept peeking at Jackson.

"You're an optimist," Brad said. "That's an admirable quality to have." He sent a thousand-watt smile her way. "I recently read a book about the habits of successful people and optimism was the one area I lacked."

Brad listed the traits, expounding on their benefits. Many of the traits were the very same ones she'd put on her Mr. Perfect list. Yet, as Brad's voice droned on, Nan's mind wandered.

Jackson leaned against a high stool with one knee bent to cradle the curve of his guitar and his other leg stretched out in a relaxed stance that oozed a sex appeal sure to melt any female in the room.

She was looking right at him when his gaze singled her out of the crowd. Nan automatically tightened her hold on Brad's shoulders and inched herself closer to him, looking for any sort of a lifeline to save her from the nebulous sea she fell into whenever Jackson was around.

Brad didn't seem to notice. He stayed on beat like a metronome and told her about a speech he planned on giving at a medical convention the next week. Nan nodded her head and tried to focus on what he was saying.

"The day I was born, my parents declared me a genius. From that point on, every moment of my life was planned out for me to be the best at everything. I think doctors should apply this philosophy in their treatment of patients. To achieve optimum healthcare, a patient needs to make a plan for it when they are young and adhere to it everyday of their life. Anything that doesn't fall into the plan's guidelines should be discarded."

Nan blinked. She was a planner, but…surely she didn't sound as fanatical about plans as Brad did. "Isn't that extreme? Didn't you do fun things as a kid like make mud pies or watch a silly movie?"

"Mud pies? Not hardly, I excelled in golf and chess. When my family traveled abroad, I had my own tutor and became proficient in the native language of the country we stayed in. Time doesn't stand still for anyone. If you're not learning or achieving, you're being left behind. If you aren't constantly choosing healthy then your body will suffer. I plan on raising my children that way from birth."

Nan drew a deep breath. She'd grown up with practically nothing, but she wouldn't trade the lazy afternoons she'd spent daydreaming under the ancient oak tree near her family's trailer for what Brad described. Did he ever enjoy ice cream treats and chocolates? Have pretend tea parties in a mud hole, or go on cloud watching picnics with messy hot dogs?

The beat of the music changed. The drummer tapped out a fast tempo as the band launched into *Johnny B. Goode*. Brad stopped dancing and pulled her off to the side of the dance floor."

"I don't do fast," he said and Nan nodded.

She felt so off key with Brad. What was wrong with her? Maybe she was coming down with a virus. She felt a little dizzy. "I could use a drink," she said over the music.

"Me, too. I'll be right back."

Brad left for the cash bar before she had the chance to tell him what she wanted to drink. Then she relaxed, remembering he was on call. He'd bring back a Coke or something, she told herself as she watched him. He didn't saunter and he didn't march, his determined stride fell somewhere between and never wavered. He cut an impressive and confident figure in a room full of people.

So why was her gaze turning back to see Jackson rather than watching Brad?

Jackson finished one song and then eased into the sensual sway of a song she hadn't heard in years. "Baby I'm-a Want You" by David Gates echoed seductively throughout the ballroom.

He'd climbed off the stage to the dance floor and walked among the swaying couples as he sang. Gasps and sighs escaped the lips of the women as he caressed one woman's cheek then ran a finger through another woman's hair.

Nan's heart pounded, her breath rasped, and her body tingled as Jackson walked her way. She told herself that she should turn and run after Brad. But she didn't, she stood her ground as he walked right up to her.

He was so close, she could feel the heat of his body, smell his arousing scent, and see the want in his eyes as he sang, changing the words of the song.

"*Lady, I want you. Lady, I need you.* You're the only one I care enough to *dream* about."

His blue eyes, full of fire, lit on hers and he seemed to slide right into her soul. It was only for an instant then he moved on, singing the original words to the song.

Nan stood still, not breathing, not thinking. Not doing anything but vibrating from the impact. For a moment, Jackson had reached out and connected with her soul, where no man had gone before.

She had to get out of there fast.

She dashed to Brad just as he left the bar with their drinks. "Come on," she said, grabbing his arm. "I need some fresh air."

Brad handed her a goblet and followed.

The air in the ornate hallway felt a hundred degrees cooler than the ballroom. Nan took a big gulp of her drink to give herself some recovery time before she had to speak to Brad. The white wine tingled all the way down. She gasped, nearly choking.

Brad pounded her back. "You okay?"

"Fine," Nan wheezed out.

"Hey, Swanson." A man who looked as if he bought his clothes on daily trips to Italy walked up. "I was on my way to find you. A few of us on the board are putting together a little weekend yachting trip. You interested?"

Brad shook the man's hand. "Steve, meet Nancy Miller. Nancy, Dr. Steve Dennison, plastic surgeon and long time friend."

Nan met Steve's handshake with a firm grip, liking his tanned sea captain smile. He was young and attractive.

He turned to Brad. "I won't take no for an answer."

Brad shook his head. "I really don't think I can. I'm head speaker at a medical convention in New York later this week. When I get back, I'll be swamped."

"It won't be until the next weekend, so you'll have plenty of time to recover." Steve held up his hand to stave off any more excuses. "Even a machine needs some down time. At least plan on coming to the party in the harbor that Friday night. We won't set sail until Saturday, but bring a change of clothes in case you decide to stay. I'm hoping to set up some challenging chess matches."

Brad's face brightened with the first enthusiasm she'd seen out of him all evening. "Chess?"

"Official timer and all." Dennison slapped Brad on the back. "I knew you had a weakness somewhere. Bring Nancy along with you," he added, nodding at her.

Brad turned to her. "Interested in a yachting trip, Nan?"

"Well I. . ." She blinked, momentarily surprised. Yachting for a weekend with several of the hospital's board members? That sounded like the cherry on top of the sundae of life. Surely over a weekend's time she could repair some of the damage tonight's dinner had done. Her chance at the scholarship and her image as the spokesperson for the Trouble Shooting Committee just might be salvageable. "I'll have to check my work schedule, but—"

"I'll smooth the way with your supervisor," Brad interjected. "We'll come Friday night, but I won't make any promises beyond that."

"Excellent. I'll see you both then." Steve started to leave then turned back. "Can you believe Weldon up there on that stage."

"Yeah, I've seen him play before."

"Who'd have thought he had it in him back in Chicago."

Brad frowned. "Did you ever hear why he quit?"

"No, never did. See you Friday night."

Jackson quit what? Apparently Brad and Jackson knew each other. This came as a surprise to Nan. She planned on asking Brad as soon as she found some fresh air. She was still feeling a bit faint and her headache had worsened. She shouldn't have had that gulp of wine, and ditched what was left on a tray before they exited the building.

Drawing a deep breath, she leaned against the white portico pillar. The rain had stopped, but thunder still rolled across the night sky. Even the usual salty, night- cool breeze from the Atlantic bowed low, subservient to the storm. The air was steamy and still.

"Nan," Brad said, leaning close enough to surprise her. "I'm going to kiss you." He looked as if he was waiting for her approval and she nodded, feeling more that just a little off.

He pulled her into his arms and pressed his mouth to hers, passionately and she moved closer to him, looking for a spark, even a glimmer of desire to light. Brad was the perfect man, intelligent, successful, and driven. Fireworks should be bursting inside her.

He leaned her back over his arm, a southern man about to devour a southern lady. Nan waited for the kiss to deepen; sure her body would catch on to what her brain was hinting.

His cell phone blared and Brad jerked upright as if hit by lightning. He shifted to grab his phone, setting them off balance and Nan barely avoided landing on her lacy decorated derrière. No thanks to Brad, he was already talking on the phone then hung up.

"That was Dr. Barra," he explained. "There's an emergency at the hospital and she wants me to consult with her."

"I understand," Nan said between gritted teeth. As Brad escorted her back inside the Yacht club, she puzzled over her irritation. She above all people understood dedication. If someone had called her about a patient, she would go without question. It took her a few minutes to pinpoint her problem. Brad had made all the right motions, acted like he was consumed with passion, but the slightest buzz from his cell and it was as if he'd never been kissing her. And he hadn't really. Jackson would have finished the kiss before answering the phone.

Bella Barracuda met them inside.

"I'm sorry about this, Nan" Brad said.

"It's not a problem." Nan nodded to Bella Barracuda, then smiled at Brad.

Brad nodded as if he expected no other answer, then started to turn away but swung back. "Oh, Nan. There's something I want you to see. Can I pick you up about six on Monday?"

"Monday?" Nan, repeated, searching through her feelings. She wasn't sure she was ready for a second date with Mr. Perfect so soon.

"Perfect," Brad said smiling. He then offered a stiff arm to Bella Barracuda. The woman snuggled against Brad and shot Nan a he's-all-mine look. Apparently Dr. Barra wanted more from Brad than consulting on an emergency case at the hospital.

Walking toward the ballroom, Nan felt the room swirl and she turned to the ladies room, deciding to rest.

"Where are you off to, sexy?" X-ray Eyes from dinner stood before her. His fleshy smile, shiny head, and ample belly invaded her personal space.

"Personal business and my name is Ms. Miller." Colleague of Brad's or not, she didn't like the man and wouldn't pretend otherwise. She stepped back and he grabbed her arm, brushing her breast in a pretense of helping her catch her balance.

Shocked, Nan angled away from the man's grip, but he held on. An uneasy panic swelled inside her.

"Wait. You look pale," the doctor said.

The conversational voices surrounding her receded, as if coming at her from a long distance. The lights dimmed and her skin turned cold, almost numb. She desperately looked for the ladies room.

"Nan! I've been looking for you everywhere."

Nan whipped toward Alexi's voice, seeking the familiar in a world abruptly foreign. She saw Alexi coming toward her, registered that Jackson was there, too. She lunged from the man's grasp, stepped back, and the world went black.

CHAPTER FIVE

Jackson scooped Nan up into his arms before her head hit the floor. Pulling her close, he glowered at the man she obviously had been trying to escape. "What in the hell is going on?"

The man held up both hands innocently. "Dr. Knapp, head of radiology. The lady stumbled and seems to have fainted."

Jackson didn't think it had been so simple. He'd seen panic on Nan's face before she fainted.

"Come with me," Alexi said, her pregnant body cutting a wide path through the crowd.

Jackson sent Dr. Knapp a look that said the man would be taking his life in his hands if he followed. The seconds it took him to get to a private room ticked too slowly. While common sense told him Nan had fainted, he couldn't help but remember another time and his failure.

"What do you think is wrong?" Alexi asked even as Nan stirred in his arms.

"I don't know." Jackson settled her on the sofa and assessed Nan's condition. Her pulse and respiration, though slightly rapid, were steady, and still within normal range. Her skin worried him; cool and clammy to his touch and her dress was still damp in places. He ran his fingers up from the pulse at her throat to her forehead. Only then did he notice Nan watching him.

"What happened?" he demanded.

Her brow furrowed.

"Did that jerk—"

"Calm down and give her a chance to talk," Alexi said, laying a hand on his shoulder and angling closer to Nan.

Jackson stamped on the emotion threatening to escape. This is why he didn't get involved. This is why he kept his distance. He released Nan's shoulders and stood up to put space between them, but kept his eyes trained on her.

Nan swallowed hard then spoke. "I'm not sure what happened. All of a sudden I became dizzy and cold."

"Are you allergic to anything? Any other symptoms? Nausea? Pain? Difficulty breathing?" Jackson fell back into a mode he'd thought he'd left behind years ago. He paced as he spoke.

"No." Nan sneezed. "Though I must be more addled than I thought. You're beginning to sound like a doctor."

Alexi handed Nan a tissue. "He—"

"Just normal questions anybody would ask," Jackson said, interrupting Alexi. The past wasn't anybody else's business but his. "You probably fainted because you sat in a freezing room in a wet dress instead of going home and changing like a sensible woman."

Out of the corner of his eye, he saw Alexi soothe her hand over the blue dress elegantly adorning her eight-month girth. His body broke out into a sweat.

Alexi felt Nan's forehead. "I know the feeling you described. I became dizzy and cold when I first became preg—" She clamped her hand over her mouth, suddenly realizing what she'd almost inferred.

Nan sat up quickly. "Well that's one problem I can definitely rule out." Her laugh sounded forced. "Unless Superman slept in my bed and then zapped my memory."

Her gaze met his, and she blushed. Guiltily? But why? Unless she lied. Brad Swanson? He didn't want to think of her with someone else. It wasn't acceptable.

Well fool, what did you expect when you pushed her away? He could admit to himself now that was what he'd done New Year's Eve in Salty's Bar, why he'd turned down a recording deal with a music producer. He'd been weighing the pros and cons of signing on the dotted line all day, until Nan had started talking about all the wonderful opportunities he'd have. The overwhelming feeling that the mill of success was about to pull him under its grinding wheel again descended on him and he'd torn the contract up. Then asked Nan if she was ready to rent a hotel room for the night. Nan had walked.

Nan slumped back. "It was probably the effects of white wine on an empty stomach and too little rest."

If she was sleeping with Swanson then it was his own fault. He shouldn't have pushed so hard.

"Fool," Jackson muttered, speaking to himself again.

Alexi and Nan looked at him, telling him he spoke aloud. He scrambled to explain. "You should take better care of yourself. Are you sure you're not having any other problems besides dizziness?"

"Positive. I just needed to rest a minute and then I'll go home." Nan stood.

"Sit down," Jackson ordered. "You've just fainted and you think that I'm going to let you drive home? He checked his watch. "As soon as I finish this last set, I'll drive you both home."

Nan blinked and sat. Jackson had been more emphatic than the situation called for, but she could see his point. She was still a bit dizzy, but wasn't about to admit it. "That isn't necessary. I'm sure I'll be fine after a few more minutes rest."

Jackson drew a deep breath and Nan braced herself for his argument. Instead she heard him exhale, before he finally said, "Please."

A battle the size of WWII launched itself in her stomach and the tinges of a migraine headache that she hadn't had for years intruded. How could she resist him? Letting him take her home wouldn't be like going out with him again. "I'll call a cab," she said, making one last ploy to save herself.

Jackson scowled. "You'd trust an absolute stranger to drive you home more than you'd trust me?" His eyes glittered.

"Not wanting to impose doesn't suggest I don't trust you." It was herself she didn't trust.

"Then wait for me," Jackson said and left the room.

~~*

*T*he door slammed shut behind him with the finality of a trap snapping closed.

"Curiouser and curiouser," Alexi said from across the room.

Nan glared. "A lot of help you were. What happened to women's independence? Sisterhood and all that rot."

"Too busy watching the fireworks. You and Jackson spark like a match to dry tinder."

"Yeah, well I grew up listening to Smoky the Bear. Forest fires kill." Nan rolled the tension from her shoulders. The man was as touchy as a hound after a porcupine encounter. "I sense some heavy emotions running hot beneath his way-too-casually-cool surface. He's never shown them before."

"He's a hard man to get to know. He keeps everyone at a distance. Even Jesse." She leaned her head back to rest against the chair's ample cushion. "You know when you first met Jackson, even a blind man could see the sparks fly between you two. I told Jesse that if any woman could reach his brother, it would be you. I still think he's one man you shouldn't have let go." Alexi eyed her with a determined angle to her chin.

Nan bit her lip. How did she tell Alexi, a woman who'd always had everything, that no matter how much appeal Jackson held, if he didn't want to move forward and share goals in life, she couldn't afford to involve herself with him?

She wanted to own her own home. She wanted to travel. She wanted to send her children to good schools. She wanted success, and she wanted the hope that came with working every day toward a brighter future. A man like Brad could help her in that direction. A man like Jackson would only drag her back to what she had left behind.

"Things between us just didn't work out. We aren't going the same direction in life."

"Moving in opposite directions can make for explosive collisions, like me and Jesse for example. While parallel motion can get pretty dull. From the hot and heavy looks between you two, I bet your paths are destined to intercourse, uh, I mean, intersect. Why avoid it?"

"Cute," Nan said dryly. "Jackson isn't the man for me."

"Hmm," Alexi said, clearly not believing. She rolled to her feet. "I'm going after some crackers, decaf, and water. You sure you're feeling better?"

Nan waved Alexi away. "I'm sure."

Alexi left and images of "intersecting" with Jackson filled Nan's thoughts. She had no idea geometry could be so interesting.

. .

An Indiana Jones-like Jackson, visiting professor in mathematics, walked into her classroom. She stood, precariously balanced on a stool, reaching for an overhead-projecting screen that stubbornly refused to lower. She froze, her heart fluttering dangerously. In the three months he'd been at the university, her hemline had risen three inches in hopes of catching his eye. She could tell by the look he leveled over the rim of his sexy glasses that she finally had his attention.

"I like your line segments, Professor Miller," he said.

She wanted him, had wanted him from the moment she'd seen him. "And I 'love' the way you work a problem, Professor Weldon."

He locked her classroom door before he crossed the room. She stayed on the stool, frozen with anticipation. He slipped off his glasses as he approached.

"You say that as if you have a problem for me to solve, Professor Miller." He slid his hand up her leg, then pressed the inside of the back of her knee, making her fall into his arms.

"I do, though it's more like a puzzle than a problem," she said, breathless with the feel of his hard chest against her.

"Puzzles require more time and ingenuity than simple problems. You've intrigued me. Do tell."

She licked her lips, readying her mouth for his kiss. "Can two objects on a horizontal plane be both parallel and perpendicular to each other, Professor?"

"Let's see if we can find out." He cleared her desk as he laid
her upon it. *Papers, books, and tests flew, but she didn't care. She
knew the highest-grade possible was about to be made in her
classroom.*

"Top grade coffee and a pitcher of ice water, coming right up."
Alexi plowed into the room.

Top grade? Coming? Nan blinked back to reality, then
slumped back onto the couch muttering, "He was and I was."

"Did you say something?"

"No. I'll take the ice water first."

"I thought you were cold."

"That was before." Before the Jackson invasion.

*W*rapped *in the warmth and* scents of Jackson's jacket, Nan
watched him slide back into the car after seeing Alexi inside her
door. His movements fit his demeanor, terse and tense.

Before he started his pick-up, she placed her hand on his arm.
"How does Alexi look to you?"

"Tired. Why?"

Nan shrugged, dropped her hand from his arm, and breathed.
Something she had a hard time remembering to do around him.
"She'd shoot me for mentioning it, but her ankles were pretty
swollen tonight. I don't think it's anything to immediately worry
about, but I told her to lay off the salt and increase her protein.
She promised to go in early for a check up. I don't like the idea of
her being alone this late in her pregnancy. Anything can happen."

Jackson expelled a heavy breath and ran his hand through his hair, mussing the raven-wing layers. "You think she's showing signs of preeclampsia?"

Nan's brow stretched with surprise. "How did you know that?" Jackson had astutely picked up on a possible complication few people outside the medical profession would know about unless they personally knew someone stricken with it.

"How doesn't really matter. Do you think Alexi is in trouble?" Jackson's face in the almost moonless night was more shadow than substance.

"No. Not exactly. I do think the potential is there."

"Jesse left a message on the answering machine a few minutes ago that his flight had just landed in Savannah. He should be home inside of thirty minutes. After I get you home, I'll call and check. My bro and me are going to have a long talk. Alexi's too far along for him to be out of town."

"I agree. I'll call her tomorrow and see how she's doing."

Jackson started his truck and backed out of the drive. Nan turned her attention to the shadowed scenery to escape looking at Jackson. The he-who-she-shall-not-name tactic had failed miserably.

The effects of the earlier storm had faded completely. The world had settled back into a comfortable status quo. Salt and the scent of the sea laced the night breeze whipping in the open window. Through the passing live oaks and historic cottages of Tybee Island, Nan caught glimpses of silver waves cresting in the Atlantic before Jackson pulled onto Highway 80 and headed west. Unfortunately, for Nan, her world was far from returning to status quo. It was as if the storm had blown her life off course, tossing her back into Jackson's dangerous proximity.

The atmosphere between them was tense and fraught with expectation. It was as if a live wire danced between them and neither of them knew who it would zap next.

During the two months they'd dated, more often than not, she'd sat at a table watching Jackson and his band play. Her seven A.M. work shift and every-other-weekend work schedule tended to curtail their dating time. His night owl lifestyle hadn't meshed well with the demands of her job.

He'd also kept every moment so damn sexually intense, that she didn't think a thing was missing from their time together until the euphoria wore off. Then she'd been able to assess where Jackson was going with his life and where she wanted her life to go.

Things had crystallized for her on New Year's Eve, sitting with him in Salty's Bar. He'd just torn up a recording contract from a country music producer, telling her he had no interest in accomplishing more with his life than twanging out a tune in a local bar, late nights, and sleeping till noon. Then he pretty much asked her to share his bed for a while.

She'd left then. Left before she lost more to him than she could afford. He was a man going nowhere and after watching her mother waste her life on a man just like that, Nan wasn't going to make the same mistake.

She had best remember that. But instead of keeping up the safe silence, Nan dug at Jackson's stony wall. Maybe she couldn't get him out of her head because he was somewhat of a mystery she'd never solved. She knew there was more to him than he let her see. She also knew there was more to his past than he was willing to share. Maybe if she satisfied some of her questions, she could move on past him.

"You were worried about Alexi even before I said anything. What do you know about eclampsia. Have you noticed something that I've missed?" she asked as he pulled into the drive to her apartment and cut the engine.

The chirp of crickets, a passing motorist, and an occasionally barking dog filled the silence. Jackson folded his arms and adjusted his long legs in the cramped cab. "She's my sister-in-law. I..."

Nan thought she would turn blue from holding her breath, waiting for him to finish his sentence. He didn't.

"Yes?" Nan prompted.

"Nothing," he said, shaking his head. She could practically see the wall slide back into place.

"Come on, I'll walk you to the door."

Sighing, she slid out of his truck, attempting to maintain her dignity in the short dress, though after the view Jackson had caught earlier it was kind of a moot point. The dizziness had run its course and the coffee with extra sugar and cream had taken the edge off her headache.

She followed him to the door, deciding that she'd find out more about Jackson's past, and how Brad and Dr. Dennison knew him.

To what end? Her mind whispered. Nothing she could learn would change the direction he was going, which was opposite hers.

She shoved her key into the lock. Irritated with herself for even wondering about him.

Jackson closed his hand over hers on the knob. The jolt of his touch tingled all the way to her toes; they curled.

"Nan, about earlier—"

"No. Let me say something." She turned to him, angling her neck to see him. "I didn't mean to hurt you when I walked out of Salty's."

Jackson shrugged. The yellow glare of a street lamp, barely muted by the eaves of her porch, cast a revealing light upon the square lines of his stubble-rough jaw and lean face. He frowned, his eyes intense. "I was out of line about you baiting your hook tonight."

Nan pressed her finger to his full lips, closing her eyes at the pleasure tingling through her. "What I think is that we both want different things in life. You can't deny that."

"No," he said, grabbing her hand and pulling her toward him. "But neither can I deny this."

Jackson was like the storm, all wild, knock-you-off-your-feet power. His mouth closed over hers with hot, liquid passion. He did nothing more than cradle the nape of her neck with his hands, bury his fingers into her hair, and kiss her deeply. Yet, her heart pounded with dizzying force and a flood of aching desire pooled in her center.

After one long, soul-wrenching kiss, he groaned, and kissed her again. Varying his need, he nipped lightly at the corners of her mouth, tasted the tender flesh of her bottom lip, and then dipped deeply into her mouth again.

Drawn beyond the safety of her common sense, Nan demanded more from him. She leaned into him, wrapped her arms around his neck, and pulled her body close to his. His coat gaped open, and her satin-draped cleavage brushed his chest. He pulled her closer, close enough to feel the hard ripples of his chest against her aching breasts. Close enough to feel his muscled thighs against her legs. He answered her demand with one of his own, then leaned back against the door and urged her closer still.

She didn't hesitate to follow. As months of longing broke loose, she pressed tightly against the growing ridge of his arousal. He growled deep in his throat, slid his hands down her back, and cupped her bottom, lifting her up and pulling her hard against his sex. The hem of her short dress bunched and the rough material of his jeans rubbed her thighs. From the breath of air against her bottom she knew that only her lace underwear separated the bare flesh of his hands from her most intimate parts. Still she didn't care. She wanted nothing between them.

Jackson pulled his mouth from hers, breathing hard. "Damn, Lady, I still want to make love to you," he said softly. "That's something I can't seem to walk away from." He set her back on her feet, slowly easing his hands from beneath her dress to rest on her shoulders. His blue eyes were so dark with desire; they were blacker than the night, and more electric than a crack of lightning.

"We went through this before, Jack. I can't—"

He stopped her denial with a gentle, firm kiss. "Don't say anything. Think about it again. Just you and me together. No strings. We'll get it out of our system and move on."

He opened her door. She stepped inside, still stunned by his kiss and the depth of her want for him. Instead of dying out over their months apart, desire had mushroomed, grown larger, more needy. What was she going to do?

"I'll come by and take you to get your car tomorrow."

"Thanks, but you don't know what you're offering. I'm working the early shift, and from what I remember, you don't do morning. I'll just catch a cab."

Jackson frowned. "I do mornings, sugar. In fact, I'm very good at mornings."

She tingled at his words, but started to protest. He staved off her reply by brushing her lips lightly with his thumb. Automatically her tongue slid out to taste his warm, slightly salty skin. He pressed his finger to her tongue, lingered in its moistness a moment, then slipped his thumb to his own mouth.

Nan watched his tongue lick the same spot she had. Watched his pleasure in tasting her where she had tasted him. She closed her eyes against the potent suck of desire making her want to pull him to the ground and love him till time ceased to exist. When she opened them again, he was gone, only the roar of his truck echoed in the night. Jackson had forgotten his coat.

Warm silky fur rubbed against her ankle and a plaintive meow dispelled the feel of Jackson's lingering touch. Nan sighed, bent down and picked up Shakespeare.

"No Romeoing for you tonight, sir. Seems as if there's enough of that going on already." After locking the door, she wandered into the kitchen to feed Shakespeare. Now that Jackson was gone, her common sense seemed to be returning. She'd done the right thing three months ago. She didn't need a relationship going nowhere.

"Remind me to make it to the grocery store tomorrow." She dumped a can of tuna in Shakespeare's dish, then scoured the refrigerator for something for herself, but nothing seemed to satisfy.

Shakespeare finished his meal and adjourned to her bedroom. Nan followed. The nights had become longer since she'd stopped dating Jackson; she'd eaten less, slept less, and worked more.

Shakespeare groomed himself on the slipper chair next to her bed. Nan cleaned up and settled into reading "A Midsummer Night's Dream." But her concentration eluded her. She closed her eyes to drift to the land of dreams and lovers, where Puck's fairy dust made the impossible happen.

Jackson's kiss lingered upon her lips and thoughts of him plagued her all throughout a restless night. The devil stood on her doorstep. She had her hand on the doorknob, and her eye at the peephole, looking at him for all she was worth, and he looked good. Come morning she knew she was going to let him in the door.

CHAPTER SIX

At five A.M. *Nan rolled out* of bed groaning. Even after coffee and a shower, she didn't manage to get both eyes open until the doorbell rang.

She hurried to answer it, her mind a muddled maze. Wet hair wound up in a purple towel and her damp body wrapped in a fuzzy robe that had seen better days, she peered through the peephole and blinked twice. The devil had arrived.

Juggling several lunch bags, Jackson ran an impatient hand through his hair and rang the doorbell again, then rapped his knuckles on the door for good measure. Eye pressed to peephole, Nan jumped at the sharp sound.

She cracked the door open and stuck her nose into the slit. "Jackson?"

"Morning." He grinned enough to flash the dimple in his left cheek. The rough edge of very little sleep laced his deep voice; its intimacy conjured up images of waking in his arms on a lazy morning. *After* making love.

"What . . ." was the only word she could manage to say as she furrowed her brow.

He held up the white bags and dangled a set of keys. "Breakfast and transportation. Remember?"

"MMMM." Nan drew a deep breath, catching the scent of cinnamon and fresh soap. His black hair gleamed damply in the porch light, giving evidence he'd recently showered. A dark shadow on his square jaw let her know he'd skipped shaving, as a man in a hurry might do. The morning air hung heavy with the essence of spring and still carried a whispery breath of winter's chill. Jackson wore his customary dress, a snug fitting black T-shirt, muscle-hugging jeans, and mirrored sunglasses. Her mouth watered at his appetizing appeal.

"Well, sugar? As much as I'm enjoying your interest, it's chilly and I like my buns at least warm if not hot."

"Buns? Oh, my. Um, I forgot to give you your jacket last night." Nan unlatched the chain and pulled the door open.

"Jacket wouldn't help these." He held up the scrumptious smelling bag. "Though, I like the direction of your thoughts." Jackson brushed his way in before she could move back. He grinned like a man who had decadent things on his mind as he waved the bags under her nose. "Cinnamon buns, darlin'. You know, of the big, hot, sticky, *sugary* variety you eat for breakfast?"

"Of course," Nan said, pretending she'd never even considered anything else. She pulled the edges of her robe closer, a little self-conscious. "I love buns. Um, cinnamon buns."

"You look better than the pastries."

Nan pushed at the towel wrapping her head. "I, uh, thanks. If I look better, they must be really messy."

"You look delicious." He lifted his sunglasses off and pointedly slid his gaze over her.

Her body quickened and flushed, tingling in all the places she'd dreamed he touched. Acute awareness plowed through the cotton field of her mind. Awareness of him, of the heavy yearning in her breasts, and of the throbbing heat in the center of her desire. She tugged the front edges of her robe closer; the material skimmed her naked breasts. Her movement brought his gaze to her chest, and her nipples tightened.

His pupils dilated and he slowly lifted his gaze to hers. Throat dry, she swallowed, catching her bottom lip between her teeth. Almost as if the scene played in slow motion on a movie screen, he tossed his glasses on her hall table, dropped the bags to the floor, and swept her up against his hard, lean body.

"Damn," he muttered as he lowered his mouth to hers. She burned everywhere. Her hands left behind the modest job of keeping her robe closed and sought the heat of his broad shoulders and silky hair. He deepened the kiss, bending her back over his arm. A shock of pure pleasure ripped through her and she fought to keep a grasp on her sanity. His lips trailed down her neck and pushed her robe open. Nan refused to open her eyes; refused to acknowledge that this wasn't a fantasy. This was real.

"You are so damn beautiful," he said. Cool air and his heated breath brushed over her breasts and she knew what he was seeing, knew without looking that she lay naked and open to him. The dampness of his tongue slid along her chest and inched closer to her aching nipple. Then heat shot though her as she felt him suck her nipple into his mouth.

Nan gulped in air. Blood roared in her ears. Her back arched and his burning hand slipped beneath the robe, cupping her sex. She moaned. He felt so good. Oh, how she needed his touch there. She reached for him, pulled upon his shoulders, pressing her sex against his hand.

His groan came from deep in his throat, primal, sexual, and needy. "Let's take this to the bedroom, sugar."

A bed in a room with no window to a future her mind screamed through the sensual haze enslaving her.

"We can't," Nan mumbled. He nipped her breast and she moaned. "I have to go to work."

"Double damn," Jackson whispered as his mouth left one breast and moved to the other. His finger slid against her, pressing into her feminine folds and she moaned with need.

Nan knew that in another second she'd be lost. Work, patients, responsibility, everything would cease to matter.

She straightened her back, forcing his mouth back up to her neck. "I can't. I need to dress," she said, pulling back from the fire consuming her alive. She pushed on his shoulders and he straightened. They stared at each other. They'd gone further than they had before. The fire between them had burned hotter than ever before. He was breathing as heavy as she and looked as stunned as she felt. He clenched his jaw; his full mouth fell into a grim line, telling her how much his restraint was costing him.

Without a word he set her on her feet and pulled her robe closed.

Nan scrambled for something to say. "Uh, you'll find fresh hot coffee in the coffee maker, cream in the fridge and sugar on the table. I'll...I'll be out in a jiffy." After I take fifty cold showers, she thought as she turned and ran.

Jackson reached for Nan as she left. Then let his hands drop when she disappeared into the bedroom like a fuzzy rabbit running from a fox. He drew in several ragged breaths of air, counted to ten; then forced himself to retrieve the breakfast he no longer desired.

He stood in the entryway for a long moment, uncomfortable as hell. He didn't even have room for air in his jeans.

Slowly the red haze of desire eased and he began to notice his surroundings. Taking note of everything he passed on his way to locating the kitchen. There was a multitude of plants everywhere—palms and trees and flowers, potted plants, hanging plants. You name it; Nan had it.

The kitchen was no different. Amongst the plants, shades of soothing blues, bright whites, and cheery yellows greeted him in the wallpaper, counters, and curtains. He ran a curious look about, interested in what his surroundings could tell him about their owner. She liked to care for things.

When he'd dated her, he'd avoided knowing personal details, including going to her apartment. Sharing things like that led a woman to believe he had more to offer than what he gave between the sheets. So why was he here now? Just to give her a ride.

So why the buns? Just to share a breakfast?

No. It was about damn time he started being honest with himself. He was here because he couldn't get Nan out of his head. He wanted her in his bed. He wanted the fire between them to burn him alive, to make him forget. Because when he was kissing Nan, nothing else mattered, not even the past. And that felt good.

It was a sexual thing. Nothing else.

Frowning, he thrust himself into the busy work of setting up a cozy breakfast at Nan's dinette table. He popped the buns into the microwave to warm them, then set out two mugs of coffee.

He had to bide his time this time around. Maybe with a little room to breathe, she'd see things his way. They could explore hot sex without getting caught up in issues of goals and futures. The woman needed to loosen up and live the day for the day, and he was the man to show her how to do it. Hot, sticky cinnamon buns were the first step. Too bad she had to be at work this morning.

A slight noise from the door had him spinning around ready to give Nan the sensual breakfast of her life. Instead he met wide yellow eyes that seemed to say; "I know what you're up to."

The fluffy gray cat flicked its tail and bared its teeth, as if to tell Jackson his plan was doomed. Jackson bared his teeth, too, returning the favor. "What? You don't think I'm the man for the job?"

"Meow," the cat replied. The microwave beeped and Jackson pulled the steamy buns out, breathing deep of their rich aroma. He looked back at the cat. "These tell a different story. Before breakfast is over I'll have her eating out of my hand. Wait and see."

Jackson set the buns on the table. Just as he was about to sit down, the cat hopped into the chair. He gently brushed the cat back to the floor. "Sorry bud, this is my place this morning. You go find somewhere else to lounge."

The cat flicked its tail and left the kitchen. Turning his attention back to breakfast, Jackson realized he'd forgotten to get cream from the fridge.

"The buns smell wonderful," Nan said as she walked into the room.

She brought with her a light fragrant cloud of enticing honeysuckle and mint freshness, reminding him of the honeysuckle bush not too far from the old cabin he lived in. Sometimes on steamy, summer afternoons, he'd lay out by the creek and revel in the warm sun and sweet smell.

A flash of making love to Nan in the hot sunshine, in just that spot, shuddered through his mind. He blinked, bringing Nan back into focus. She stood before him cool and collected. The complete opposite of the wildly abandoned woman he'd kissed moments ago. Dressed in efficient pristine nurse whites with her luxurious sable hair pulled into a neat bun, she looked very professional and very reserved.

"You smell wonderful, too. I love honeysuckle." He grinned at her and she smiled back at him. He recalled pulling the centers from honeysuckle flowers as a kid and licking the sweet nectar.

He wanted to taste the sweet nectar of Nan's center. She'd *taste even better.*

"Pardon?" Nan frowned and walked to where he was staring mindlessly into the open refrigerator.

He cleared his throat. "Uh, the buns, I bet the buns will taste even better." He shifted his gaze back to the task of finding cream, but the contents of the refrigerator blurred. Nan was too close for rational thought. He hooked his thumbs into the pocket of his jeans to ease the swelling tightness.

Maybe he should have just stayed in bed this morning. A man needed all of his wits if he was going to woo a woman like Nan into his bed. And he didn't know if he was up for *that* this early in the morning.

"Can I help you find something?" Nan leaned in beside him, peering into the fridge, wreaking more havoc on his already scattered brain cells.

"Yeah." Jackson exhaled roughly and centered his gaze directly on hers. Her mouth formed a surprised "O" and her pupils dilated, leaving her irises a warm honey brown. He wanted her with a rawness that left him nearly undone. He straightened as she did. They ended up only inches apart. She didn't back away, and he took that as a good sign.

Without moving his gaze from her face, he said, "Your choice. You can either help me find cream for the coffee or we can find your bed and get this craziness in our blood out of our system now."

Nan stepped back then, and Jackson cursed himself for a fool. He had all the subtlety of a bulldozer. It was a wonder she didn't kick him and his buns out of her apartment. "Nan, I'm sorry, I didn't mean to sound so crude. It's just all night I—"

"We need to hurry," she said, business-like.

His jaw went slack with surprise. He didn't have to hurry; he was already ready. "I can do that. Which way to the bedroom?" He reached for her.

She sidestepped away. "No. I, um, mean breakfast. Here's the cream." She grabbed a carton from the fridge. He stepped back as she firmly shut the refrigerator door. "I have a planning meeting I need to attend before my shift starts and I have to— Shakespeare! No!"

A suspiciously satisfied meow sounded across the room. Jackson looked over. Shakespeare sat on the table licking his left front paw. Bits of crystallizing white sugar clung to his whiskers.

"He should have horns on his head," Jackson muttered, glaring at the cat.

Nan laughed and shooed the cat out of the kitchen.

Cat-lick-denuded-cinnamon buns were all that was left of the sensual breakfast he had planned. Hell, he should have stayed in bed. Then he looked at Nan; saw the sparkle in her eyes; the sexy curve of her smile, and changed his mind. Buns or no buns, he was glad he had come.

Breakfast didn't go exactly like he'd planned. They had had to whip by the bakery and get coffee and fresh buns to go. He now had a pleasantly satisfied sweet tooth and a sticky steering wheel to show for it.

Forty quick minutes later, he pulled his pickup next to Nan's lonely hunter-green BMW at the Savannah Yacht Club.

Nan turned to him, hesitant. "I really appreciate this morning. The breakfast and the ride, well, it was very thoughtful. Thanks."

"You're welcome." He liked how she looked in the early morning. Though she was too pale, giving evidence that she spent more time working than she should, he liked how the bright sunshine glinted off the golden lights in her brown hair. An inner glow in her dark honey eyes challenged the new day and drew him to her. Nan seemed to look at life much the same way he had a lifetime ago, fresh, optimistic and hopeful. Everything he wasn't now. He had no business wanting her, wanting to touch and feel the breath she gave to life. But he did.

She opened the door to get out, and he did the same, walking around to her. She unlocked her door and leaned deep into the car to drop her tote bag onto the passenger's seat. The crisp material of her white pants stretched across her bottom, outlining the conservative, full cut of her panties. The complete opposite from the underwear she'd worn last night. He grinned. Next time he found Nan in a compromising position on the hood of his pickup, he wouldn't be so quick to rush her inside, even if it was storming. There was something hot and elemental thinking about making love to her in the rain. "You look better in a uniform than any nurse I've ever seen."

She straightened then frowned. "What are your comparisons? The nurse in *One Flew Over the Cuckoo's Nest*? I think waking up this early in the morning has you delusional."

He opened his mouth to tell her he'd seen plenty of white uniforms, then shut it. That part of his life was over.

"Well, thanks again. It was, um, good to see you." She seemed a little nervous as she turned to get into the car.

"Yeah. Real good." He caught her shoulder and turned her back to him. "Not so fast, you have sugar on your mouth."

"I do?" She reached up to brush away the crumb, but he captured her hand in his before she could wipe it away. He leaned down and laid his lips over the spot and licked. Sweet heaven.

Nan stiffened slightly. "Jackson, we can't."

"We can't?" he whispered back and slid his mouth more in line with hers. He waited a moment to see if she'd pull away. When she didn't, he ran his tongue across her bottom lip, softly, slowly, coaxing.

Her answer came in her sigh of surrender as her palm flattened against his and their fingers intertwined. Her skin heated and electrified his nerves, sending a shock straight to his gut. Her lips parted, and he kissed her. Not hard, as the blood racing through his veins urged, but tenderly, like the sun's warmth in the early morn. A deep moan worked its way up the back of his throat as she sank into the kiss, wrapping her arms about his neck.

When he could no longer hold back his desire, he gently set her back on her feet, drew a deep breath, and tucked her head into the crook of his shoulder.

After a moment he stepped back and cupped her chin to brush his thumb across the last crumb of sugar clinging to her mouth. Her lip trembled beneath his touch. "I meant what I said last night. I want to make love to you. You and I would be incredible." He took her left hand and kissed her bare ring finger to its tip. Then he nipped the sensitive pad with his teeth before covering it completely with a soothing combination of his mouth and lips. "We're both free, consenting adults. We can, sugar. We definitely can."

CHAPTER SEVEN

*S*he could.

She had to.

Next time Nan saw Jackson, she'd tell him they couldn't start seeing each other again. No more hot buns in the morning, no more kisses. Since he'd left her off at her car after a sticky bun breakfast yesterday, he'd intruded into her every thought like a movie star filling up the big screen. His voice, his every movement and every word lay amplified in her memory.

"Breathe," Nan encouraged her patient.

The young woman's flushed face contorted with pain, and she cried out. Up until this point she'd remained focused on her determination for as "natural" a birth as possible. Now in the Transition Stage, the woman wavered.

"I can't," the woman moaned. "It hurts."

"I know, but you're almost there. You can do this." Nan squeezed her patient's hand, giving what support she could. The father, who'd originally planned to be his wife's birthing coach, had been banished to the waiting room. The man fainted every time his wife had a contraction. Nine times out of ten, it seemed to Nan that when a woman needed a man the most during life's trials, the man let her down.

"I'll breathe with you, remember what they taught you in Lamaze, focus and breathe. He, he, he, ho." Nan guided her patient in the short and long breath patterns until the woman's contraction eased. Then she bathed the woman's flushed face with a cool cloth and received a thankful smile before the woman shut her eyes to rest a minute.

Nan checked the fetal monitor and her patient's vital signs on the various machines. Once she determined that all was well, her mind immediately turned to Jackson. Before she'd run into Jackson Saturday night, sensual thoughts of him had been a problem, but since he'd kissed her again, her imagination had run completely amok. His preposterous proposal for sex had wiggled in the back of her mind like a worm at the end of a fishhook and she felt akin to a hungry fish, a very hungry fish.

A fish that would just have to stay hungry. She wouldn't see him again. Much less get naked and live out all of her fantasies. What would be the point?

Getting into a relationship without even the plan of a future commitment would lead to nowhere but heartache alley. Even if Jackson came around and tried to make a go of a relationship, he still wasn't going anywhere with his life, so the ending would be the same. That path had destroyed her mother. Passion didn't put food on the table and clothe children.

So no matter how Jackson made her feel, *she couldn't.*

Relieved she'd finally settled the issue; she drew a deep breath.

Candy stuck her head into the birthing room. "How's she doing?"

"Good. We're at nine centimeters. Contractions are running a little over two minutes apart. Is Dr. Schwartz here yet?"

"Yes, she's scrubbing up."

"Good. I think this one's going to come in a hurry."

The woman in labor popped her eyes open and struggled to sit a bit straighter. "Before lunch?" she said hopefully. "I'm starving. I don't think I can face another ice chip."

Nan smiled as she adjusted the mechanical bed higher. "Candy, call dietary." Nan checked the chart for the doctor's orders. "She can have a regular diet after she's had the baby."

"I'll do it right now. Stop by the break room after the blessed event. You won't believe what's been going on all morning." Candy dipped back out the door before Nan could question her.

An hour later, Nan left her patient the proud mother of a healthy baby girl. She ran down to the cafeteria and grabbed a deli-bag for lunch, then headed back up to the break room next to the Nurse's Station to eat. Not only did she feel the beginnings of a headache coming on, but after Saturday night's fainting disaster she'd decided to lay off coffee and chocolate bars for lunch. On her way through the nurses' station to the break room, Nan immediately noticed the aura of excitement buzzing from her co-workers.

Candy angled up from her seat and motioned for Nan to join her. "Hurry before you miss them. We think they're getting ready to break for lunch."

"Who?" Nan murmured, walking toward Candy.

"Prime filet," one of the other nurses said, keeping her eyes fastened to the picture window directly across from the table. Surprisingly, everyone on break sat on the same side of the table instead of around it facing each other as usual. Whatever they were looking at through the big picture window held their rapt attention.

"Prime what?" Nan placed her tray on the table to the left and opposite them, since there was no more room on the other side and pulled her chair out.

"Prime everything," came Candy's dreamy reply.

"Especially the one on the far left," Darla said. "Oh, honey. He's Prime rib, prime buns, prime cut. No doubt he's got a prime p—"

"Pectoral muscles," Candy piped in. Everyone at the table looked naughtily at each other then burst into laughter.

Nan shook her head and turned to see what had sent her co-workers off the deep end. Her knees gave out, and she sank hard into her chair. Not more than twenty feet out the window stood a group of six men, all congregated by a huge water cooler on the back of a pickup truck. A work crew. It was Monday and groundbreaking day for the hospital's new children's wing. Six dirty, sweaty, well-muscled, young men. The one on the left, the tallest of the group, was in the process of pouring a huge cup of water over his familiar head and Nan's stomach clenched. Rivulets sluiced over Jackson Weldon's chiseled face, down his broad shoulders, and over his ripped torso. He was naked from the waist up. He shook his head vigorously, and ran his hands through his dark hair before getting more water and scrubbing his arms.

"See," Candy said, a little breathless. "Great pecs."

Jackson turned his back and donned a blue denim work shirt.

"Great buns," said Sarah.

"Yeah, Jackson's are the best," Nan said without thinking. Her tone conveyed the familiarity of a lover, probably because she'd fantasized about him so much. She looked quickly at her friends, hoping they were too distracted by the view to notice.

No such luck. Every one of them zeroed in on her. Nan gulped her diet Coke. She was in big trouble. Her headache began to pound.

"You know him!" Candy said, her eyes rivaling saucers for size. She glanced at Jackson again and then at Nan. "You know him intimately?"

Face red, Darla fluttered her hands with excitement. "Oh, oh, oh, this is like finding the Diet Coke man naked in your hot tub—it's just too good to be true. You have to tell all. Where did you meet him? What did you say his name was?"

Every eye in the place looked as if she was their fairy godmother about to make their every dream come true. She loosened her tongue and plunged ahead before her cowardly denials could speak up. These women had chosen her to be their voice for very real problems, she couldn't lie to them. "His name is Jackson. Jackson Weldon. He's my best friend's brother-in-law. I met him at her wedding a little over a year ago. You know how it goes. He was best man and I was the maid of honor and I caught the bouquet and he caught the garter and we had to do the picture thing where he puts the garter on me."

All of her co-workers nodded, their gazes full of expectation. "That's how I met him," Nan said, wincing when her voice warbled a little. Standing up, she went to take her leftovers to the trash, only to discover she hadn't eaten anything yet.

"No, no, no," Candy said, getting up from her chair to shoo Nan back into hers. "You're not getting away so fast, besides, you need to eat. You're looking a little pale. From your tone of voice, you sound as if you need us."

Nan was sure she had to be beet red.

"Candy's right," Sarah said. "All joking aside. If you need to talk we're here, girlfriend. I'm sensing some major things left unsaid. You've always listened to our woes and bolstered us up when we were down. It's about time you counted on us for once."

Nan blinked. Had she done that, only helped and never shared? Had she kept herself isolated? Yes, a small voice inside of her peeped up and then grew louder. Nan drew a deep breath. "We dated then stopped dating because he wants a live by the moment kind of thing and I didn't want to go down a nowhere road. He wants to date again." Nan glanced out the window, only to find that the men had left, gone to lunch apparently.

"I knew it was too good to be true. All those great looks can't make up for a love'em and leave'em mentality. You did the right thing," Darla said.

~~*

*N*an walked in from work and saw Jackson's sunglasses on the table in the hall. She picked them up, her body tingling with the memory of his mouth and his hands upon her naked breast, touching her, making her feel more of a woman than she'd ever felt before.

Geez, when had her practicality turned to melodrama? She needed a damn cold shower. Marching to her bedroom, she tossed his mirrored glasses on her dresser and glared at them. How dare he mess up her life like this? All this sex stuff was driving her crazy. She didn't want a cold shower. She wanted a hot bath. Defiantly, she stripped and filled the tub with piping hot water and honeysuckle oil.

Sinking into the heat she glared at Jackson's glasses peeping at her.

No one knew she was here, and she'd never tell a soul that she had come. She had saved years for this. The small town where life kept passing her by was a thousand miles away. They all thought she was nursing a sick friend, instead, she was nursing her starved soul. She lay on a cushioned chair on the beach, nude, soaking up

*the sun as the breeze caressed her like a lover. During the week
she'd been here, her skin had tanned to a sensual dark and her
peach nipples had turned golden. Her whole body glistened and
waited, wanting more than the breeze could satisfy.*

*She knew he watched. He had every day. The man whose
beach house was next to the one she rented. She'd seen him come
and go in his expensive cars. Seen him on his deck watching. It
made her feel deliciously naughty.*

*Suddenly, something blocked the sun's heat and she opened her
eyes. He stood there, raven-haired and tanned. He was nude as
well, only his eyes were hidden behind the mirrored glasses. But
she didn't need to look into his eyes to gauge his appreciation. He
advertised it as only a man could. And my, did he advertise well.*

*She felt a moment of uncertainty, as if she shouldn't be here.
But all of her life she had waited, waited for that moment of
excitement that stayed just beyond her staid grasp.*

*This wasn't about love. Love always passed her by. This was
sex—pure and simple. This was about the moment, and she forced
herself to grab it even though her heart thundered at the thought.*

*"You want me, baby. Don't you?" She ran a finger from her
lips down between her breasts.*

*"Depends on what you're offering, sugar." He leaned over
and followed her finger with his. She had to force herself to stay
still beneath the heat of his touch.*

*Her blood roared in her ears and liquid fire licked at her
desire. What did she say now? Her mind went blank.*

"A seat?" She slid her legs to one side so he could sit down.

*His answering laugh was deep and full. "That'll do for a
start." Instead of sitting where she'd made room for him, he ran a*

hand down her leg, caught hold of her ankle and slid her leg back to rest along the edge of the chair.

"This suits me better," he said as he nudged her legs off each side of the chair and sat facing her, his knees to her knees.

She gasped and sat up straight. She was completely open to him and he took his time lifting his gaze to hers.

"What's your name, sugar?"

She licked her lips, her mouth dry. "Nan. And yours?"

"Just call me Jack." He cupped her breasts in his hands and thumbed her nipples. She gasped again, automatically arching to him.

"Relax, sugar. We aren't going to do anything you don't want to do." He gently pressed her back against the lounge to where she was almost lying down in from of him. "Today, I think we won't worry about anything else except tasting each other."

His hand slid from her breast and moved down the soft expanse of her stomach until his fingers disappeared into the curls of her sex. "You'd like that, wouldn't you sugar? You'd like me tasting you, making you hot, so hot all you can do is—

An insistent knock reverberated through her apartment. Nan sat up from her bath, shocked and her body throbbing. Someone impatiently knocked on her door again. Her eyes flew to Jackson's sunglasses on her dresser. Was he back to get them?

Pulling on her fuzzy robe, much as she had done just the other morning, she glanced through the peephole and opened the door with a sense of disappointment. "Brad?"

Brad looked up from his watch and frowned. "Nan? You're not ready?

"Ready?" she said, shaking her head confused. She was ready but not for Brad. "For what?" She opened the door wider and Brad stepped inside.

"Our date. Remember Saturday night at the banquet, I told you I wanted to show you something. I believe I said I'd pick you up at six. Surely you didn't forget. That would be so unlike you."

"Sorry, I guess I did. I had a hectic day at work."

"That's rough. Can you hurry? We've an appointment with the real estate agent in twenty minutes."

Nan felt as if she'd drifted into the Twilight Zone. "I'm afraid you've lost me."

"I've bought a house. Well, I will have by tomorrow afternoon. The real estate agent is giving me one more walk through before I close on it. I'd like you to see it and give me your opinion."

A house? They'd shared one kiss and he wanted her opinion of a house? Nan opened her mouth and shut it. She supposed it would be rude to decline.

"I'll be ready in a minute." She swung around and headed back to her bedroom where she threw on some clothes, ever conscious of Jackson's mirrored glasses watching her as she dressed to go with Brad. She could still feel the heat of that damn beach.

For the next two hours, she was privy to exactly what money could buy when you had money to burn. The experience gave her a headache and she was thankful to get back home.

"It's perfect, don't you think?" Brad pulled up before her apartment and shifted his Mercedes in park.

"Yes," Nan said honestly. The house she'd just seen with Brad had been perfect. With large picture windows and thousands of square feet, the house was a marvel of upscale architecture and design. The mini-mansion came completely furnished from fine china in the kitchen to the linens on the antique beds. So why did the house leave her feeling as if something very important was missing?

"Experts put the whole package together. All I have to do is move in."

"It's lovely, but doesn't it bother you that you won't have things around that you've chosen?"

"Not at all. I wanted a perfect show place, besides decorating is a waste of time. Only a man who chooses to spend his time productively can make his mark in the world. That's one thing that impressed me about you. You have a reputation for being the most disciplined and organized nurse in the hospital. They don't hand out the Lois Emerson Merit Award to just anybody and you've managed to get it two years in a row. You know how to plan."

Nan rubbed her temples a moment. She expected a man like Brad to have certain expectations for a mate, just as she did, but he sounded as if he'd come up with a list and was measuring her up to it. "Do you think you can plan every detail of life?"

Brad's eyes widened with surprise. "Of course. Don't you?"

Nan opened her mouth, ready to deny she'd ever approach life with such cold calculation, and promptly shut it when Jackson came roaring up to her apartment on a Harley. He parked directly in front of Brad's Mercedes. Nan's mouth watered. Jackson was as smooth and addictive as melt in your mouth chocolate.

"What's Weldon doing here?"

Unjustified guilt rushed up her cheeks. That Brad took her to see a house he was buying clued her in that his interest in her ran deeper than their relationship called for.

She had no doubt that the kisses she'd shared with Jackson wouldn't make it onto any of Brad's approval lists.

In fact, kissing Jackson had to rank as one of the ten top stupidest things she'd ever done on her own list. But her lists were different from Brad's list. She wasn't as cold and calculating as Brad seemed to be. Brad looked at her, waiting for an explanation as to why Jackson was here.

"Uh, maybe he's here about Alexi. She wasn't feeling too well at the hospital benefit. How do you know him?"

Brad didn't answer her question as he exited the car and came around to open her door. Offering a tense smile of thanks to Brad, she walked over to Jackson

Brad was right behind her.

"Is Alexi all right?" Nan shouted over the motorcycle's rumbling engine. The deep sound vibrated through her body. He wore jeans, black leather chaps, black boots, and a black cotton Tee that had shrunk to a touch-me-tight fit.

Jackson slid off his helmet and ran his hands through his wild black hair. Her fantasy of making love on his Harley while wearing nothing but his black leather jacket came back in spades. She frowned at the unwelcome flush of heat that being this close to him on his Harley triggered and shouted her question again. "Is Alexi okay?"

"Just left her and Jesse. She's fine," he said. A frown of irritation crossed his brow. "Sorry to interrupt your hot date. I came to get my sunglasses off the hall table. If the door is unlocked, I'll just grab them and be out of your way."

"I'll get them. They're in the bedroom." He killed the engine just as she finished her sentence making her last word ring through the air. A dead silence followed.

"Bedroom?" Brad said from just behind her. She could see the question in Jackson's devilishly amused gaze, and she could hear the even bigger question in Brad's surprised voice.

"I didn't want Shakespeare to gnaw on them," Nan muttered.

"What?" said Brad.

"You're kidding, right?" Jackson asked, amusement fading.

"I'll be right back." Nan bit her tongue as she turned around and rushed to her door. Though she dreaded leaving them alone together, the thought of facing Brad that second was worse. What was he thinking? How could she explain about Jackson's glasses being in her bedroom? Considering her fantasies, she had little doubt what Freud would have said about the maneuver. Her headache edged closer to a migraine as she fumbled with the door.

Shakespeare *had* found them. He lay curled up on her dresser with the glasses pinned beneath his paws. Nan quickly snatched them and hurried back. The moment she stepped outside, the world sort of faded before her eyes, and she had to grab the wall to steady herself. A wave of dizziness swept through her. When her vision cleared, she saw Jackson watching her, a serious expression on his face.

"What's wrong?" He took the sunglasses from her and placed a steadying hand on her arm. "You look like you're about to pass out."

"It's nothing. I just got dizzy there for a moment."

"Like at the benefit?" His thumb brushed the inside of her arm.

Nan brought her hand up to her head, escaping his touch before he short-circuited her thought processes again. "Not really. I have a headache. I shouldn't have run."

"Did you eat today?" He brushed her hair back from her face. There was no way she could hide from his direct gaze. "When was the last time you had a checkup? Do you have frequent headaches?"

"Yes, I ate lunch. I'm not sure when my last checkup was. And I suffered migraines as a teenager, but not since. I probably need to relax and get a little fresh air." She looked over Jackson's shoulder. "Where's Brad?"

"Lover boy left for the hospital to the tune of his cell phone." Jackson placed a hand on each of her shoulders and ushered her back inside her apartment, gently squeezing the muscles at the base of her neck. "You're tight as a banjo."

He worked miracles on her neck for a few minutes, then guided her to the big easy chair in her living room and pushed her softly down into its pillowy depths. He stood in front of her and resumed rubbing her shoulders, letting her head rest against his stomach. Her plan to tell him they couldn't see each other wavered like a mirage before her eyes. She couldn't quite grab hold of it right then. His moves were so smooth it turned her blood to liquid honey. He felt like heaven, and he smelled even better.

"So, did you have a date with Swanson?"

"Not really. He took me to see a house he's buying."

Jackson's hands on her neck stilled. "House?"

"Yes, in Garden Hills. He wanted me to see it."

"Bet it's just what you were looking for."

Nan shrugged off his hands and stood. "What's that supposed to mean?"

"Nothing," Jackson muttered.

"For your information, the house was perfect, but I'd never buy it for myself. A house is something that should be a home, a place for family to grow and a reflection of their lives. When I buy a house, it won't be a showplace. What about you?"

"I'm a renting man. No hassles."

No commitment, Nan thought. He slid on his mirrored sunglasses before she could read his expression. A big scratch slashed across one lens and a tuft of cat fur was caught in the nosepiece. Jackson sneezed.

He removed the glasses and glared at them for a long moment, picking off the cat hair. "Sticky buns and sunglasses. Is there anything your cat doesn't eat?"

"Mice. I think the Tom and Jerry reruns he watched as a kitten ruined him."

Jackson shook his head. The next thing Nan would probably say was that she had the cat in therapy. "Come on, let's get you some fresh air." He grabbed her hand and pulled her up.

He should be marching his booted feet out the door without her, but for some damned reason he couldn't seem to walk away from her. Seeing her with Brad grated against Jackson's bad side. He wanted his kiss to be the last thing Nan thought about before she went to sleep. He wanted his touch to be the one lingering on her lush body. And what was Brad showing Nan a damned house for? Garden Hills, no freaking less.

Nan slowed her step. "Where are we going?"

"Wherever the bike can take us. You can't beat a good ride for clearing your head."

"But I'm wearing a skirt."

Jackson turned and ran his gaze over her. She was back to wearing her below the knee skirts and her preppy-crisp shirts. The short, skin hugging dress she'd had on at the benefit had been an aberration, but what about the black satin underwear? The thought that she might just have it on started blood pooling south of his belt.

Damn, the woman was driving him crazy. He knelt and ran his hand up the smooth skin of her leg, taking the hem of her skirt up too. He forced himself to stop before he reached the object of his thoughts.

Nan gasped, but didn't pull away and Jackson took that as a good sign.

"It hikes up good so you shouldn't have a problem. Come on. You need to loosen up a bit." He tugged her hand a little more urgently this time. He had to get out of the apartment quick. He wanted Nan to loosen up all right. He wanted her to be coming apart in his hands several times over and that was just to start with. Seeing her with Brad again had added urgency to his desire to get naked and naughty with her.

CHAPTER EIGHT

*W*inding down the highway with Nan's bare thighs hugging his, the feel of her breasts smashed against his back, and her arms wrapped tightly about his chest did little to ease Jackson's urgent need to bed her. From the way she clung to him and the tentative way she leaned into a curve, he could tell this was her virgin ride. He could also tell that she liked it a lot.

Deciding to enjoy the moment, he put his nagging thoughts aside and savored the feel of the bike and the woman. Over the past few years he'd gotten better at letting everything go and just feeling the moment. It'd been the only way he could survive.

An hour later he pulled to a stop beneath the shady arms of a gnarled oak tree skirting an empty stretch of beach. With the moonlight and the waves to serenade them, the evening was prime for seduction and he was more than ready for a little sex on the beach. Easing down the kick stand, he flexed his shoulders to rub against Nan's breasts and heard a soft gasp of excitement. Seven minutes, he gauged. They'd be well on their way to heaven in seven minutes.

Oh hell, Nan thought as her beach fantasy from earlier came flooding back. *Just sex. Grab the moment.* She wasn't naked and oiled at the moment, but she was definitely hot and bothered. Every part of her thrummed from the ride and the feel of Jackson's back rubbing her breasts. No, she told herself as she sucked in the salty air. Forget that. It was just a fantasy.

She forced herself the concentrate of the beautiful tableau before her. Night had fallen and a cool spring breeze blew lightly in from the ocean. A chorus of crickets and frogs joined the luring music of the sea sweeping to the shore and moonbeams danced upon the silver crests of waves.

The ride had been exhilarating and erotic. Her hair had escaped its neat chignon to hand in a wild mass about her shoulders and her breasts and body ached for more, as if the ride had vibrated something loose inside her.

Sliding from the bike, Jackson helped her off then leaned back against the seat to look out at the sea. "You like the ocean?"

"Love it, though I can't remember the last I stopped to see it at night." Nan turned to the ocean, welcoming the taste of salt in the air and the cool breeze. She burned for his touch and needed to get her mind on something besides having sex on the beach. Beating back her hormones, she searched for some functioning brain cells. "Uh, when did you start working construction?"

"I've done it on and off for a while. Last month, the band decided to just do occasional performances, so I started working for Jared and James more often." Jackson put his hands on her shoulders and started to softly massage them.

Another electric jolt sizzled through her. "Like it?" she asked, only capable of forming two syllables.

"Hadn't thought about it. It's money for a while. You like nursing?" He pulled her back, and she leaned against his hard body, feeling the heat of him to her core.

"Um, yeah. Being able to uh, help people is great, but, um, the staffing problems, uh, make the job needlessly difficult." She sounded as if her mind had gone kaput. Thankfully, he stopped the sensual, rhythmic caresses on her shoulders and she breathed with relief. But that only lasted a second before he spun her around to face him.

The wind ruffled his dark hair like the hand of a lover and the moonlight caressed the strong planes of his face, playing shadows over the full curve of his lips and the cleft in his chin. She tumbled headlong into her desire for him.

He brushed his lips over hers. "You should work less and do a few things like this."

She tried to save herself by talking. "I have a list of fun things. I just haven't gotten to them yet."

"Nan, throw the damned list away and just do it."

Before she could respond, Jackson pulled her up against him and started kissing her with the hottest need she'd ever felt from a man. Every part of her that wasn't already throbbing from the ride tingled. She met him kiss for kiss.

The man was so smooth he slid inside a woman and invaded her every pore. By the time they came up for air, she was plastered against his side and his right hand cupped her left breast, teasing her aroused nipple with the pad of his thumb.

She moaned with pleasure, and swore she heard him growl before his mouth came down hard on hers. At the end of his second kiss she was ready to drag him into the sand. Never in her life had she been this needy, not even when all of her teenage hormones had raged. She was a woman over ready for a man and it seemed the only man her body wanted was Jackson. In her book the mind was supposed to dominate the body, but Jackson was rewriting the pages. Right that minute, enough hot, heavy sex to get him out of her system sounded really good.

"I want you." She pulled up his shirt, caressing his bare skin.

He groaned, going after the buttons of her shirt. Pushing the cups of her bra to the side, he exposed her breasts, and leaned over to gently nip her aroused peaks, then eased her nipples with the

brush of his tongue. Nan's knees buckled from the intense
pleasure. He caught her with his left arm and shoulder and slid his
right hand up her skirt to cup her sex over her underwear. It was
hard to tell which was hotter, his hand or her. He started to rub her
lightly, an easy, but insistent back and forth motion over her sex.
Her hips rocked with him, pressing against his and the hard, jean
clad muscle of his thigh. Lost in her need, she arched to him,
wanting more. He gave her more. Sliding his hand beneath her
panties, he eased his finger into her sensitive groove. A cry of
excitement escaped her; her heart pounded so hard she thought she
would faint from the pleasure.

"Let's go for a ride, sugar," he said gruffly. Cupping her
bottom, he pressed her sex tighter against his fingers and rubbed.
At the same time, he teased her lips and the tips of her breasts with
light sucking kisses. Nan shook with the release rocking her soul.
She continued to moan, and Jackson buried his face in her neck.

"Damn, woman. I can't seem to stop myself around you." He
took her hand and pressed it to his erection. He was as hot as the
midday sun. "There's a whole lot more to come."

A blush heated her cheeks, but she didn't move her hand.
Instead, she cupped him, and he pressed himself harder against her.
Already she wanted more from him, more of him. She moved her
fingers to the snap of his fly.

Jackson tried to suck some air into his lungs so he could think.
Nan in no way resembled the woman he'd put on his Harley
earlier. Her neat bun had become a wild mane. Her prim skirt was
hiked up to her hips and her modest shirt hung open, letting the
moonlight bathe her full breasts. She'd never been more beautiful.
He wanted her. Wanted to lay her back into the soft sand and bury
himself deep inside of her again and again. He could still hear the
pant of her breath and the cry of her release echo in his mind.

Three months ago, two days ago, hell even two minutes ago, he would have done just that. But having had a taste of her, he wanted more than just one roll in the sand. Seeing her in Brad's Mercedes and watching the man walk behind her with a proprietary air irked Jackson. She didn't belong with Brad.

He threaded his fingers through hers, and pressed her hand against his throbbing erection. He couldn't ever remember needing a woman as much as he needed her. In the three months since she'd left him behind in Salty's Bar, he'd had plenty of time and opportunity to find out that it was Nan he craved and no other. A good month or two in the sack should work her out of his system. He rubbed her hand against his fly, then lifted her fingers to his lips. Her skin was soft and silky and the musk-like fragrance of her sex clung to his hand. He breathed deeply of her, wanted to taste her, and almost lost hold of his new resolve. He started buttoning her blouse.

"If I go any further, sugar, you'll hate me in the morning. I want you choosing me when you're thinking straight and not when I've bulldozed you into my bed. Forever isn't in the cards, but I want more than just one night. Come to Jesse's birthday party Friday night, and spend the weekend with me working out this craziness in our blood."

"But—"

He touched his finger to her lips, stilling her protest. "Wear that black underwear you had on the other night. Now hop on. I need to get you home before I change my mind."

She didn't argue, and he made fast time getting her home. The ride wasn't the same, though. She held herself stiffly from him and didn't say anything as he walked her to the door, helping her unlock it. He didn't mean to hurt her feelings. She had to know how much he wanted her.

Nan opened her door, turning to him, and he leaned over to kiss her, whispering softly, "Tonight was incred—"

"A mistake." She planted a finger in the center of his chest and pushed him back.

"What the hell?" He rubbed his chest, thoroughly confused.

"I'm not sixteen, I'm not drunk. I'm a thirty-year-old woman who isn't a pushover. I don't need you deciding how I'm going to feel in the morning. Thank you for the ride." She slammed the door in his face.

He stood there for a minute stunned. How in the hell had he become the bad guy when he'd tried to do the right thing? He muttered and cursed as he stomped back to his bike.

Sitting on his seat like he was king of the road was Shakespeare.

Jackson glared at the beast, swearing horns sprouted from the cat's head as he watched. The cat dug his claws into the bike's leather seat and hissed when Jackson moved to take him off. "Damn! Go easy on the seat, will ya? Let's have a man to cat talk here. You crossed the line when you licked my buns, and it pissed me off that you scratched my glasses, but unless you want to be strung up as shark bait stay off the bike."

Jackson heard Nan gasp. She'd come back outside. She ran over and snatched up her cat. "Don't threaten Shakespeare."

He was a fool. He should have taken Nan when he had the chance. If he'd had a damn lick of sense they would still be at the beach going hot and heavy. "I didn't threaten the damn cat, I just laid out some ground rules."

"His name is Shakespeare. Why don't you like him?"

"I didn't say I didn't like him." How in the hell had she come to that conclusion? He rubbed his hands over his face. "I don't even know the cat."

"Shakespeare."

"Shakespeare then. I don't know what has you so mad. I don't think you're a push over. But I do want *you* in my bed for longer than just the spur of the moment. I want to make love until we're both in a mindless oblivion. So you think about that before you write me off that approved list of yours and maybe I'll see you Friday." He mounted his motorcycle and roared off. Hell, women weren't from Venus. Their damn reasoning was so far out there, they had to be from Pluto at the very least.

Nan hugged Shakespeare to her breast. Considering Shakespeare had probably gouged a hole or two in Jackson's seat, the man had shown remarkable restraint. But it irked her he was making her choose to have an affair with him rather than just sweep her off her feet. And what in the world possessed him to tell her that she had an approved list?

He'd probably done her a big favor tonight. Had probably saved her from making a mistake. Maybe she'd be more grateful after a cold shower. So what if he would have been right about her regretting things in the morning. At least she wouldn't have this unfulfilled ache inside.

~~*

*T*wo days and numerous cold showers later, Nan wasn't any better off and she wasn't in any better a mood. She pulled up to Alexi and Jesse's house and told herself she was relieved that Jackson's truck and his damned bike were nowhere in sight. Every day outside the nurses' station she saw him working, caught the gleam of sunshine on his tanned muscles and had to listen to the ohhs and ahhs of her co-workers as they ate him alive with their hungry gazes. Nan was loath to admit that deep inside she was eating him up with the best of them. In the space of seventy-two hours she'd mentally made love to Jackson no less than a dozen times, and they'd been on his motorcycle to boot.

Even writing all of the fantasies in her book had done little to purge him from her mind. Friday kept looming larger and larger on the horizon and her heart kept beating faster and faster with anticipation. Would she spend the weekend with him? Could she? How did one throw caution to the wind and just do it?

When she'd returned from her wild ride with Jackson Monday night, she'd found that Brad had left a message on her answering machine. He'd said he would call while he was out of town and had reminded her about the yachting party in two weeks. He ended his call telling her they needed to talk as soon as he found the time.

Be it Jackson's influence, or Brad's recent behavior, she was seeing Brad with different eyes. He wasn't just a man absorbed with his career as she'd first thought. He planned life to the point that it bordered on obsessive. And she had to wonder if she was anything more than a calculated decision on his part. Had he asked her out because he liked her, or because she'd achieved the distinct honor of being the first person to earn the Lois Emerson Merit Award twice? Was Brad even aware of her on a physical or a personal level? At least physically Jackson left her no doubt that he was very aware of her.

She was in big trouble. The GQ man with the IQ to match was having less and less appeal and the smooth southern bad boy was almost more than she could resist. She feared that rather than sticking to the high road, she was about to take a wrong fork that would lead her to a dead end. If the ride was anything like the one Jackson gave her the other night on his motorcycle, she was a goner. The wild exhilaration had appealed to her more than she wanted to admit. She had just reached the point in her career at which she felt established. Now she could look to doing some of the fun things she had listed, like taking a gourmet cooking class, or vacation to a new place, or learn a second language, or even take a creative writing class—all good safe things.

She sighed. She'd rather kiss Jackson on a moonlit beach or a sun scorching one for that matter.

Alexi stepped outside and waddled her way over before Nan could gather her thoughts and get out of the car.

"Boy, am I glad to see you!"

"Why?" Nan smiled at Alexi's method of fitting her rotund figure into the passenger's seat—a one leg at a time scoot. She'd grown larger in just two weeks.

"Jesse has hovered and fussed this week until I feel like I'm smothering. It's a wonder he didn't chain me to the couch. Believe me, this play tonight is a Godsend." Once in, Alexi leaned back and shut her eyes.

"Don't forget to buckle up." Nan backed out of the drive, turning her BMW onto the coastal road leading them off Tybee Island, back the few miles to Savannah. She and Alexi planned to stop for seafood before going to see *A Midsummer Night's Dream* at the outdoor Shakespeare Festival. "Jesse can't be fussing over you that badly."

"You don't know the half of it," Alexi gasped, short of breath.

Seeing the dark circles under her friend's eyes and the tense lines of stress on her face, Nan held her tongue and quickly drove them to the restaurant. Luckily they were eating early enough to avoid the dinner rush and were seated immediately at a table overlooking the Intercoastal Waterway. Gulls flew by, fat white clouds dotted the hazy blue horizon, and crusty pelicans hovered, looking for a tasty fish to flash on the shimmering water.

"How are you feeling?"

"I'm tired. It's harder to get comfortable at night, and once I do get comfortable enough to sleep, I have to wake up and go to the bathroom because junior here has decided to play football with my bladder. I'm out of sorts and want my baby now. I don't want to wait another month. Can you imagine how big I'm going to be then?" Alexi picked up the menu. "I'm starving. The fried shrimp and fish platter looks great, doesn't it?"

"Baked," Nan said. Alexi looked as if she'd gained about ten more pounds. "You need the protein, not the fats. And no salt. When did you last see the doctor?"

"Today." Alexi rolled her eyes. "I should have left you at home with Jesse. Scratch that. You're too gorgeous to leave at home with my husband while I'm looking like a beached whale."

"Does Jesse have a Harley?"

"A motorcycle?"

"Yeah."

"No, not since he was in high school."

"Then don't worry. Jesse is safe." Nan picked up her glass of water. She had to go and open her big mouth didn't she? Now she'd have Jackson on her mind the rest of the evening.

"My goodness, I think there's more to the story than Jackson said."

Nan choked on her water. "What do you mean by that?" she wheezed out.

"Just mentioned he gave you your first ride the other night. Did you enjoy it?"

Nan swiped her napkin off the table and dabbed the perspiration off her flushing brow. "It?"

"The bike."

"Oh, the bike. Yeah, it was…great."

"What else?" Alexi narrowed her eyes.

"Nothing else, absolutely nothing," Nan squeaked. "Tell me what's going on with Jesse."

"I think you're lying through your teeth. Jackson had a long talk with Jesse the day after the hospital benefit and Jesse hasn't left my side since."

"I assume that this talk was about leaving you at home alone. I have to agree with Jackson on this one. You're too far along in your pregnancy. Four weeks is nothing when it comes to babies. We get women into the Labor and Deliver Department all the time that go into labor well before their due date. We fuss because we love you."

"I know. I worry, too. About the baby and the delivery and if everything will go all right. And then there's afterward. Will I be a good mom?"

"You'll be a great mom." Nan leaned forward and grasped Alexi's fingers. "I don't mean to scare you. Just keep in close contact with your doctor and do as she prescribes."

"Do you think I can get a prescription for Godivas?"

"We'll share a box and a bottle of bubbly in about six months."

"Six months? That's too depressing. Let's change the subject. If you're biking with Jackson where does that leave Brad?"

Nan shrugged. She'd wondered the same thing herself. "I'm not sure that I'm really anywhere with him. He took me to see 'the perfect' house he's buying, then left town saying he would call.

We're supposed to go yachting the weekend after next with Dr. Dennison. You know the plastic surgeon who keeps the aging young?"

"I've heard of him. Are you going to go?"

"I'm not sure. Part of me wants to and part of me doesn't. Brad seems to have this checklist of perfect traits for a perfect mate and perfect kids. He has everything all figured out, planned to the last detail. There's very little room in his life for the human factor."

"Human factor?"

"You know, the fun, the spontaneity; the concept that it's okay to be less than perfect. I don't think I would enjoy life very much if I had to constantly measure up to something. Yet on the other hand I'd be completely miserable if I didn't have goals. Go figure."

"You want to live in the middle and not in the extremes."

"Put that way, it makes sense."

"If you ask me, people living in the extremes seem like they're going to fall off the edge."

"Speaking of living on the edge, the only information I get about Jackson comes from you. He's very adept at leaving little time for conversation. We hardly talk."

"That good, huh?"

"That frustrating. I consider myself an intelligent woman until Jackson is around. Now I don't know what I am, or much about him. Is he still grieving for his wife? How long ago did she die?"

"About four years ago. The family doesn't talk about it much, and since I'm new to the family I haven't done much pushing on the subject. Jesse keeps saying Jackson just needs some time and we need to respect that. I think it goes deeper."

"In what way? Was he driving? Was he in the accident?"

"No and yes. He was with her, but she was driving. It happened in Chicago. After the accident, he left his internship at Chicago General and moved back to Georgia."

Surprise hit Nan at first, but then once she recalled all the little details the dots connected. Dennison's question to Brad, Jackson's behavior when she fainted, and his knowledge of preeclampsia when she described some of the problems Alexi was having. "It takes a lot more than just a drifting good-timing attitude about life to become a doctor. So why is Jackson out hammering nails and strumming a guitar now?"

Alexi shrugged.

The question plagued Nan throughout the play and for the next two days. Why had he given it all up? Was he so devastated by his wife's death? She watched Jackson work outside the Nurse's Station's window by day and began to note little things that showed her he had probably been a very good doctor. It was in the way he looked at the people around him. She sensed he really saw them, and listened to them. And when he was with her, he had left her no doubt he was very aware of her. Brad made a brilliant surgeon, but was he aware of her as a person?

During the nights, she dreamed about Jackson's passion, his kisses, and the depth of the desire between them. What in the world was she going to do? The man was not only consuming her thoughts but was encroaching upon her heart as steadily as the ocean swept across the shore. The weekend loomed. What would she do?

CHAPTER NINE

Nan threw her black book of fantasies on the bed and paced across the room. The last two fantasies she'd written had scared her. They were just as sensual as before, but another element was easing into the text that was decidedly more personal.

Her pen had filled the pages of the book with her physical wants, and secret sensual desires, desires she never even knew she had. All of the fantasies centered on one man, Jackson. And she'd been okay with that. A woman would have to be dead not to respond to him. But the stories were starting to become more than just about sex and the emotional needs emerging frightened her.

If she didn't leave now, she would be late to Jesse's birthday party. D-day had arrived. It was Friday evening and she still hadn't made up her mind whether to stay the weekend with Jackson. Part of her wanted to stay, play out her fantasies and get him out of her system and another part of her feared she would lose more to him than she could afford. Like her heart. No, it was just sex. She wouldn't let it be anything more than that. She'd take the plunge and then she'd be able to settle down with a respectable man out living life rather than hiding from it as her father had done.

It was just sex she told herself again as she stuffed her fantasy book back under her pillow and snatched up an overnight bag, cramming things into it. Minutes later, she turned the corner to the hall and encountered a flurry of activity.

"Shakespeare!" Nan wailed. Miracle of miracles her casserole on the hall table remained unscathed, but the wrapping and ribbons on Jesse's present were flying in the air like fur in a catfight.

"Meow." Shakespeare flicked his tail, then jumped up and sat on the present as the paper rained down on him.

She glared at him. She didn't have any more wrapping paper and she didn't have time to stop and buy more. "Maybe Jackson's idea of a few ground rules wasn't so bad. I won't string you up for shark bait, but you won't get any tuna treats either. You're lucky Mrs. Brodrick next door is going to feed you this weekend."

Shakespeare purred as she picked him up and she couldn't resist giving the silly cat a hug before she set him down. Even as a kitten he'd gone from one disastrous mess to another, but she loved him anyway. The thought stopped Nan in her tracks. What if she had had a list of traits she expected her pet to have? What if she had expected Shakespeare to live up to her perfect idea of a cat? Would she have him to love now?

Disturbed by the new idea and the thought she may have done just exactly that to Jackson, she gathered everything and wrestled her way out the door. The phone rang and Nan popped her head back inside. Brad's voice piped over the answering machine. Had he called at any other time this week, she would have welcomed the chance to speak to him. But he hadn't called and now that she was on her way to see Jackson, she didn't want to talk to Brad. She locked the door.

~~*

Sitting on the porch of his parent's farm with his three brothers, Jackson took a long swig of beer. Party balloons and crepe paper hung from one end of the wooden beams to the other and inside he could hear the comfortable chaos of his mother bustling about getting ready for the shindig. That was one thing that could be counted on in life. Emma Weldon knew how to have a country hoe down better than anybody did.

Out back, his father had BBQ ribs and pork cooking over huge spits. John Weldon's BBQ stood unmatched in the south. Picnic tables were draped with bright red and white checked cloths, and bales of hay had been spread over the southern red dirt to make the ground just right for two stepping to the twang of a hot fiddle.

He should be happy with his life the way he'd set it up. He had no cares, no responsibilities. He did what he wanted, when he wanted. So why in the hell was he so insistent on tangling up with Nan? Why not just let her go?

Even if he were of the mind to have an ongoing relationship, she'd be a bad choice. She'd already walked away once and he had no doubt she'd do it again. Not that he could blame her. Few people could live life as casually as he chose to live it these days and he'd never go back to his old ways. Not for anything. So what in the hell did he expect to get out of this weekend?

Nan. He wanted her. For so damn long after Amy died he'd felt nothing but pain, then the pain sank into a sea of numbness and he'd developed a take-it or leave-it indifference about life and women. At least he had until Nan appeared. Indifference was one thing he'd yet to feel about her.

What would he do if Nan didn't show? It had nearly killed him to ride away last Monday, and he'd tortured himself with thoughts of her all week. Every day that he worked on the hospital wing, he was aware she was inside, behind the closed doors. Did she know he was out there?

"What's gotten into you lately, big brother?" Jared came up and punched Jackson in the arm.

"Ouch." Jackson rubbed his shoulder. "What are you talking about?"

"You've cut your hair for one, and you've shown up for work every damn day this week." Jared parked his large frame smack dab in front of Jackson, crossed his arms, and planted his booted feet in an I'm-not-going-to-move-until-you-fess-up stance.

"You're also on time for the birthday party," James, Jared's twin joined in. Hell, Jackson thought, his younger brothers were like bulldogs when they got a hold of something.

"You never cut your hair until Mom hog-ties you to do it."

"You haven't worked a week solid in years."

"And you're never on time for a party. In fact you were an hour late to your own birthday party."

James leaned in, taking a big whiff. "You smell good."

Jared squatted down. "I think I've figured it out, James."

James joined Jared to stare at Jackson's boots. "He gave his boots more than a spit shine. Those suckers are gleaming."

They looked at each other, grinned, and spoke at the same time. "A woman."

Seeing that his brother Jesse, who sat grinning on the porch swing wasn't going to be any help, Jackson hiked his bottom up on the rail behind him and gave his brothers a light kick, knocking them onto their butts. "Don't sell the construction company, guys. The world isn't ready for you two No-Shit-Sherlocks. We're Irish and we're Weldons. There's always a woman."

"True," Jared stood, brushing his backside.

"Yeah," James concurred, opting to stay seated on the floor, and leaning his back against the porch post. "But when a man starts changing his routine, then the woman is more than just 'a woman.' Right, Jesse? It hasn't been too long since Alexi turned your routine upside down."

"Yeah," Jesse agreed. "There's one more thing you all need to add. We're Irish, Weldons, and too damn stubborn for our own good. A boot shine and a hair cut aren't going to be worth a flip in the long run."

"Hell," Jared said. "Alexi has ruined Jesse for life. The man's going philosophical on us."

Jackson looked over to where Jesse sprawled. Jesse's comment had been directed right at him. Things between them had been a bit uncomfortable since their talk after the hospital benefit. Jesse wanted to know more than Jackson could say.

Jared let out a wolf whistle. "Ooo wee. Here comes a babe. Who is she?"

Jackson swung his gaze out to the driveway. Nan had just stepped from the car. She turned her back and leaned in, apparently to gather a few things out of the passenger's seat. The short skirt she wore rose up. Jackson's beer bottle fell from his hand, clattered to the floor, and spewed over with foam. Nan never wore short skirts. This one covered the essentials, but just barely. Jackson was on his feet in a second.

James scrambled up from the floor. "Remember from Jesse's wedding? It's Alexi's friend, the nurse. Man, I'd love to have some of her TLC."

"Yeah, she looks as if she has a bedside manner to die for. Give me some mouth to mouth, baby," Jared added.

Jackson stopped at the end of the porch and glared at his brothers. "Hit on her and I'll plaster you both to the wall."

James and Jared held up their hands and backed away.

"Guess we found 'the woman,'" Jared muttered.

"No, shit Sherlock," James added. "Why is it our brothers find all the babes first?"

Jesse stood. "Bide your time, boys. The way Jackson's going he won't have her for long."

Jackson turned away disgusted. It didn't matter what Jesse thought. Jackson wasn't looking for long term anyway. He crossed the driveway, making sure he kept his body between the view of the porch and Nan's barely covered bottom.

"Need help, sugar?" He came up behind her, close enough that when she backed out to stand up her bottom slid nicely against his fly.

She gasped, but he didn't feel the least bit sorry. He'd waited too long for her already.

"Here." She turned around and stuffed a package into his hands that looked as if it had been through a paper shredder.

"Don't tell me. Shakespeare helped you wrap it."

"He did a good job, don't you think?" She picked up a casserole dish and her purse, leaving a large tote bag still in the car. She wore her hair loose in a mass of fiery waves that smelled like sunshine and honeysuckle.

"That cat is a master," Jackson said, leaning closer. His gaze zeroed in on the overnight bag and his already hot blood revved up. If he didn't miss his guess, Nan had come prepared to spend the weekend with him.

~~*

*A*lexi stood at the head of the table and patted her stomach. "I have an announcement to make."

"Little late for confessions, Lexi," James called out.

"Looks like Jesse has made you a walking announcement," Jared added.

Laughter followed the remarks and Alexi joined the cheer.

"She looks good," Nan said to Jackson. He sat in the lounge chair next to her with his long legs stretched out and his arm across the back of her seat.

Jackson brushed his thumb against the bare skin of her arm. "When I talked to her this morning, she said she was feeling a lot better."

Nan snuggled into his embrace. Every nerve in her body crackled with awareness, and she had to fight the whole evening long for coherency.

Any single woman would have a hard time staying sane around the Weldon brothers. They were all raven hair, hot-eyed temptation in boots. And they left no doubt the devil had made it to Georgia and spawned four men guaranteed to lead a woman astray.

Nan couldn't get his passion out of her mind. Pretending for three months that he didn't exist anywhere but in her fantasies hadn't helped. So maybe making love would. Maybe once she knew his touch completely, then she could get on with her life—a been there, done that, sort of thing. So why did she feel that she wasn't just throwing caution to the wind? Why did she feel as if she were blasting caution all the way to outer space?

Alexi clapped her hands to quiet the laughter and the jokes to finish her announcement. "John and Emma, and Dad," she said getting the attention of her in-laws and her father. "Jesse and I found out today that you're going to have a grandson."

Nan saw Jackson's mom and dad smile and hug. By Alexi's father's grin and puffed chest, you'd think he was the one having the baby. The sense of family between the Weldon's went straight to Nan's heart. She had no family, no parents. She'd have no moments like these and it hurt.

Alexi continued. "Next, Jesse and I would like for Jackson and Nan to be the baby's Godparents."

Nan sat up in surprise, a rush of joy flooding her heart. She and Alexi were close friends, but that Alexi would entrust her with so dear a responsibility, touched Nan's heart. She heard a moan of pain next to her and looked at Jackson. She couldn't tell exactly what he thought about being a Godparent, but it didn't look good. He had his face buried into the palms of his hands and he was rubbing his eyes.

Nan suddenly realized everyone was waiting for her to respond. She stood, sort of blocking Jackson from the eyes of the group. "I'm honored. I only hope that I'll be as good a Godparent to Jesse junior as Alexi and Jesse are friends to me."

"Thank you," Jackson said as he stood up next to her. His voice was gruff and filled with tension. Once the crowd moved their attention back to Alexi and Jesse, Nan brushed her hand through Jackson's jet-black hair. What about being a godparent caused him anguish? "Are you okay?"

Her caring touch seemed to surprise him. He caught her hand in his and brought her fingers to his lips. The need in his eyes went way beyond the physical. Nan saw into his soul and she saw a man in pain.

He drew a deep breath. "Yeah. Let's dance, sugar."

As he pulled her into his arms and she felt the beat of his heart against her cheek. She knew then, she would spend the weekend with him. She had to have answers to her questions and a weekend of just sex, might help her get him out of her mind. Sort of like a hair of the dog that bit her type thing.

A slow song played softly, and she melted into his embrace. His touch held as much magic and warmth as the moonlit summer night. He pulled her close to his hard muscle and everything inside of her reached out to him. She had no idea how long they swayed or if the music changed.

"Let's go," Jackson whispered in her ear.

"Where?"

"To dance. I know a better place and a better song."

From the smooth, deep sexy rumble of his voice, Nan had no doubt that the time had come to go with Jackson to his cabin. She followed him, but kept in the background as they said good night. She felt a bit odd, though at thirty it shouldn't bother her that others knew she was leaving the party with Jackson. When they stopped to see Jesse and Alexi, Nan could tell they were both worried about Jackson.

"We need to talk," Jesse said to Jackson. Nan watched the men's intense blue gazes measure each other.

Alexi stepped forward, her brow creased and a troubled depth lay in her eyes. She hugged Jackson. "We didn't mean to upset you. We should have thought to ask you in private."

Jackson patted Alexi to comfort her, but stepped back from her after a short hug. "You surprised me. I'll need to think about it. I can't promise anything," he said to Alexi and then turned to Jesse. "I don't have any more to say."

"We still need to talk. I'll call you later."

"Later then." Jackson took Nan's hand. She quickly leaned over and gave Alexi a hug.

"Call me," Alexi whispered and Nan nodded.

Jackson led the way from the party out into the darkened perimeter. Nan searched her mind for the best way to ask him what lay behind his dark moments. "Jack, why—"

"Shh. I've been aching to do this all night, all week." They'd reached the driveway. He pulled her up against his body and lowered his lips to hers, effectively staving off any questions. He kissed her thoroughly with a needy, tender roughness that had her desire burning. She panted for air by the time he ended the kiss as a shivery with anticipation tingled and burned through her erogenous zones like a flash fire.

"Follow me, sugar." He released her and walked to his Harley, looking way too calm for her peace of mind. He seated himself and gave her a questioning look. She hadn't moved.

"You coming?"

Jackson clearly thought she was having second thoughts. Trouble was she was having second, third, and fourth thoughts about making love to him on his motorcycle. She couldn't wait to get him where she wanted him and if she didn't hurry she was going to strip him naked right there in his parent's yard. Smiling, she turned around, and walked to her car, making very sure she added enough hip action to her stride to cause the hem of her skirt to bounce.

As she followed him, she realized that for the first time in her life she was headed down a road that she had no idea where it would end, but she was having fun.

~~*

Ten minutes later, they pulled up in front of a small cabin. Jackson reached her car and opened her door before she could. A grin tugged her lips. He obviously wasn't giving her any room to change her mind and kept brushing tantalizing circles on her hip as he walked her to his door.

"I didn't realize that you live so close to your parents."

"Actually, it's a cabin on the backside of the farm. I like it here, very private, very secluded. Besides my parents, the nearest neighbor is a mile or so away." They walked up onto the quaint little porch and Jackson unlocked the door. "Wait here," he said, then disappeared inside, shutting the door.

Nan blinked in surprise. She expected Jackson to be tearing her clothes off by now, just as she wanted to attack him. Instead, she was left standing alone on his porch. After what seemed like an eternity, but had probably only been a minute, Jackson came back and opened the door.

"Okay, you can come in now." He pushed the door wider.

The furnishings were sparse and it appeared to be a one room deal with a four poster bed in one corner and a small refrigerator, microwave, and hot plate in the other, but that wasn't what drew her attention. About the room there were dozens of lit candles emitting a spicy aroma. A bottle of champagne sat on ice in what looked like an old cow milking bucket, and spread out on the little dinette table were small dishes of cheese, crackers, whipped cream and strawberries. She blinked away threatening tears. He'd obviously gone to a lot of trouble to plan their evening, and the romantic simplicity of his gesture reached deep inside of her, touching her heart. "This is wonderful," she said, her voice husky with emotion.

"No, you're wonderful." He flipped the power button on his boom box and soft, slow music filled the small room. "Come here, Nan."

Nan liked Jackson's wonderful a whole lot more than Brad's pleasant. She dropped her purse and walked into Jackson's arms. For a long moment he hugged her tight and then he began to sway and step to the music. She released a sigh of pure pleasure. He felt so, so good.

His voice was low at first then grew to a deep sexy timbre as he sang to her, dancing intimately beneath the flicker of candlelight. He stepped true to the beat of the song. Her step lagged a bit as she relaxed into him, but that seemed to be okay with him. He just molded himself to her, and kept on dancing, and the longer they swayed, adjusting to each other, the more in tune they moved.

When they'd dated before, their relationship had been casual and looking back on it, Nan had to admit almost impersonal. There'd been no sticky bun breakfast, motorcycle rides, or romantic candlelight. His band had been doing a six-week stint at a local bar and she'd gone to see him sing. They'd done a movie or two, ate dinner a few times, and spent a lot of time kissing. Jackson had been angling to get horizontal and she'd been set on something more than heating up the sheets. Between his night schedule and her day one, there'd been little time.

So what made the difference this time? Why was she here, about to make lo—have sex with him? They weren't officially dating. Jackson was still angling for the horizontal and as far as she could tell his hot sheets were never going to lead to a warm home and hearth.

Was it because no matter what she'd done she hadn't been able to get the man out of her mind? Or was he different? Did she see a vulnerability to him she hadn't seen before? She supposed she was here because of a combination of those things and because she had to have an answer to all of the questions Jackson provoked. And yes, the fantasies were part of it, too. He stirred something deep within her she hadn't known existed, a part of herself she was almost afraid to face.

The music changed and his voice deepened. Her heart started to beat faster as her body became more and more aware of his heated muscles and musky scent. It was the song he'd sung at the hospital benefit. As he had before, he changed the words. "Lady, I want you. Lady, I need you. You're the only one I care enough to dream about."

Nan shut her eyes and drew in some air. If he only knew how much he had filled her dreams. He kissed her next, his lips warm, his breath intoxicating. Tenderly he massaged, working his hands up to the back of her neck and inside the collar of her blouse. Her blood raced until stole all of her thoughts and all of her doubts away. For better or for worse, whether this would be a mistake or not, she couldn't fight her attraction to this man any longer. Be it a day, a week, or a month, she had to have an answer to what he made her feel.

The liberation to enjoy the moment hit her blood stream like a heady aphrodisiac. She kissed him, threaded her fingers through his silky hair, and pressed her body close to his. His fingers trailed from her nape to the pulse pounding in her throat, then dipped lower. She arched to him and he opened the first two buttons of her blouse. His mouth followed his fingers, and his tongue tantalized her skin all the way to the front clasp of her black bra.

"You're beautiful," he said cupping her breasts through the cotton of her shirt and bra. "So hot, so soft, and smooth."

She moaned. Never in her life had she felt so sexy and free. He stepped back, his demanding gaze met hers, and he sang another verse, again using his own words. "Lately I've been thinking. Lately, I've been hoping that you'll share with me everything you've got to give."

Deep inside her the need to meet his demand on an equal level stirred. Not only did she want to be seduced, but she wanted to do the seducing, too. She released her hold on his shoulders and without moving her gaze from his, finished unbuttoning her blouse, letting it slide off her shoulders to the floor. She then did the same to his shirt, touching his chest, his nipples, running her finger down the trailing line of soft black hair disappearing into the waistband of his jeans. She reveled in the play of candlelight on his smooth sun-darkened skin, kissing and licking wherever she could.

He placed her hand over his erection. "Lady I need ya. Lady I'm dying. Can't you see what you're doing to me?"

"Me too," she said softly. Taking his hand she placed it on the bare skin of her thigh, and then guided him up under her skirt to settle over the heat of her sex. Her action seemed to snap his control. He groaned and time became a whirlwind.

He quickly removed her skirt and bra, trailing tiny kisses over her shoulders, leaving little love bites on her waist. When she stood in nothing but her heels and her black lace underwear, he backed away from her, circled her, and then moved toward her like a hungry lion about to devour. "You're beautiful, and so damn sexy," he growled.

She stopped him with a hand to his chest. "Your jeans," she whispered. "Take them off."

First went the boots, then the jeans, leaving only his briefs.

"Everything," she said as he started her way. "Take it all off."

He stopped a second, raised his brow at the insistence in her voice then followed her instructions. When he finished, she moved, walking around him. From the broad curve of his shoulders to the narrow flare of his hips, he was all man, hard muscle, jutting erection. He was elemental male and beautiful.

She moved up behind him and pressed herself to him, snaking her hands around to cup and stroke his arousal.

He groaned, leaning back into her and rocking his erection in her hands. "Are you trying to kill me?"

She laved the back of his ear with her tongue and whispered, "Maybe I want you. Maybe I need you. Maybe you're the only one who can satisfy me."

"Maybe?" he growled. He shot out of her teasing embrace and whipped around. The next instant he wrapped his arms around her waist and lifted her up. In four steps he crossed the room and tossed her on the bed, then he pinned her to the soft mattress with his hard body.

"Maybe?" he asked again just before his mouth found her nipple and he began to suck and tease while his hand located her other breast, massaging it to a throbbing peak. Then he devoured her. There was no other word for it. She couldn't think, all she could do was feel.

He soothingly laved each nipple with his tongue only to pluck it to an aching point with his fingers again and again. He had her writhing with need, arching up from the bed with her desperation to have him inside her before he moved lower. Her exquisite torture had only just begun.

He covered her lace panties with puffs of hot breath, making her feel his heat, making her anticipate his touch. Then he turned her over and maddeningly moved back up to the nape of her neck. Little love bites sizzled down her spine and pooled into a hot, wet, burning heat between her legs. She was on fire and he was the only man who could save her.

She wiggled against him, her face nuzzling the mattress, even as her hand dug desperately into the sheets. "Jack, now," she called to him, needing him inside her.

"Maybe?" he asked, softly, infuriatingly and started to knead her buttocks.

Paybacks were both heaven and hell.

"Ever since I saw you up against my truck in this," he slid his finger underneath her underwear. "I've been burning like a man on fire."

Nan jolted with pleasure, her hips lifting off the bed. That was it, she couldn't take anymore. She flipped over, pushing her underwear off and pulled him down.

Amusement gleamed in his blue eyes. "Maybe?" he asked again.

She sighed. "No maybes about it. Make love to me, Jack."

"Never thought you'd ask, sugar." He sat back on his knees, slid on a condom he'd had under his pillow. She welcomed him as he covered her body with his, driving satisfyingly inside her.

Nan arched up to him, and he pushed deeper. He was hot and needy and determined to thrust her to heaven. She felt as if he went straight to her soul. His hands cupped her breasts, teased her nipples, caressed her everywhere and just when she thought she would shatter from the pleasure, he slid his thumb over her sensitive, needy heart of her sex. Within three strokes she came apart and shuddered against him with the force of her release.

"Keep on riding, baby." He latched a hand on each side of her hips and drove into her, grunting with sheer sensual pleasure over each stroke. His movements sent her spiraling higher and higher and she cried out from the intensity. He groaned, sounding thoroughly satisfied, and the world was swept away in a series of bright colors. The very core of her being shuddered uncontrollably with pleasure so deep that stars shot before her eyes until she collapsed into a spent pool of quivering flesh.

Neither of them could speak, they could hardly breathe. Jackson curled up behind her, wrapped her in his arms and kissed her temple. She fell into a deep sleep and for the first time in what seemed like forever, she didn't have to write a single word in her little black book.

~~*

A long time after Nan's breathing fell into an even rhythm, Jackson lay close to her lush body, threading his fingers through the silky auburn hair strewn across his pillow. The momentary exhaustion of sexual satisfaction had passed and he was already hungry for her again, but it was a nice hunger.

It didn't surprise him that sex was different with Nan than it had been during his brief sexual encounters since Amy died. Two brief, stolen moments when he'd indulged his physical needs and had hoped drown his pain, but he'd always walked away dissatisfied and guilt-ridden. But things with Nan were different. He wanted her with a fire previously unsurpassed in his life. Something about her drew him, pulled at him, so he just couldn't walk away.

But it was still just sex. By having her he'd get his want out of his system and they could both go back to their comfort zones. She was a mover in life, a person who'd never be content to drift. Sort of reminded him of what he was like before med school, before the accident.

Always with the memory came the screech of tires and Amy's horrified cry. A sharp pain wrenched inside of him and he rose from the bed, careful not to wake Nan. He wanted to be alone to wrestle the demons back into the black pit deep inside him. Slipping on jeans, he blew out the candles and stepped out onto the moonlit porch with his guitar.

Most nights, when the memories were more than he could bear, he'd play all night beneath the stars. Music eased his soul and kept some part of him alive. Eric Clapton said it all. Jackson sat on the steps and began playing "Tears in Heaven," so low the sound was a whispered prayer in the night, for only in music could he let go of the pain in his soul.

He wasn't sure how many hours he'd played that song, but a quiet sniffle from the door interrupted his reverie. He looked up to see Nan standing in the moonlight, her wild hair a dark swath against her creamy skin and the white of the sheet from his bed. He didn't need to see the tears in her eyes to know they were there. "Why are you crying?"

"The song. It reaches into the soul and connects."

"Yeah, it does." The song connected inside of him, and kept him with the living. That she picked up on its depth connected them. The moment hung soft and sweet in the air, and her as yet unspoken questions fell as thick as the dew on an early summer morning.

Damn. He didn't want her questions, because he had no answers he was willing to give. What he carried inside him was his own private hell and nothing less than he deserved. He didn't want her pity. He wanted her hot and wild and he wanted to be deep inside her. For in those few moments of pleasure, he could forget his pain. He could forget the anger and self-loathing raging inside him.

Setting the guitar aside, he stood and walked to her then picked up a corner of the sheet and gave it a little tug. "Let go," he said gruffly. "I want to see you naked in the moonlight. Outside, right here beneath the morning stars."

"Outside?"

He heard the excitement in her gasp and his groin tightened in response. The night he'd found her nicely laid against the hood of his truck had lingered in his mind and suddenly he knew what he wanted. He caught the sheet as she slowly released it. For a few minutes he just admired the shadow of her womanly body touched by the streams of moonlight. "Don't move," he ducked inside and snatched a condom. Then he went back to her. Scooping her up, he walked from the cover of the porch.

"Where are we going, Jack? Are you sure nobody passes by?"

"Yeah, I'm sure. Close your eyes and relax. Don't peek. I want you to tell me what you feel and I'll tell you what I see. Can you do that?"

"I can try. What do you have in mind?"

"Trust me," he murmured. Seeing Nan shut her eyes had to be the biggest turn on he'd ever gotten. He reached the hood of his truck in three strides. "I'm going to set you on your feet a minute. Don't move and don't peek."

"Okay."

He spread the sheet over the hood and then he picked Nan up and set her on it.

"When am I supposed to start telling you how I feel?'

"Now, sugar," he said inserting himself between her legs.

"Well, the grass was wet and tickled my feet. Beneath my bottom I feel a damp sheet over cool metal. I feel you in front of me. I feel your jeans against the inside of my legs. So, I'm naked and you're not, right?"

"Yeah, can you picture it in your mind? All your sweet nudity silvery in the moonlight and I'm half dressed. Doesn't that make you feel a little bit naughty?" He leaned forward and kissed her lips before she could answer.

"Yes."

"Does it feel good?"

"Yes."

"It's going to feel even better." He cupped her breasts and teased her responsive nipples, enjoying their softness beneath his molding fingers. "I see your breasts. They're rounded and just right to fill my palms. I see you arch to me, and the pleasure of my touch."

"I, uh, I feel the heat of your hands. I feel excited when you touch me, when your rougher skin caresses mine."

He leaned over and sucked on a nipple.

"Ah, I feel fire. A smooth fire that makes me burn."

He did the same to her other breast, laving and plucking until she placed her hands on the hood of the truck and completely arched her back to offer him more. "I see a woman so damn beautiful in her need that no artist could ever capture her essence. I see your breasts aching for my touch; you're lifting them to me. I like it. Lay back, Nan. Lay all the way back."

She did as he asked and he stepped back to view her. "Move your arms out to the side and let your legs relax, sugar. Open them just a little wider for me."

"I, um, feel the cool night air all over, but I still feel hot. I feel strange."

"I see a woman ripe and open for loving. Do you know what that does to a man?" Her breasts jiggled as she sucked in a breath.

"No."

"It makes him burn, sugar. I can see your heart beating in the pulse at your throat. I can see your breasts move as your lungs fight for air in your excitement. I can see the triangle of dark hair between your legs and your sex open and waiting for me. It makes me want to be and do everything. Do you want that from me, Nan?"

"I'm not sure. I feel vulnerable."

He moved up and slid his hands down her calves, pushing her legs open enough to place a kiss on the inside of her thigh. "You like that, sugar?"

"Yes."

He kissed several places higher. "How about that?"

"Yes, oh, yes. That's so smooth, makes me want more—more of your touch, more of the pleasure of your mouth."

"There's more. Lots more." He pushed her legs apart, and kissed her feminine flesh until she writhed.

"Jack, oh, Jack. I need you inside."

"Soon, sugar." He tightened his grip on her hips and held her prisoner to his loving until she arched and shuddered, crying his name to the stars.

By the time she stilled, Jackson thought his erection was going to bust right through his jeans. He reached down, popped open the button, and slid down the zipper. A sigh of relief escaped him as his throbbing penis sprang free of its confines.

"Let me." Nan moaned and tried to sit up to reach him.

"Let me," he said. "Just turn over and relax for the ride. I've been thinking about doing this since I found you bottoms up on my truck's hood."

"You sure?"

"Lady, count on it." Jackson helped her turn over then rolled on the condom and gently eased her down until he smoothly slid inside her. As he thrust in and pulled out, she moaned and her muscles tightened lovingly about him. Pure pleasure washed over him like a benediction from heaven. He'd thought God had forsaken him into an eternal hell until he'd made love to Nan for the first time. And now that he was making love to her again, he could feel the heavens open up for him. He pushed harder and higher until she cried out again and again as her sheath spasmed around his dick, sucking him beyond all control. The orgasm ripping through him thrust him to a new plateau and staked a claim on ground he never meant to explore as his heart squeezed tight. He picked her up and cradled her in his arms as he carried her back to bed. Making love to Nan was messing with his mind.

CHAPTER TEN

The early morning sun dappled through the oak leaves and dotted flecks of gold across the rippling creek. Nan lay back upon the old quilt Jackson had spread along the grassy bank. She couldn't remember ever getting up and doing nothing but enjoying the breeze in the air and the warmth of the sun. She always had something planned, something on her daily agenda to do. Were she at home right now, she'd be cleaning out a closet, or organizing a drawer, or clipping coupons, anything to keep her life moving opposite the direction she'd grown up.

Jackson slid the basket of food they'd brought from the back of his motorcycle. He'd been quiet this morning, sort of withdrawn, which made for an odd morning after. And she couldn't seem to forget the raw pain she'd heard in his voice when he sang so quietly on the porch last night.

"What?" Jackson stopped at the end of the blanket. "You're looking at me as if you've lost your best friend."

Nan shook her head and forced a smile on her face. "Hearing you sing last night. I just wondered why you chose that song?"

Jackson focused on the basket in his hand as he set it down. When he looked up he had a casual grin on his face. "Didn't you know Eric Clapton is a guitar player's god? I play a lot of his stuff. It's a beautiful song."

Nan sighed. Instinctively she knew there was more behind what she heard last night. "It's a moving song and you sang it with heart."

"I strive to please my fans. Where are the strawberries and cream? I'm starving." He reached for the basket.

Nan snatched it away. "I'm starving, too. You might just have to fight me for them." She reached into the basket and started setting the stuff out.

Jackson stretched out on the blanket and shut his eyes.

"What? Are you giving up without a fight?"

"Nah, I'm planning my strategy. I have the champagne." He held up the bottle. "And as I see it, we have breakfast this morning because I put the stuff in the fridge last night. You owe me."

"Hmm." Nan took a bite of cheese. The champagne would be good. She didn't think she had ever indulged herself so much before. She remembered last night and a blush heated her cheeks. She looked Jackson over, the dark shadow of his beard, the long wave of his hair, the sensual curve of his lips, and the capable way he moved his hands. No, she'd never been so wild, nor had she ever had such sensual excitement and fulfillment. "Okay. I'll trade you ten strawberries and five pieces of cheese for a glass of champagne."

Jackson lifted a brow. "That was easy." He pulled the foil off the top of the bottle and began working the cork.

Nan smiled. "There's more."

Jackson stopped mid cork popping. "More?"

"I'm afraid so."

"What more?"

Nan looked over at Jackson's bike and deepened her smile. "Just something I've been thinking about."

Jackson turned his head, puzzled. "What?"

"Nope. I won't tell. You're going to have to trust me."

He frowned. "Trust you?"

"Um, hmm."

"Let me get this straight. For ten strawberries and five pieces of cheese, I'm supposed to give you a glass of champagne and something else that has yet to be disclosed?"

"That's right."

Jackson uncorked the bottle and poured a glass of champagne. Nan triumphantly reached for it, but he didn't hand it to her. He drained the whole damn thing in one smooth gulp. "Nope. I won't do it."

"What!" She sat up like a beanpole, indignation pumping into her. "You don't trust me? After what I did last night!"

Jackson laughed. "Not only are you gorgeous when you're naked on the hood of my truck, but you're gorgeous when you're pissed. I didn't say I didn't trust you. If I'm going to set myself up for undisclosed services then I demand to have half of the strawberries, half of the cheese, and you neglected to mention half of the whipped cream."

"Oh." Nan sat down with a poof and a tingle. Every time she thought about their love making last night, the juices inside her bubbled with excitement. "If you get half of the food, then I get half of the champagne, and that includes the glass you already drank."

"Deal," Jackson said. He poured two glasses of champagne and handed her one. For the next hour they worked their way through strawberries and cream, champagne and cheese. A definite buzz worked its way through her bloodstream.

He refilled her glass. "This last one is yours, sugar. And you have to drink it like I drank the first one."

She saluted him and drained the glass then sat up proud of her accomplishment. "This is potent stuff. I feel kind of Ring-Around-the-Rosy." She giggled then popped her hand over her mouth. She never giggled.

"Ring around the what?" Jackson leaned forward and brushed an errant strand a hair from her face.

She captured his finger in her hand. "You know. The old nursery rhyme." She sang what she remembered of it. "In kindergarten, back when I fit in with the crowd, the girls would get together and hold hands. Then we'd run in a circle until we were dizzy and fell down."

"I don't remember it. My brothers and I were probably more interested in chasing lizards back then."

She scrunched her nose. "Lizards. Yuck."

While she held his finger, he aimed it at her chest and pushed until she fell over backwards onto the blanket. He followed her down, then took his other hand and traced the V of her shirt over the top of her breasts. "Luckily, since then I've discovered the merits of women."

"We're much better than lizards."

"Much. All sugar and spice." He leaned over and kissed her and she closed her eyes, reveling in the sensations swirling through her. "Now that I've gotten half of the strawberries and cream and you've gotten half of the champagne, what undisclosed services of mine did I barter?"

Nan drew a deep breath, an action that brought her breast in contact with Jackson's arm. He rubbed his forearm against her then moved his hand down to cup her. Through her clothing, his thumb zeroed in on her nipple with unerring accuracy.

"Did you have something like this in mind?"

She wet her lips with her tongue. "That's part of it."

"There's more? " He moved to her other breast.

"A lot." She took a deep breath. "You got the truck. I want the motorcycle." She watched Jackson's expression change to puzzlement.

She reached up and slid her finger under his shirt to toy with his nipple. "You gave me a ride on your truck last night. I want one on your bike this morning."

"The bike, huh?"

"Yes."

"So, how long have you been thinking about that?"

"I'm not telling."

He laughed. "I have my ways at getting to the truth." Jackson angled up from the blanket and moved over to his Harley. He walked all the way around it as if he were examining a racehorse. Then he stopped and looked down at her, his expression unreadable.

"You're sure we won't get interrupted?" She looked around. A thatch of lazy oak trees cut them off from the dirt road they'd traveled to get here and nothing but wild flowers, tall grass, and a broken barbwire fence met her gaze across the creek.

Jackson grinned and raised a brow. "Fairly, but isn't that part of the appeal of making love outside rather than in your bed, sugar? Doesn't the fact that you can't be a hundred percent sure excite you?"

Nan laughed. "I'd be mortified if someone saw us."

Jackson shrugged and stepped away from his bike. "Well, if you aren't willing to take the risk…"

"Take your shirt off," she demanded, sitting up to watch him. Whether it was too risky or not, be it the champagne at work, or maybe she'd just lost her mind completely. Whatever the reason, she wasn't going to pass up the opportunity.

He grabbed the edges of his T-shirt and slowly pulled it up over his head, tossing it her way. Nan caught it and snuggled it, breathing deeply of his cologne.

His boots followed, landing with a "thunk" at the edge of the blanket where she sat. Her blood began to pulse and heat dampened the skin between her legs. She shifted on the blanket, hoping to ease the building tension inside.

Sun glistened off of his broad shoulders and the blue-black waves of his raven hair. She wanted to explore the length of his muscled body over and over again. She couldn't seem to get enough of him.

When his hands moved to the button of his fly, her mouth watered, and her heart began to race. She had fantasized about making love on his Harley, but she'd never thought about *how* to do it. He slid the button open and zipped down his fly. The bulge emerging told her he was as turned on as she was as he shucked his jeans and briefs.

"Come here, sugar," he said his voice so deep and smooth that its silken vibrations wrapped around her center and shook her. She stood and walked to him, not even sure her legs could make the distance as champagne and desire swirled through her. She came to a trembling stop before him. He reached around and gently pulled the bands holding her hair back. Threading his fingers through it, he spread it about her shoulders then unbuttoned her blouse. "You know much about bikes, sugar?"

She managed to shake her head. Her blouse came off and her bra quickly followed. The light morning breeze tickled her skin as the warmth of the sun beat soothingly on her bare flesh. She felt totally decadent to be naked in the daylight, and her nipples immediately hardened to sensitive points. He cupped her breasts and rubbed the pads of his thumbs over them. Pleasure shot through her and a low moan vibrated in her throat.

"You treat a bike right and she'll always give you a smooth ride, sugar." He leaned down, kissed her left nipple and drew it into his mouth, sucking her into a whirlwind of hot desire. Her hands clutched at his shoulders as she arched to his pleasure giving mouth. A second later he released her and stepped away.

"Oh." She wavered, her toes curling in the grass for balance. She looked up at him, trying to decipher what he wanted. He had a man-on-the-move smile on his face and a deeply sensual gleam in his blue eyes. He hadn't shaved when he'd showered, so a dark shadow shaded his square jaw and the cleft of his hard chin. He looked like a desperado, wild and wicked as he moved behind her and slid up against her bottom. She could feel his erection pressing against her, feel the heat of his breath upon her neck, and the pleasuring tingle of his touch as he ran his hand over her hip and along the waist band of her jeans. She sucked in her belly willing and wanting him to snap them open and strip them away. He did so in a flash and didn't stop until she was completely naked.

"Before I ride, I always make sure she's in prime condition." Still playing with her nipples, he brought his other hand between her legs and gently rubbed her dewy flesh then slid a finger into her wet passage. "I get her ready to ride."

Nan moaned. "I'm ready, Jack. So ready."

"Bikes are finely tuned, and respond to your slightest touch."
He took her hand and ran it up the leather and steel handlebars,
over the gadgets on it to the center of the bike. Once he reached
the leather seat, he splayed her hand upon its cushioned softness,
pressing her hand in place before moving his up to brush over her
jutting nipples. Then he took her other hand and brought it back,
placing it over his shaft. Nan eagerly stroked him, filling her hand
with his pulsing hardness.

"Not yet, sugar. We need to make your fantasy complete." He
stepped away from her, took his leather jacket off the back of the
bike and threw it over the handlebars. She watched, fascinated as
he climbed on and situated himself on his bike. His arousal stood
ready and waiting, as was the look in his eyes when he spoke.
"Your turn, sugar. You'll find a condom in the back pocket of my
jeans."

Now that the time had come, a slight awkwardness spread over
her as she retrieved the condom, but her curiosity was too great to
call a halt to this game. Condom in hand she approached him. He
leaned over and kissed her, the stubble on his face causing her skin
to tingle. She fumbled the condom in place, her nervous fingers
caught in the thin Latex, and Jackson reached over, helping her to
smooth it along his hard sex. She wanted him inside her now, but
the reality of doing it on his motorcycle was a lot more
complicated than making it happen in her dreams. "How?" Nan
murmured, wondering what to do next.

"Climb on in front and face me, rest your backside on my
jacket." She did as he directed and he helped her get balanced.
"That's it," he said as he settled her legs on either side of him.

"Now move forward and rest your feet on the bottom of the
back bar."

"You sound as if you've done this before," she accused.

"No." He cupped her bottom, lifting her up as she moved closer. "But I've thought about it. A lot." He pulled her down on top of him as he pushed his erection upward penetrating her instantly, deeply.

Nan moaned with pleasure, pressing her breasts against his chest.

Moving his hands to the handlebars of the bike, he rocked his hips a little, urging her up. "Now, hold onto my shoulders and you take us for a ride, sugar. I'll hold the bike steady; you're in the driver's seat."

Tentatively she levered up and slid back down, amazed at how easily she could move.

Jackson thrust up watching the sunlight set Nan's auburn hair ablaze with fiery lights. She was so hot and so damn sexy that all he could think about was getting deeper and deeper into her. He wanted to keep thrusting and thrusting until they both went crazy with desire. "That's it. Yeah, just like that. Slow, steady, and hard, sugar," he murmured, rocking his hips harder and harder. She was a wet dream come true, and he wanted to be the man with whom she came apart.

Last night, the numbness that had ruled his body for so long had faded. How could he remain indifferent with a woman like her? Her full breasts rubbed his chest and bounced with her every move. The sun kissed her naked flesh to a peachy glow, and the hot heat of her sex nestled in red-blonde curls grabbed his erection, smoothly milking him to an excitement that had his blood rushing like the wind. She was taking him for a ride and as before, being with her was unlike being with anyone else.

Her honey eyes were darkened with secret desire and slanted to a love-me-baby angle. And her lush mouth, parted with the force of her desire, seemed ready to take anything he had to give. He pumped into her harder, forcing his hands to keep the bike steady when all he wanted to do was to grab her and pump them both into insanity. "How long, sugar? How long have you been thinking about this?"

"Three," she gasped.

"Three whole days, huh." He smiled pushing up into her and reveling in her slick, smoothness.

"Three months." Her breath caught and her muscles tightened on him and he couldn't hold back any more.

"Months? Damn, sugar, you're killing me. That's it, come with me." He thrust into her one last time and her convulsing orgasm sent him over the edge. He jerked with the force of it, his spasms moving him deeper into her, and still it wasn't enough. When she settled in his arms, her breathing a heavy, rasping in the air, he stayed buried inside of her as he slid off the bike and carried her to the quilt. Lying on top of her, he kissed her tenderly, breathing in her essence and loving the feel of being intimately connected. He was in trouble. His erection was gearing up for another hard ride and his heart was revving up his blood to fuel the action.

The sound of a plane had him shift and his thigh suddenly felt damp. "Damn," he sat up quickly to see. The condom looked intact, but his leg was just a bit too wet.

"Oh my Gosh!" Nan bolted upright in a panic. "I don't believe this."

He slid the condom off and placed it with the used paper plates to be thrown away. He didn't see any fluid leak from it, so he figured they were safe. "Don't worry. Odds are that it won't matter."

"Won't matter! Don't you hear the plane? They're going to see us like this!"

Jackson switched gears from the possible condom leak to realize Nan was upset about being seen naked from the air. "You won't be anything more than a speck on the horizon to the pilot."

"Even being a naked speck is mortifying," she said. "They'll know what we've been doing."

He found her flustered embarrassment as endearing as her wild streak had been a turn on. She was a mixture of black lace and prim nurse's whites. The roar of the plane drew closer. He rolled over on top of her to cover her body with his. "The only thing the pilot can see is my backside. You're safe."

"I want clothes," she grumbled, wiggling.

He kissed her and neither of them knew when the plane finally flew over. Nan was a wonderful distraction and he had packed another condom in the other pocket of his jeans. This time they went green and made good use of the trees for support.

"*You cook a mean steak.*" Nan sat back in her chair and folded her napkin after dabbing her mouth.

Jackson had already polished off his dinner and sat with his legs stretched out, sipping the last of his beer. Physically there wasn't any part of Jackson she hadn't had the pleasure of seeing or touching. They'd spent the morning sun bathing naked on the quilt by the creek, and the afternoon in his bed. They'd both gotten sun today. Jackson's tan had deepened, making his teeth flash white when he grinned. "My motto with meat is if I can't grill it then I don't eat it."

"I wondered how you did without a stove." She couldn't imagine living such a makeshift way every day, but he had turned out an excellent meal. A fresh salad, and microwaved potatoes and veggies went with their steaks. "The steak was heavenly."

"No. The steak was good. You're heavenly." He leaned over and kissed her soundly.

She moaned. Making love again right that minute would kill her because she was already so replete. She'd lost count how many times they'd made love since she'd arrived last night. But with Jackson making the moves, she couldn't deny him, and was ready to die for pleasure.

He didn't move in for the kill this time though, he stood up and tugged on her hand. "Let's go sit on the porch."

He sat on one corner of the swing and placed a long leg across the bench seat, leaving his other leg planted on the porch. He patted the wood between his legs. "Sit here."

She snuggled into him as he wrapped his arms around her, spooning her against him so they could both look out at the starry night and see the moonbeams peek through the clouds at the hillside. A chorus of crickets and frogs sang in the distance.

"This is beautiful. Quiet and peaceful. We haven't seen anybody all day," she said surprised to feel the contentment inside of her. She'd grown up in the country, and was no stranger to it. Yet her memories of it were different. The dark had always been too dark, the crickets too loud, and the isolation too acute. Moving to the city, having a career, and being hemmed in by people rather than land had been something she'd yearned to do for as far back as she could remember.

"In the four years I've lived here, you're the only person who has been to my cabin. No reason for folks to stop by, this is private property and my family respects my privacy."

His words intrigued her. Was she special to him? Jackson had made love to her with a passion and tenderness unlike any other, yet she'd never met a man so against making any type of a commitment to anything. "Don't you get lonely out here?"

"No." He tensed, and she wondered if he would continue. "I grew up with three brothers whose mission in life was to crowd into anything their older brother got to do. I like quiet. What about you, any brothers or sisters?"

"Nope. I'm it, which was probably a good thing."

"How so?"

Nan shrugged. She didn't talk about her childhood much; it pulled her down and made her sad. "Between me and my father, my mother had more than she could take care of."

"You never say much about your folks. Where do they live?"

"They don't." She breathed deep, and forced herself to speak. "My father drank himself into an early grave and my mother worked herself into one trying to get help for him and feeding me. After they died, I left the broken down trailer they'd rented and moved to Savannah, eventually working my way through nursing school."

For a long moment Jackson remained silent. "I'm sorry. Men who can't take on the responsibilities of caring for a family shouldn't have one." His voice cut harshly through the night.

"I don't think my father planned it that way. He caught the tail end of Vietnam. When he came back, he was never the same. His platoon was massacred, and only he and one other man survived. My father and the other man had a run in with a land mine. They called for a chopper to medi-vac them out. Shortly after that, a North Vietnamese sniper team ambushed his platoon, and my father blamed himself for their deaths. He thought that the land mine explosion and the chopper helped the Vietnamese to pinpoint his platoon."

"But he couldn't have known."

"Maybe, maybe not. I'm sorry it happened, but he let it ruin his life and took my mother with him. She loved him with all of her heart and soul, but it wasn't enough."

Jackson hugged her tighter. Nan lost herself in her remembrances of the past. Few had been happy. Most had been anguished with constant problems. He pushed the swing with his foot and they swayed softly in the evening breeze for a while. After a time she spoke again.

"Jack, tell me about your wife. What was her name?"

He tensed. For a long time he didn't answer and Nan wondered if she had made a fatal mistake. He was just opening up to her. Would he completely withdraw from her now?

"Her name was Amy. I suppose you already know she was killed in a car crash four years ago."

"Yes."

"There's not much to say beyond that. We married when I was in school, which made life rough, but we stuck it out. What about you, ever married?"

"Me?" Nan blinked, surprised. Didn't he realize she would have already shared something like that with him? "No."

"That explains it."

"What," Nan said, her brow furrowing.

"Why I'm such a lucky man. Rumor has it that once a woman marries it ruins her for great sex."

Nan elbowed him in the stomach. "Typical male reasoning. It isn't marriage that does it. It's the pile up of the demands of being a mother and a wife. Plus the fact that men either never learned the art of romance and seduction, or forget how to light a candle after the wedding. Women need more than just sex to keep a fire burning."

Jackson cupped her breasts and stroked her nipples through the cotton of her shirt. "You sure about that?"

Nan moaned, yet managed to capture and still Jackson's hands. "That helps, but I'm positive about the other."

He laughed. Leaving their hands entwined, he set the swing in motion again. "You said something this morning that I wanted to ask you about. Why was kindergarten the only time you felt like you fit in?"

"It was the only time that not having what the other kids had didn't bother me." She shrugged, reluctant to bring back the memories. "Whether it was in their mind or in my mind, when I grew older, I always felt outside the circle."

Jackson released one hand and picked up a strand of her hair, toying with it between his fingers. "I know what you mean."

She arched her neck to look at him. "How? You had a big family. Great parents. This huge farm."

"That didn't count for much when we were growing up. We're Irish. My father works in a shipping yard and my grandfather was a peanut farmer. Blue-blooded folks used to refer to us as "wrong-side-of-the-tracks-Weldons. I think that drove all of us to achieve more and more. Jesse has his own security agency. James and Jared their own construction company. And for a while I spent a great deal of time pursuing a different career."

"Medicine?"

His muscles tightened like a twisted rubber band. "Who—"

He unfolded his arm from around her and she caught his hand in hers. "Alexi told me, but before that Brad mentioned that he knew you from Chicago. You are a doctor?"

"I was a doctor."

Nan waited a minute, hoping Jackson would explain more about why he left the medical field. He didn't, so she pushed further. "Why'd you leave medicine?"

"Let's just say I changed my mind and drop the subject."

"But—"

Jackson pulled his hand from hers, pushed her forward, and slid off of the swing. "There aren't any buts." He paced across the porch, tense and agitated. "You want to go out for a drink or something?"

She didn't. She wanted to sit right here and talk. She wanted him to open up to her, to let her beyond the wall he kept erecting whenever they ventured too far past the physical realm. But he'd already withdrawn. Were she to push further, he'd only shut her out more. The past twenty-four hours in Jackson's company had taught her some things about him and herself. The time had brought them closer. In fact, she didn't think she'd ever been closer to a man. She'd never ventured into shared fantasies' territory before. Had never known that side of herself until she'd met him. They'd shared laughter and sex beyond her wildest dreams. She thought about her little black book.

Well, maybe not *beyond* her wildest. She'd never had so much relaxing, pleasurable fun, but underneath there lay a tension. And like now that tension reared its head.

"I've been tired lately. We were up really late last night and I have to be at work by six Monday morning. It's already after ten.

I'll regret another late night. In fact, I was thinking about heading home around noon tomorrow so I can get things done and still hit the sack early."

Jackson walked back her way and lifted her chin with his finger to bring to gaze to his. "You've fainted once and nearly did a second time. Have you seen a doctor yet?"

"Not yet."

"Promise me you'll see one soon."

"I promise. So to answer your question, I'd rather stay here. Why don't you play? I love listening to you."

He seemed relieved at her suggestion and quickly settled down with his guitar, playing a variety of songs. His voice in the night both comforted and thrilled her. In music she heard his yearning and need. It reached out and grabbed her heart, tugging so hard she could feel herself falling headlong into him.

Much later his song turned to kisses and his kisses turned to loving, and she had a hard time imagining what it would be like never to touch him again.

~~*

Nan woke up Sunday morning to an empty bed and the steady drizzle of rain pattering on the cabin's roof. Several places about the room Jackson had set cans to catch leaks from the ceiling. The drip-dropping sound reminded her of the trailer she once lived in. Her mother had always planned to move to a better place, but that never happened. Her memories of the way things had been were so strong she had to fight to keep her perspective. This wasn't the past, but many things about Jackson's cabin needed a little bit of care; the torn fabric on the arm of a chair, a drawer set askew, and the wood needed polish. What she hadn't seen yesterday, she saw today. She'd find it depressing to live amidst the disrepair, too much a reminder of the past.

Getting up, she went in search of Jackson. She found him out on the porch asleep in the swing. His guitar lay beside him. His rugged, harried appearance told Nan he'd been awake most of the time she'd slept. He looked so alone, so solitary that he seemed as far away from her as the stars. She turned to go back inside, not wanting to disturb him.

"Don't go." He sat up and moved his guitar off the swing.

Nan walked back and joined him. The hem of his T-shirt she wore rode up and she tugged it down a little, but Jackson reached over and stayed her hand with a caress. A slight chill hung in the damp air and raindrops splattered the porch's edges.

"Rough night?" Nan asked.

He shrugged. "The usual."

"Want to talk about it?"

"Not really. Do you want breakfast? I can run into town and pick up more buns."

Nan smiled. "Shakespeare would be crushed that we left him out."

"That's good."

Nan glared at him and he raised his hand to deflect the killer look. "Okay. I take that back. I'll even buy him one. How's that?"

"Much better. I wonder what time it is?" She stood up. What had been relaxing yesterday was making her feel antsy today. She had the need to do something, anything she could term as productive.

"I think there's a clock on the microwave."

Nan blinked. He *thought* there was a clock on the microwave. Wasn't time important enough to *know* where a clock was? She shook her head and wandered back inside the cabin. Stepping between the cans collecting water drips, she moved over to the microwave and read the time twice before she believed it.

"Jack. It's already eleven thirty." She rushed around, picking up things she usually kept neat and stuffing them into her tote bag.

Jackson stuck his head in the door. "What's wrong?"

"It's eleven thirty."

"So?"

She turned around and stared at him. "Half the day is already gone. There is so much to do."

"Like?"

"Like get ready for work next week. There are uniforms to iron and groceries to buy. My violets need replanting, and there's probably dust all over my furniture. I'm going to have to take a rain check on the buns."

Jackson looked at her like she'd grown a second head. "Glad you could spare the time yesterday." He slammed the door and the doorknob tumbled across the floor.

Okay. Just because he didn't sleep last night and was in a sour mood didn't mean she had to lose her cool, too. She counted to ten. Then when looked at the doorknob, she counted to fifteen before she finished gathering her things. Jackson was sitting on the porch swing, messing with his guitar when she walked out. He looked up, watching her intently as she went over to him. Somehow this wasn't how she pictured their romantic interlude ending.

"Your doorknob broke." She meant to say something else, but those were the first words that leapt from her mouth.

Jackson shrugged and strummed out a chord.

"What are you pissed off about?"

"Nothing."

"It doesn't look like a nothing to me."

"Your dust is gathering."

"Damn it, Jack. You're not being fair. There are things that have to get done. The world would be a sorry place if they didn't get done. A little dusting around here wouldn't hurt."

"You weren't thinking about dust yesterday or last night as I recall. Why the big change this morning?"

"Sex doesn't make the world go around."

Jackson looked up from his guitar then. He didn't say anything, just looked at her and raised a questioning brow.

She blushed. She couldn't deny he had made the earth move under her feet. "Well, not all the way around."

Jackson set his guitar aside and stood. "Sure about that, sugar?" he asked advancing.

Nan stepped back and planted her hand in the middle of his chest. She could barely hold back the groan. He felt so good and now that she knew intimately the magic he could make, she'd lost all resistance to his charm. If he maneuvered her into bed now, she'd be there all day. "Dinner," she piped, her voice creaking in her suddenly dry throat.

"I'm hungry," Jackson murmured. He took her hand from his chest, brought it up to his mouth and nibbled. "Hungry for another taste of you." He brushed his tongue over her finger.

Nan stepped back and moaned as an electric streak of desire shot up her arm. "Not now. Tomorrow night. My place. I'll cook dinner for you."

His gaze focused on hers over the top of her hand. Her invitation seemed to stop him cold. Was he surprised? Or had she scared him? Now that she thought about it, when they'd dated before, she had never invited him to her apartment. She supposed it was her way of assuring they didn't end up in bed. But on the other hand, he hadn't asked to come in either. Not until he'd brought her the sticky buns.

After a long moment, he breathed deeply then spoke. "Tomorrow night, your place?"

"Yes." Nan licked her dry lips. Why did she feel as if her heart hung on his answer? This weekend was meant to explore her thoughts about Jackson, possibly get him out of her system, not to entrench him deeper inside of her.

He released her hand and stepped back as he ran his fingers through his hair. This didn't appear to be an easy decision for him and Nan wondered why. It wasn't like they weren't somewhat involved. They'd just spent about as intimate a weekend as two people could.

"Okay. What time?" he finally answered.

"Six," Nan said, suddenly having the urge to smile.

"Six it is." Jackson moved forward and swept her up in a mind-boggling kiss. She felt in that moment as if he'd made more than just a physical step her way.

CHAPTER ELEVEN

"*I expect you to be on your* best behavior tomorrow night. Paws off the food and absolutely no snack attacks on any of Jackson's personal belongings," Nan instructed as she finished watering her plants and checking them for signs of trouble.

Shakespeare blinked at her and deigned to give her a flick of his tail. She wasn't sure she had his cooperation at all, but she let it go. She had other things to worry about. Like what she was going to say to Brad. The message he'd left on her answering machine Friday night said he would call her when he got in tonight. At ten o'clock, her "night" was just about over with considering she had to be up at five in the morning.

She'd already decided she'd tell Brad they couldn't date any more. She just hadn't figured how to say it. Did she owe him an explanation? Her mind kept turning circles, looking for answers. At ten fifteen she couldn't stay up later and called Brad. She got his answering machine.

"Brad. This is Nan. I'm afraid I won't be able to go next weekend for the yacht party. As it turns out, I'm working then. When you get back, we need to talk. Good night."

Nan hung up the phone. She couldn't break off with him via the answering machine, so canceling their date was the best she could do for the moment.

As she lay in bed thoughts of Jackson swam in and out of her mind—him at the beach, at his cabin, the places and the ways they'd made love. The way her body ached for him now was so much worse than the ache she had had before. Having him only intensified her need for him. He was coming for dinner, beyond that she had no idea. Making love to him only made her want more things from him. A vivid fantasy took shape and she pulled out her pen and little black book.

A masked, black-clad pirate stood on the bow of a ship that had just captured the frigate she had sought passage on. She was on her way to England to marry a stranger—Lord Weldon to whom she'd been betrothed since birth.

Her heart pounded with fear as the scurvy pirate who'd forced her from her berth dragged her by her bound hands to the masked man. An icy wind whipped about in the cold drizzling rain, making her shiver.

"I'll take her from here," the masked man said turning to her. He looked dangerous, dressed all in black. His eyes gleamed blue from beneath his mask and his damp raven hair blew wildly about his broad shoulders.

"Aye, Black Jack. She's a feisty one and a beauty as well. She'll warm your bed better than a tavern wench any ol' day."

Black Jack caught hold of the rough rope wrapped tightly about her wrists. "This won't do." He drew a dagger from his belt.

She flinched, painfully pulling against the binds. Tears brimmed in her eyes as he forced her closer to him.

"You'd do well to fear me," he said, his voice a deep, almost unnatural rasp. Then amazingly, he cut the ropes. She fell backward, but he was faster. He caught hold of her waist and pulled her up against him.

Her blood rushed in response to her hammering heart. She feared him, but his hold on her was gentle, his body warm to her cold, rain dampened state.

"You need ropes of silk to bind you." Lord Weldon looked through his mask at the woman with whom he was betrothed. Some of the anger in his heart eased. The old salt hadn't lied. She was beautiful. Still, no amount of beauty was worth the price he'd have to pay to fulfill a near twenty-year old promise his deceased father had made.

Lord Weldon smiled; his plan was working well. In capturing the king's ship he would finally reclaim a small portion of the money the king owed his family and had refused to pay these past ten years. And once word reached England that his bride to be had been taken captive by pirates, no one would blame him for not marrying the girl. He'd set her up in her own home, provide for her, and avoid the perils of the marriage bed. Though from the full bosom pressed so softly to his chest, those perils were a bit less than he'd imagined.

With all the hard-edged pirates he'd hired, he'd have to keep her confined to his quarters to assure her safety. And considering the spark in her eyes, she'd have to be tethered to keep her there. The thought of her bound to his bed, a slave to his desires aroused some dark fantasy inside him. He'd never take an unwilling woman, but the idea of a woman pretending to be unwilling until his touch swayed her, caused his blood to pump. Very little in life excited him anymore.

His betrothed recovered enough to push back from his chest and to fight his hold. He smiled as he pulled a silk handkerchief from about his neck to bind her again. Maybe by the time they reached port, this beauty would want to share in his fantasy. She would have to be blindfolded. He couldn't chance her connecting the Pirate Black Jack and Lord Weldon.

~~*

The alarm clock rang and Nan fought the silken binds to free herself, her body aching for another touch from Black Jack's magical hands. Her eyes popped open at the thought.

Lord, have mercy! In her sleep she had wound her sheet about both her wrists. Untangling herself, she pulled out her black book and started to write. When she finished, she knew she was in big trouble. Not because of the fantasy and not because she'd almost made that fantasy come true by binding herself in her sleep. Nope, she was in big trouble because of where this fantasy had ended up. The unwilling Lord Weldon had eventually married her.

Nan bounced out of the bed and rushed off to work in record time. If she kept herself busy, kept her mind focused on the million and one demands of her job, then maybe she could stay sane until Jackson showed up for dinner. This just sex relationship was more that she bargained for. Her need of Jackson should be diminishing not increasing.

The Labor and Delivery Department was insane and seeing Jackson working outside the Nurse's Station window all day nearly drove her crazy. She didn't have time for anything more than a Coke for breakfast, and lunch consisted of a bag of chips as she wrote in her patients' charts.

She was starving by the time she left work and part of her hunger had nothing to do with food. She stopped at a lingerie shop to appease some of her appetite and then dashed to the grocery store. There she spent double what she usually did, which wouldn't be a big deal if she could remember half of what she bought. All she could think about was Jackson and what she'd bought to tantalize him with. She also bought him a little plant to brighten up his cabin.

A brisk breeze whipped in from the ocean and a line of dark clouds hovered in the distant horizon. Rushing home before the storm, she put a roast and a potato casserole in the oven and checked the asparagus soup she had prepared yesterday. She would serve the soup cold and add a spinach and vinaigrette salad to complete the main meal. For dessert she had snatched a Chocolate Decadence Cheesecake from the grocery's freezer.

Hurrying to the bathroom to take a final assessment of her appearance, she looked in the mirror as she spritzed on her favorite light perfume. Her mind a convoluted mess with one clear thought. She'd married the man in her fantasy. Repeatedly. Was it some sort of sign that she was supposed to really marry Jackson?

"But I can't marry Lord Weldon," she blurted out to herself.

Eyes wide, she clamped her hand over her mouth. Okay, she could handle this. Talking to a mirror as if the fantasy she had had last night was real was no biggie. She was completely in control of her life. She was a mature, consenting adult. It was just sex, right?

She was…she was…deranged. She decided to call Jackson and reschedule after she went to therapy. That should take about six months. Six months was good. Maybe by then she'd be able to carry on an intelligent conversation and not see a masked pirate lover lurking around, or a Harley, or remember the hood of his truck, or hear guitar music. Okay maybe she needed a year of therapy in Siberia to cool down her attraction to Jackson.

Though the leopard-print underwear she'd bought and wore gave lie to her intentions, she still walked over to the telephone to call Jackson and cancel. The doorbell rang before she could make it. He was early. Jackson was never early.

Jackson rolled his shoulders, marveling at the relaxed ease he felt. For the first time in forever, he'd had a damn good day. This just sex proposition with Nan was just right. He couldn't wait to have her again, but that hunger would ease. Just give it a little time and he'd be back to his normal self. Still, he thought, maybe things would be a little different from now on. The possibility of another damn good day on his horizon seemed to be something he'd have to adjust to.

Back in med school and during his internship, he had had too many things to do to feel any type of ease, ever. Recently, he had done just what he had to do to get the job finished, but today things had been different.

He'd enjoyed the warmth of the sun on his back, the fresh breeze blowing in from the Atlantic, and the low-key camaraderie involved in the shared task of building something tangible and worthwhile with his own hands. There was a certain satisfaction in construction. Nothing like the rush of handling medical emergencies in the ER, but then he didn't have to deal with the patient who didn't survive, or the constant pressure of having a person's life rest on your decisions. And without medicine, he didn't have to deal with the constant reminders of Amy and his own failure.

Jackson wasn't sure what made today any different than every day for the past four years, but being with Nan had to be part of it. He lifted an impatient gaze to the gathered clouds, showering him with a misty rain. At this rate he'd be soaked before she answered the door. He shifted the wine and spray of honeysuckle blossoms he'd clipped from the bush next to the creek and aimed his finger at the doorbell again. What was taking her so long?

She opened the door just as he hit the buzzer and she jumped about three feet. She appeared tense, harried, and as needy as he felt. She looked him up and down twice, started to say something, but couldn't seem to get the words out.

Her full lips parted and she seemed so adorably kissable he couldn't wait another minute. He'd been thinking about kissing her all day long.

"Here." Stepping into her apartment, he handed her the wine and the honeysuckle, then he wrapped his arms about her hips and lifted her to his kiss. She managed to move the wine bottle to the side, but the honeysuckle lay squashed between them. He didn't care; she met his kiss with sock-smoking enthusiasm. She tasted like heaven itself and he delved deeper into her sweet mouth.

Jackson didn't even think to ask Nan or to say anything, all he could think about was having her. He set her on her feet, shifted his arms and swooped her up, just barely remembering to kick the front door shut with his boot as he carried her back to her bedroom. She kept kissing him and he kept kissing her; they hardly had time to breathe.

He laid her on the bed and stepped back. Her eyes were dark with passion, her mouth open and ready for more of him, and her breasts rose and fell intriguingly with her every breath. She wore a feel-me silky brown blouse and an enticing short white skirt.

"I've been waiting all day for you," he said softly as he loosened her hand from the wine bottle and set it on the floor. Then he took the fragrant honeysuckle spray and placed it on the bottom of the bed.

"Me too," she confessed. "You, uh, wore all black."

"Yeah. Does that bother you?" He placed a knee on her bed and leaned in close enough to cup her breasts in his hand.

"Um, nnooo. You're sort of damp."

"Yeah. Let's work on getting you damp, too." He flicked his thumbs over her rising nipples. Just then an alarm rang from the kitchen area, and Nan jumped up from the bed lickety-split.

"The roast."

"Roast?" He was roasted all right.

"It will burn if I don't turn off the oven."

"I can relate," Jackson muttered.

"Huh?" Nan looked back at him as she walked to the door.

"Nothing. Just hurry."

"Okay. I'll be right back."

Jackson flopped back on the bed and accidentally knocked the pillows askew. He was in the middle of seducing her and the woman remembered a roast in the oven? Maybe he was losing his touch. Maybe he was losing his mind. He turned over on his stomach and groaned. Having an affair with Nan was like jumping into a forest fire. He was doomed to burn and he'd known that beforehand. How long did it take to turn an oven off? He opened his eyes and before him was an open black book.

A diary? Frowning, he sat up and placed the book on her bedside table. Would taking off his boots seem too presumptuous? After the way he'd carted her into the bedroom, she would expect he'd take off his boots—and maybe a few other things as well. He leaned over to slip off his boots and did a double take on the open page of the black book. The name Lord Weldon jumped out at him and he picked it up. Was Nan doing some sort of genealogy research? If so she was clearly barking up the wrong Weldon family tree. He didn't have any lords in his ancestry. He looked at the door, thought about reading it without asking then changed his mind.

"Nan," he called walking to the door holding the book. "Who's Lord Weldon?"

"Oh my God!" Nan froze in the middle of transferring the potato casserole from the oven to the table. She couldn't move; she couldn't speak. Her heart raced and the room swayed like a banana boat in a hurricane. The heat of the casserole burned through her insulated gloves and still she couldn't move.

Jackson entered the kitchen. "Nan?"

She shut her eyes. She couldn't look at him. She couldn't breathe, and she could feel the blood rushing from her head.

"What the hell!"

Nan barely felt Jackson take the casserole from her, but his expletives came through loud and clear though. "Ouch, damn, sonofabitch, that's hot! What kind of crappy potholders are these?"

His grip on her shoulders was firm as he pushed her down into a kitchen chair and shoved her head between her legs. "Take a deep breath, Nan."

"I can't," she gasped.

"Are you hurt? Are you sick? Why can't you breathe?"

"You, you. You read my story! How, how could you?"

Jackson pulled her head back up and Nan sank into a sea of embarrassment. "Just let me drown."

"Drown? You're not making sense." Jackson studied her face a minute then furrowed his brow. "What story?"

Nan sucked in a lung full of air. "You mean you didn't read from the black book?"

Jackson stood up and retrieved her black book from the floor where he must have dropped it to rescue her. "You mean this?"

"Yes." She reached for it and he snatched it back.

"Not so fast. I didn't read it, but when I moved it off the bed I saw Lord Weldon's name on the page. If you want this back, you're going to have to explain that. And let me warn you, I won't buy into any coincidental theories."

Nan bit her lip. She was in a fine pickle and it was her own fault. She crossed her arms, tapped her foot, and glared.

He raised his eyebrow. "Not talking, huh?"

"Nope."

"Well, I guess I'm just going to have to read for myself. He flipped the book open.

Nan jumped up. "No!"

Both of Jackson's eyebrows shot up this time. "Who is Black Jack? Just exactly what are you writing about me?"

"It's not about you."

"Not about me? The scarlet blush all over your face tells a different story. What gives?"

The game was up. She was either going to have to shoot him, tell him what she was up to, or stab him with the meat thermometer. Since she didn't have a gun, her best option was out. The thermometer was still in the roast across the kitchen and her legs weren't steady enough to carry her that far. She sat back down in the chair. She'd have to tell him.

"Please, let me have it back, Jack. It's just a book of little short stories that I think about and write down."

He grinned. "Really?"

She watched in amazement as he handed the book back to her. She took the book, her fingers so numb she couldn't feel its leathery binding. Embarrassment burned through her every nerve.

"Short stories, huh." He sat in the chair across from her. "That's really cool. I didn't know you were interested in writing. Tell me about it."

She blinked and felt like such a fraud. Could fantasies be considered short stories? "I've only started doing it recently. It's nothing much."

"Don't underrate yourself. Every great writer starts somewhere."

In her mind Nan saw Hemmingway and Steinbeck turn over in their graves. "This isn't exactly what made the classics."

"So, am I the good guy or the bad guy in the story?"

"Both," Nan managed to rasp out.

"If I'm in it, you've got to let me read it." His blue gaze could have rivaled a puppy in the window of a pet store.

She scrambled for an excuse. "It's not ready for someone else to read yet. I just wrote it last ni—"

"Last night? This sounds interesting. Please, I promise to keep in mind that this is just a rough draft."

She tightened her hold on the book. Were the tables reversed, and Jackson had written something about her, she didn't think she would be as calm and as reasonable as he was. In the last fantasy she only suggested a scenario about making love to Jackson rather than describe it as she had in many of the others. Could she live with it if he read just one?

She opened the book to the last story and shoved it to him. "You can only read this one. I'm going to put dinner on the table."

"Why don't I put dinner on the table and then read while we eat. You are either going to sit right here or go lie down. Those are your only two options."

"But—"

"No buts. Next time we go out to eat when you've worked all day. Did you make that appointment with the doctor yet?"

Nan narrowed her eyes at him. "I'm not an invalid. I can cook, and I can put dinner on the table. I just became dizzy for a minute."

"You know that as many times as it has happened over the past weeks, it's more than that. Don't avoid the issue. Have you made that doctor's appointment?"

"Yes." She wasn't lying. She had. She had a checkup scheduled three weeks from Friday. After noting her poor eating habits today and getting dizzy, she was pretty sure her whole problem was nutrition. Sometimes when it came to healthcare, doctors and nurses were the worst. They consumed more coffee, ate the least balanced diet, and in the past probably smoked more cigarettes than the average person.

"Good." Jackson stood, laying the black book on the table. "Before I start putting out all of this delicious food, where's Shakespeare?"

Nan grinned. "He's asleep in the magazine basket by the television."

"Then it's safe?"

She nodded. "He's too well mannered to attack the table when we're sitting at it."

He looked at her as if she'd just told him the sun was green. "I've learned not to take anything for granted where he is concerned. Now what do I do first?"

"Soup. It's in the fridge."

Jackson was efficient and within a few minutes he had dinner on the table and had fetched the red wine he'd brought. Lighting the multi-candle centerpiece was the last step and they began eating, both so hungry they didn't really talk for a while.

"Are you a gourmet cook or what? This is great."

"Thanks. I've yet to take a class or anything, but about every other month I pick out a new recipe to fix, and once a month I try and go to a different restaurant. That way I'm always experiencing something new on a regular basis instead of getting into a rut of eating the same thing all the time."

"There you go again." Jackson shook his head smiling.

"What."

"Goals and plans. They're a cure-all to you."

"You know what they say about an ounce of prevention."

"Yeah. I just hope that nothing comes along and detours your whole life."

"Things like that happen to everybody. Life is never easy. I'll just come up with a new plan. I always have. I bought you something." She jumped up and retrieved the plant. "It's to brighten up your cabin."

"Thanks," he said, though his voice sounded dubious.

"It's an African violet. They're supposed to bring happiness to those who keep them."

"Sometimes nothing can do that," he said, but before she could reply, he picked up her black book.

She reached for her wineglass, was tempted to down the whole thing, but then set it back down. Wine wasn't going to help. It was a good thing she had already eaten most of her dinner, because she suddenly lost her ability to swallow.

Jackson read, his expression moving from puzzlement, to interest, to a sexy grin. It didn't take him long before he finished. He set the book down, forked the last bite of his roast and potato casserole then picked up his wineglass. He didn't say a damn thing about the story.

Finally, she couldn't stand the suspense any longer. "Well?" she demanded.

"Well, what?"

"I told you they were stupid." She sat back, strangely let down. As if she had bared part of herself and been rejected.

Jackson set his wine down with a clunk. He stood and started taking off his black shirt. Nan glued her hungry gaze on him. When he'd first shown up at her apartment, damp with rain and dressed in all black, he'd looked so much like the pirate Black Jack that she'd nearly attacked him. If she'd been able to move she probably would have attacked him. Her mouth watered and her stomach tingled with anticipation. Jackson taking his clothes off was a good sign, but he stopped after removing his shirt and came to stand directly in front of her.

"How are you feeling?"

She licked her bottom lip. "Good."

"No dizziness or anything like that?"

She drew a deep breath, centered her gaze on the dark triangle of hair on his chest and followed it down to the waistband of his black jeans. "Nope."

"How's your pulse?" He took her wrist and laid his forefinger against her vein. "It feels a little fast." Instead of releasing her wrist, he wrapped the sleeve of his shirt around her wrist and tied it there.

She shot her gaze to his face. Only then did she see the deeply sensual gleam in his eyes. She could imagine just such a gleam in Black Jack's eyes. Her heart sped faster and her stomach clenched with an influx of butterflies. "I don't think—"

He leaned over and gently kissed the words off her tongue. "Don't think, Nan. Just feel." He stood and then pulled her up with her tethered wrist. "Do you come willingly to my bed wench, or do you need convincing?" He ran his finger down the center of her chest.

Oh, my! Nan blinked. Jackson seemed to become the pirate Black Jack. Answering words burst from her. "Never, you scurvy scum."

Her answer seemed to disconcert him. "Scurvy scum?" he repeated, wincing.

She nearly grinned. "Tis how I see it. A man who has nothing better to do than to take the hard earned fruits of other people's labor is a scurvy scum."

A loud, enraged meow sounded from her bedroom followed by intermittent thumps.

Jackson looked at her and she looked at Jackson.

"What is that cat up to?" he muttered moving toward her bedroom.

"I'm sure it's nothing," she answered following.

"I left my new sunglasses in the truck and I didn't bring my motorcycle."

They entered her bedroom to find Shakespeare jousting with Jackson's boots. The cat charged, swiped out his razor sharp claws just as he passed the boots. The boots reeled then noisily thumped back to the floor and Shakespeare charged again.

"Stop," Jackson thundered with enough volume to shake the walls. Shakespeare skidded to a halt so fast his tail end keeled over his head causing him to flip in the air. Once he righted, he stood still, crouched on his paws.

"Don't touch the boots again. If you do, I'm going to have to bring my brother's dog to visit you. His name is Brutus. Got it, Shakyboy?"

Shakespeare meowed with abject humility. Then almost as if he was bowing to leave the presence of a king, he backed out of the room. Nan blinked with surprise. Shakespeare had never shown such contrition. Was she raising her cat wrong, failing him somehow? Up until now Shakespeare owned the house and *let* her live there.

To her surprise Jackson didn't even go examine the gazillion scratch marks on his boots. He scooped her up and tossed her onto the bed.

"Now, that I've dueled with that scurvy pet, let's see to you, wench." He smiled slowly then, and drew a pack of condoms from his back pocket, tossing them beside her. "I think we're going to need all of these tonight, wench."

The condoms bounced. Twelve? Nan's mind boggled. It was a good thing she didn't have to work in the morning. But surely he didn't plan to use them all tonight. She drew a deep, anticipatory breath. Whether she could manage such a feat or not, the very thought of experiencing such an odyssey of pleasure at his hands was an aphrodisiac. The smell of honeysuckle lay sweetly in the air, and the spray of blossoms he'd brought her lay forgotten on the edge of her bed. She should have put them in water.

"We were discussing stealing fruits weren't we?" he asked.

"Yes, you knave."

"Stealing fruits sounds good to me, especially if the fruits are yours, my lady."

He made a damn good pirate, Nan thought as his voice and its silky smooth vibrations thrilled her. Before she could think of a witty answer or manage to squirm out from under his hard body, he slipped his shirt up through a wooden slat on the headboard and wrapped the other sleeve around her other wrist, tying it loosely.

"Your fruits are worth any risk, sugar," he said, straddling her as he began unbuttoning her blouse.

Blood rushed through her and pooled between her legs. Her heart beat faster, and her body became fevered with sensations. She tugged on the shirt binding her, and had second thoughts about this little fantasy. "Uh, Jack, I don't think that this—"

He leaned over and kissed her softly at first then more deeply. "Don't think sweetheart, just feel." Pulling her blouse open, he groaned when he saw her leopard print and black lace bra. "Nice," he murmured, fingering the lacey edges.

She sucked in a deep breath, arching her breasts closer to the heat of his touch. He snapped open her bra and her breasts sprang free. With her hips pinned beneath him and her arms bound above her head, she was totally vulnerable to his touch, to his whim. Maybe this wasn't a good...

"Now, let me tell you what I think about your story," he said softly. Taking a velvety honeysuckle flower, he traced her nipples. "By the way, your fruits are magnificent."

Then he took the flower and pulled the center of it out. Honeysuckle nectar lay gleaming on the small stem he held. Nan watched fascinated as he placed the nectar on the tip of his tongue.

"So sweet, so tasty." He pulled out two more blossoms and did the same. This time he covered her nipples with the nectar. "Let's get back to your story and save the fruit for later."

She gasped at the arrow of pleasure shooting straight to the heart of her desire. "My story? Fruits? Oh, uh, not fair. I don't want to talk about my story right now. Fruit is good. Let's have some more fruit. Maybe stealing them isn't so bad."

He laughed. "How about story and fruit." He cupped her breasts, molding them to the center of her chest and then leaned down and brushed his tongue across their pebbled peaks, sucking off the nectar. "Delicious."

Her hips involuntarily lifted off of the bed, pressing her hot need to him. "I can't think."

"That's good, just feel," he said sitting up and releasing her breasts. She felt the loss of his touch immediately and ached for more. "Your story made me feel. I wanted to know more about the woman and the man. I wanted to know what had happened in their past and what would happen in the future. Did he tie her to his bed? Did she make love to him before they'd reached port? Did he let her go afterwards? The story turned on both my body and my mind," Jackson said.

Starting with her bound wrists he feathered light touches over her skin, moving his way down her arms back to her breasts. "And thinking about you tied like this made me hot." He rolled her nipples gently between his thumb and forefinger.

A groan of exquisite pleasure escaped from her. This time she couldn't stand it. She arched even higher and her breath lodged in her chest as she shuddered with desire.

"Are you hot, Nan?"

"Too hot," she gasped.

"I'm burning too, sugar. Burning up for you." Moving off of the bed, Jackson shed the rest of his clothes. As he came toward her, she went to touch him, but couldn't. She wiggled against the ties in frustration. She was about to ask him to let her go when he grabbed her ankles. Lifting her legs, he slid off her sandals, then ran a finger down the sensitive skin of her insoles. Before she could recover, he started nibbling the inside of both of her legs, bending them as he moved his way up until his mouth came down and covered the hot yearning flesh between her legs.

"I'd always heard there was more than one way to skin a cat, sugar," he said as he hiked her skirt up to her hips and slowly slid her leopard print underwear down.

Nan giggled then gasped and groaned in response to all of the delicious things Jackson did to her. She couldn't take anymore. "I'm skinned, Jack. I don't feel I can stand anymore. I'm on fire. Let me loose."

He kissed her deeply and reached up with one hand to release the wrist he had loosely tied. Free, Nan sat up and pushed Jackson over onto his back. She attacked with her mouth and hands, placing kisses and little touches everywhere and giving his erection as much loving attention as he'd lavished on her.

She was lost completely in her need for this one man. Ever since she'd met him, he'd been the only one to consume her thoughts; he'd been the focus of her needs. She wanted him to feel, too. To feel his way out from behind that wall that kept him a prisoner. His breath was ragged in her ear and his hands trembled as he touched her. Still she wanted more from him and gave more and more of herself.

"Now, Nan. Ah, sugar, I need you bad." He grabbed a condom and soon slid his sheathed erection inside her. "I need you now." He withdrew a little and dove deeper. "I need you tonight, tomorrow, next week. I've never needed like this before."

She sighed with the pleasurable pressure filling her. This was the way things were meant to be between a man and a woman, the passion, the pleasure, the exposure of their vulnerable selves and the acceptance of each other's flaws and humanity. This was a part of what love was all about. Wrapping her arms around him, she matched his every move as he rocked them to ecstasy and beyond.

As they lay tangled together, gasping for air, Nan knew Jackson had somehow pirated away her heart.

"The Old Salt was right," Jackson muttered.

"What Old Salt?"

"The scurvy pirate in your book."

"Oh." She snuggled closer to Jackson then her eyes popped open. "Right about what?"

"You can warm a bed better than a tavern wench."

"What!" She smacked Jackson in the chest and started tickling him.

"I...couldn't...resist...," he said in between laughing and defending himself. "Seriously, I think you should write the whole story."

"I will," Nan said in a huff. "Only I think she's going to outsmart Black Jack and tie him to his bunk one night when he's had too much rum."

"Tie him up, huh?"

"Yep."

"You'll have to research the logistics of that first. Did you know that I make good research material?"

"I'll need to consider my prospects when I get ready, but I'll keep you in mind."

Jackson flipped her onto her back and covered her with his body. "I'll just have to make sure you don't forget," he said and then proceeded to make her forget everything but him.

CHAPTER TWELVE

The phone rang. Jackson rolled over and picked it up, forgetting he was at Nan's place.

"Turn off the alarm." Nan moaned and buried herself under the blanket. "I don't have to work today."

She'd been completely exhausted after they'd made love a second time and he'd felt slightly guilty for being the cause, but not sorry. Bleary eyed, he blinked at the red numbers staring at him from the digital clock across the room. Two? Who in the hell was calling her at this time at night?

Trying not to wake her, he whispered, "Hello."

"Who's this?" a gruff, tense voice demanded.

"Who's this?" Jackson countered, irritated.

"Jackson?"

"Jesse? What's wrong?" Jackson recognized his brother's voice.

"I must have dialed the wrong number. I've been trying to reach you, too. Alexi woke up with a really bad headache and I brought her to the Emergency Room. Call Nan and bring her to the hospital. They won't let me see Alexi yet."

"Jesse, we'll be there in ten minutes. I'm at Nan's."

Jackson hung up before hearing Jesse's replay. He turned over to Nan. "Nan, honey. Wake up." She opened her eyes, but just barely. "Jesse's taken Alexi to the Emergency Room. He needs us to come."

Nan sprung up from the bed. "What's wrong? The baby?"

"He said she had a bad headache. I don't know what that means yet. Let's not read anything into the situation until we get there, okay?"

He saw the worry in her eyes, saw her take a bolstering breath, and couldn't stop himself from walking across the room and pulling her into his arms. Not only was he worried about Alexi, he was worried about Nan, too. How had he thought he could share this woman's bed and not get involved in her life? He wanted her to write that story. He wanted to see her smile and laugh. He didn't want her to feel pain. He was even starting to find her damn cat amusing. It would be a long time before he'd forget Shakespeare's ass-end flip in the air. Somehow she'd staked a claim inside of him even though he hadn't believed there was an "inside" to him left. The hug lasted but a brief moment before they broke apart and quickly dressed.

They arrived at the hospital seven minutes later. As they walked in an ambulance came barreling up to the emergency entrance. The EMT in the driver's seat popped out and rushed to the rear. Jackson knew from the man's intensity that they had a serious trauma on board. When the man opened the back doors of the ambulance, Jackson heard a woman crying for help and a cold sweat broke out over Jackson's body.

Two nurses ran to help. The EMT in the back with the woman jumped out and started talking to the nurses as they unloaded the patient. Car accident was the one word Jackson discerned. He froze, fighting the memories exploding inside him as he stared at the blood upon the stark white sheets. He remembered the blood. So much blood had covered his hands.

"Jack?"

Nan pulled on his arm and Jackson forced his feet to move, but he could barely see where. They entered the emergency room waiting area and Jackson saw Jesse. His bother paced with military precision, his steps snapping upon the polished tile floor.

Jesse looked up. Seeing the fear in his brother's eyes stabbed Jackson right in the gut. He recognized his brother's fear, knew intimately the demons that ripped through a man's soul at a time like this. It was too much, the woman's cry, the blood, the fear. Jackson's stomach wrenched with pain.

He didn't hear what Jesse said. All he could hear was Amy screaming, the horrifying screech of metal, and the shattering of glass. Jackson clenched his fists, fighting against the overwhelming need to escape.

Nan grabbed his hand and he remembered she was there. The reality of his life came crashing back down on his shoulders. Had he actually thought he could get past the blood on his hands? Had he really thought he could find solace from his private hell in a woman's embrace?

He turned, fighting to focus on Nan. Tried to hear her words through Amy's screaming in his brain. Nan was speaking to Jesse. Then Jesse spoke and from a great distance he heard bits of words and sentences. "...stabilize...emergency C-section..."

Then, their voices were drowned out by the past. "Oh God, my baby, my baby! Jackson, save our baby! Hellpp Mmee!"

He jerked his hand from Nan's and grabbed his head. Pain tore through him.

"I couldn't! I tried!" He screamed back. He didn't realize he'd yelled aloud until he saw the shock on their faces. He had to get away. "I can't do this. Just forget I exist." He turned and ran out into the night.

~~*

*N*an watched Jackson leave. A heavy, sinking feeling worked its way down her gut, and a chilling numbness began at her toes, spreading throughout her body. Shock. Medically, she knew it, but never thought she'd be able to diagnose it in herself. She had sense enough to quickly sit down before she fell down.

The harrowing pain and guilt in Jackson's eyes matched the anguish she'd seen destroy her father. In fact, for a moment when Jackson had said to forget he existed, she'd thought her father had come back to life.

God, what had happened to Jackson? She sucked in air, forcing her lungs to work. She had to focus on Alexi right now. Jackson would have to wait. Jesse still stood, frozen in the same position he'd stood when they'd heard Jackson scream. Nan reached out and tugged on his hand. "Alexi. We have to think about her. Tell me again. What did the doctor say?"

Jesse turned back. His blue eyes were so like Jackson's Nan almost cried. Why had Jackson left? Why had he deserted them in the middle of a crisis? Jesse had tears in his eyes, and Nan could see he was as anguished as Jackson had been. But Jesse wasn't running out. He stood solid amidst the turmoil.

"I haven't seen the doctor yet, he's still with Alexi. The nurse just came out and said Alexi has developed preeclampsia. As soon as they get her blood pressure down and feel she is stable, they plan to do a C-Section."

"You're sure they said pre-eclampsia and not eclampsia?"

"Yes."

Nan exhaled with relief. Had Alexi gone into full eclampsia, she could have had convulsions, and would have been so unstable that a c-section wouldn't have been possible. A coma or death could have happened then. "I know you don't realize this, but this is good news. They've caught her condition early. With the advances medicine has made, she's probably going to be okay."

"Just exactly what in the hell is this condition and why didn't her doctor stop it from happening?"

"They don't know for sure what causes eclampsia. Symptoms are an increase in blood pressure, headaches, abnormal swelling in the legs and feet. Generally, what happens is that being pregnant becomes toxic to the mother. As for prevention, there isn't a lot a doctor can do until the patient starts showing symptoms. Alexi's condition has been borderline. Her blood pressure has been a little higher than normal for her, but not high enough to consider it dangerous. She's had some swelling, but not an excessive amount. Promptly getting her to the hospital was about the best thing you could have done."

Jesse shuddered. "Jackson was so right. He must have suspected something."

Nan bit her lip, trying to stave off the tears lurking just beneath the surface. Had it just been few hours ago she and Jackson had been in bed laughing and loving? "What, what was he right about?"

"Not leaving Alexi's side. He told me that if I tried to take another business trip before the baby was born, he would beat me to a pulp. Told me that nothing on this God's earth could be more important than being there for her right now. He said I could lose it all in the blink of an eye, just like he lost Amy. That's probably why he had to leave. Sometimes the memories are more than he can bear."

Nan leaned back in the hard plastic chair and swallowed the lumps in her throat. "He must have really loved her to still grieve for her so deeply."

"I think that's part of it. I also think that maybe we've respected his wish to be left alone too long. I need to call my folks and the twins to let them know what's going on."

"Okay. I'm going to shamelessly use my connections to find out more and get you in to see her ASAP."

"I went crazy when we first arrived. I couldn't get them to tell me anything. Thanks for being here."

"Don't ever hesitate to call me. I'll never let you, Alexi or the baby down." She reached out and squeezed Jesse's hand.

He squeezed back. "Thanks. I don't want to stick my nose where it doesn't belong, but give Jackson some time."

Nan sighed. "Sometimes all the time in world isn't enough. I've learned a person either has what it takes to move past a tragedy or they don't."

~~*

E*ight hours later, Nan stumbled* from the hospital the proud godparent of a six and a half pound, nineteen inch baby boy named Jake Everett Weldon. Alexi and the baby were going to be just fine. Nan shook her head in wonder, still hearing Jake wail up a storm when he was hungry. Alexi couldn't unbutton her gown fast enough for him.

Nan went to step from the curb then stopped. A tow truck pulled out of the emergency parking area with Jackson's pickup tethered to it. Was Jackson here?

She hailed the driver and he stuck his head out the window.

"This truck yours?"

"No, but I know the owner."

"Not my problem, lady. This truck has been parked in a fifteen minute parking zone since last night. The hospital says to tow 'em, I tow 'em." He started to leave.

"Wait. Where can my friend pick it up?"

"Tell him to call Ralph Butz Wrecker Service. That's B-U-T-Z. And tell him I don't take checks, ya hear?"

Nan nodded her reply. The man hit the gas and whizzed by her. If Jackson's truck had been parked all night at the hospital then where was Jackson? It also dawned on her that she needed to go back inside and call for a taxi.

"Nan, is that you?"

Nan turned to see Brad, perfectly groomed in an Armani suit. He stood half in and half out of his Mercedes. She hadn't noticed, but he'd driven up behind the tow truck.

"Hi," she said, feeling like a wreck.

"Hi. I left a message for you yesterday. You didn't call me back."

Nan frowned. "I didn't get it. What did you say?"

"My flight Sunday was delayed. I got your message about having to work Friday night and called the nursing supervisor. She was more than glad to change your schedule."

"Oh." She had to talk to Brad. It irked her that he'd taken the liberty to call and have her schedule changed without consulting her. But since he said he was going to talk to the nursing supervisor at the hospital party, and she didn't tell him not to do it, she really couldn't blame him.

"You look awful. Is something wrong?"

"Alexi had to have an emergency C-section. She became pre-eclamptic."

"I'm sorry to hear that. Everything all right now?"

"Yes."

"Listen, you look too tired to drive. Why don't I run you home?" He glanced at his watch. "I have forty minutes before I have to start rounds."

Nan blinked. Brad didn't seem as self absorbed as he had last week. He came around and opened the passenger door for her and tucked the seatbelt around her. She was too tired to insist on a cab, and wanted to get home fast, but she felt a bit awkward. She'd spent the last few days loving Jackson just about every physical way possible and until she made it clear to Brad that she...what?

Her head started to pound. It was all too complicated to sort out in the short time she and Brad had this morning. He started the car and drove out from the Hospital complex. They passed by the construction site and Nan looked for Jackson amongst the workers milling about the site. She didn't see him.

She studied Brad's serious profile from beneath lowered lashes. He was a model of efficient neatness—not a hair out of place, not a piece of lint on his dark navy suit, and on the seat between them she saw a leather bound pocket notebook with a neatly written to-do list dated today. There wasn't a doubt in her mind that in a middle of a crisis he'd be right there handling the problem.

She wondered why Brad couldn't have been the focus of her fantasies? Why couldn't he have been the man who stirred her passions? She had to tell him she wasn't going to be able to date him anymore. She had to tell him that even though he'd arranged for her to be off this weekend, she wasn't going to go yachting. And she needed to have more than just the time it would take to drive her home.

"Brad, we need to talk. Can you come to my house for dinner one night this week?"

"I'd like to tell you about the convention. You won't believe what kind of neurological breakthroughs are on the horizon. But I'm swamped after having been gone. How about I call you Thursday and we will see if I can work something out?"

The day before they were to go to the yacht party. She supposed it would have to do. "Thursday will be fine."

As soon as they drove up to her apartment, Brad got out and walked her to her door. She managed to find her keys and he took them from her and unlocked it.

Turning her way, he studied her for a minute and she almost ducked around him and dashed inside. Why was he paying attention to her now? A week ago she'd wanted him to look at her, to kiss her, now she didn't.

"You're right, Nancy. We need to talk. I guess I've been really busy lately and I have to go now too. Make sure you get plenty of rest," he said then brushed her cheek with a brotherly kiss and left.

Nan stumbled into her apartment surprised to feel tears brim her eyes. She walked back to her bed, saw it all a tumble from her and Jackson being together, saw the wilted spray of honeysuckle lying on the floor and started to cry harder. She didn't know why she was crying. It wasn't like she and Jackson had broken up, they hadn't even been together in any official capacity to break up. He'd asked her to spend the weekend in his bed and she had. She'd asked him to dinner and he'd come.

So if she was feeling pain, if she felt as if she'd made a mistake; it wasn't anybody's fault but her own. She made her way out to the couch with a box of tissues and curled into a ball. Shakespeare jumped up and Nan snuggled him into her embrace. Just as soon as she rested, she'd call Jackson and tell him about his truck.

Thirty seconds later, her left eye popped open. If his truck was still at the hospital, then where was Jackson? He never came back inside the Emergency Room, and didn't show up with the rest of the family when they had come. Her right eye popped open and she knew she wouldn't rest until she made sure he was all right.

In fact, if she wasn't so exhausted, she would have realized it before she left the hospital, would have known she needed to check on Jackson.

Getting up, she marched over to the phone, but Jackson didn't answer. Was he there and just not answering, or had something happened to him? She had to know. Besides, he left his African violet behind.

Bleary-eyed, she drove the miles to Jackson's cabin. Despite the bright summer sun, the cabin appeared dark and neglected. No breeze lifted the air and it hung hot and humid about her. She heard the distant cry of a crow and almost dreaded putting one foot in front of the other. Needless to say, she was glad Butz had Jackson's truck so she didn't have to look at its hood and be reminded of how wonderful her butt had felt on it. She kept her eyes purposely averted from his tarp covered Harley. It definitely just didn't exist as far as she was concerned. Not if she was going to stay calm and deal with this problem that had been a major problem between her and Jackson since the very beginning. He had to open up and tell her what in God's name haunted him, or she would have to say goodbye for good.

For all she knew goodbye for good may be exactly what he meant last night when he to her to forget he existed. She half expected to see him sitting on the porch with his guitar. He wasn't, but she heard the faint strum of a chord from inside the cabin. She knocked and called out. "Jackson, how did you get home?"

"I walked and hitched. Go away, Nan. I made a mistake and I'm sorry."

He'd walked? She opened the door and saw him. He half sat, half sprawled on top of the messed up bed. Like she, he still had on the same clothes he'd worn last night, but his were a good bit dirtier. Dust and mud speckled the bottom of his black pants and his shirt that he'd tied her up with hung unbuttoned and misshapen over his broad shoulders. He looked like hell. A half-empty bottle of whiskey on his bedside table didn't improve her mood; she was starting to get pissed off. He'd rather drink than talk to her or help his brother.

"I brought the African violet." She set it on his table.

"Take it back. It won't live in this cabin."

Now she was more than pissed off. "So that's it? You're sorry. You made a mistake. I'm to walk away and never darken your door again?"

He played a jarring chord. "Yeah. That's it. I never promised you more than sex."

She paced back and forth, counting each point on her finger. "Let's replay this. I walked away three months ago, because I knew that this was a mistake. But NOOO. You aren't happy with that. You have to come barging back into my life bearing sticky buns and honeysuckle sprays. You have to take me on Harley rides and bury yourself so deep inside me that you drive me to heaven. Have you ever heard of such a thing as body language? A man can promise more in his touch than he can ever follow up with his mouth. And I'm supposed to accept a wham-bam-sorry-ma'am and forget it?"

He shut his eyes and turned away from her. "You don't understand. Just let it go. It's better this way."

His rejection cut her deep and she fought back tears. "What don't I understand, damn it? What are you hiding? Were you driving the car that killed Amy?"

He tossed the guitar down on the bed and stood. He marched angrily her way, then swung around and paced to the other end of the cabin. "God no. That isn't what happened, but even that might be preferable."

"Then what? What the hell is it?"

He rubbed his hands through his wild hair. "I was freaking asleep in the back seat is what. I was so damn hung up in being the best ER doctor at Chicago General that I worked every shift I could. That left Amy alone most of the time and she wasn't happy. She decided to have kids, and suffered two miscarriages. When she got pregnant with the third, she didn't want to tell our families about it until she made it through the second trimester. She was so afraid something would happen and she didn't want everyone to know if it did. Then we were going to be coming home for Christmas, and she decided to surprise everybody. Amy wasn't feeling great and didn't want to go to the hospital's Christmas social, but I insisted. Yeah, I had to be there to make a good impression. My career was everything. I had worked a double that day and she drove while I slept in the back seat. Amy died because I insisted we go and I asked her to drive. There's nothing you can fix, Nan. Go home." Jackson walked over and opened the door.

Nan sucked in air. Tears stung her eyes at the raw pain she heard and saw in Jackson. The tragedy tore at her heart; yet couldn't he see that he couldn't take the blame for everything? She shook her head. "How do you know that? How do you know she would have lived if you had been driving? Are you psychic? Did you know there was going to be an accident that night?"

Jackson folded his arms; his reddened eyes were brutal and hopeless. "No. She died because she was seven months pregnant and when the other car hit ours, her stomach slammed into the steering wheel and ruptured her uterus. I couldn't save her and I couldn't save our baby. She died screaming for me to help her and all of my medical training couldn't. All it did was prolong her agony a few minutes more. If she had been a passenger, odds are that wouldn't have happened. Go on back to your life, Nan." Jackson left the door open and walked over to take a swig of the whiskey.

Nan wanted to scream. She wanted to cry; she wanted to shake him until it changed everything. "I'll go back to my life, Jack. But Amy's death was an accident. All of us can look back at things and see what we should have done differently." She touched his shoulder and he shrugged her off.

"Damn it, Jack. You can't waste your whole life like my father did just because hindsight is better than foresight. You're only accountable for the future. Knowing what you know now, what decisions are you going to make in your life today? Tomorrow? That's what you're responsible for." It was like she was talking to a brick wall. The dead expression on his face never changed. She had to reach him. "Would Amy have wanted you to turn your back on everything you aspired to and believed in?"

She picked up the broken doorknob still lying on the floor and tossed it on to the bed. "Is living this way some sort of testament to her and your unborn child?"

Jackson flinched, but Nan pursued. She wouldn't be able to look herself in the mirror if she didn't say what she had to say now. "Do you think shutting yourself up and never sharing anything about her does anything for her memory?"

Tears rolled down her cheeks and her breath caught in her throat. Still she forced the words in her heart out. "If I were to die, and if I had someone to remember me, I wouldn't want them to shut me away in a closet. My father spent his life punishing himself. Are you being any different? I'm not comparing him to you. What happened to you and Amy is different. Maybe at the time, if you had made different choices, the accident wouldn't have happened. You can't know that. Only God does. Hell, for all you know the same thing could have happened that night because she could have decided to go to the grocery store while you were sleeping. Would you still be blaming yourself if that had happened? All you are doing is punishing yourself for being alive. You can't forgive yourself for living and until you can do that, all you're going to do is hurt the people around you." She rushed to the door, knowing that at any minute she was going to break from the pain ripping through her.

At the last minute she turned back. "Being with you was different. I felt something special starting to grow. I've been alone most of my life and for just a little while, I didn't feel so alone. I don't think it would have lasted long. I couldn't live with broken doorknobs and not knowing where the clock is. It's okay to lounge in bed for a day every now and then. Every day would drive me crazy. Our take on life is too different to mesh. But I want you to know that you have things inside you to give. And you have something I don't have, a family. Walking out on Jesse last night hurt him. Don't throw your family away, Jack. Relationships are too precious to lose."

She started to cry. Biting her lip, she walked out the door.

Jackson followed and put his hands on her shoulders. "Don't do this to yourself, Nan. I can't be what you want. I can't make a commitment, be a father, or a husband. I had a family and I killed them. I never meant to hurt you."

Nan pulled away, her emotions like a gnashing sea, stripping away at the barriers she'd spent so long building. "No, you didn't mean to hurt me. But it wasn't an accident that we became involved. We both chose it and we'll have to live with the fall out. Even if you asked me to stick around, I wouldn't. I learned from my father that only you can help yourself. Nobody else can. Don't waste your life like my father did."

She turned and ran to her car. Her tears fell like a heavy rain and the sobs in her heart were lost in the song playing on the radio, *Tears In Heaven*.

She now knew why Jackson played the song. And part of her heart was crying tears in heaven too. Tears for what he lost and tears for what would never be between them. For even though she walked away from him, she knew she loved him.

CHAPTER THIRTEEN

She'd left the damned African violet. He didn't know what to do with it. For a long time after Nan left he stood rooted to the spot staring at the damned plant. Part of him was relieved she'd gone. It meant he didn't have to deal with her hurt. She was right. He should have left her alone. At least they hadn't gotten any more involved than they had. What lifelong consequences could just a few days have? She'd get over it. He'd get over it and everything could go back to the way it was.

And she was right about another thing. Once the newness of being together had worn off, their lives would have clashed.

But that's all she was right about. He marched over to the whiskey bottle and took an unsatisfying swig. The alcohol did nothing to help ease the bite of Nan's words. He stung all over and it pissed him off. But the biggest ache of all centered in the middle of his gut and in his already dead heart.

Why couldn't she have just left? She didn't know what in the hell she was talking about. He'd heard Amy die, crying about their baby. He'd felt their life's blood cover his hands. And *he'd* fought for their lives and failed. If there was a God in heaven, he was no friend.

Grabbing the whiskey, and a pint of Tequila for good measure, Jackson stomped out to the porch and gave the swing a good kick. It swung back and slammed against the porch railing, knocking out the decorative slats, then swung forward at a crazy angle and clipped his knee. He welcomed the pain. Taking another long draught from the bottle, he plopped down into the moving swing and the damn thing broke so that his feet were in the air and his head landed on the porch with a thump. He didn't bother to get up. By the time he finished the bottle, it wouldn't matter which end was up anyway.

~~*

"*Wake up, bro.*"

"Gos asway," Jackson managed to slur through his hangover. He forced one eye half-open, wincing at the blinding sun. It looked like there were six Jesse's standing over him.

"Not this time. Your family has a few things to say to you and you're going to sober up enough to hear them."

With a great deal of effort and trying not to move his pounding head too much, Jackson pried both of his eyes open to a slit. The six Jesse's settled into a blurry vision of Jesse, his brothers James and Jared, and shockingly, his mother, Emma and his father, John.

"He stinks worse than a brewery." James said.

"Looks like that old pig we kept out by the mud hole. How'd he get so dirty?" Jared asked.

"Nan said he walked home from the hospital, Monday night. Looks like he's done nothing but drink for two days." Jesse added a resounding curse to emphasize his disgust.

"He walked all that way. Damn. Didn't think the old buzzard had that much brawn left in him." James snorted

"Hey, watch it," Jesse said. "He's just a year older than me."

"If the shoe fits…" Jared muttered.

"I can still whip your ass any day little brother."

"Boys!" Emma Weldon shouted. "This isn't helping your brother. Let's get him out of that swing. I do declare, I've never seen such a sorry sight."

"Looks like a total loss," John Weldon said.

Jackson winced at his mother's description. He had never wanted his parents to see him this way. Had Jesse just mentioned Nan's name? Had Nurse Nan called his family trying to fix his problem? He didn't want anyone's pity; he didn't have a problem.

"You're right, he's a total loss," James said.

"I wasn't talking about your brother," John Weldon said. "I was talking about the cabin. We don't have any choice but to save your brother, but the cabin might have to just get bulldozed down. The wood is rotting."

His father's disgust came through Jackson's drunken haze loud and clear. "I can't see that he's done a single thing to upkeep the place since he moved in. This cabin belonged to your grandpa. He built it with his own two hands. It's a damn shame to see it this way."

Where in the hell was a dark hole when he needed it? Jackson wondered.

"I say we strip him and dump him in the creek," Jared said.

"Sounds good." James, Jesse, and his father all agreed.

"I'll go make some coffee," his mother added.

The conversation was just about more than he could process over the jackhammer pounding his brain. Before he could get up and tell everybody to get lost, they lifted him and carted him like a sack of potatoes. He tried to struggle against his tormentors, but was too drunk and weak to overpower their combined strength as they took off his boots, shirt, and pants.

"He must have waded through a briar patch with his boots on. Never seen so many scratches," James said.

"Shaaakspeer," Jackson said and started to laugh.

"Hell, what did he say?"

"Beats me. Whatever it was he sure thought it was funny. On the count of three, boys."

Jackson hit the water mid laugh with his mouth open. He didn't bother to shut it. The water was nice, cool. He let his body go lax thinking he could close his eyes and never wake. No such luck, somebody grabbed his hair and jerked him up.

"Ouch. That hurt." Jackson floundered, coughing. The sun was too damn bright and he had to shield his eyes to shout at his brother Jesse.

Anger lashed across Jesse's face and Jesse pushed Jackson. "Did you just try and drown yourself?"

Jackson stumbled. "Go away."

Jesse pushed again. "You want to die, bro? Is that what the past four years have been all about? I'll help you."

Jesse pushed him back under the water and held him there. At first Jackson didn't struggle. He knew his brother would haul him up in just a second. Only Jesse didn't. He just pushed him further under the water. Jackson could feel his lungs starting to burn, and a sense of urgency to breathe alarmed his brain.

He'd thought he wanted to die, but something inside him couldn't let go. He started to fight and to push against Jesse's hold. Jesse only pushed him deeper. He had to breathe, his vision was beginning to gray around the edges and he felt as if his chest was about to explode. He lashed out slugging at his brother, fighting to the surface. He finally broke through. Gasping for air, he hauled back his arm and plastered Jesse right in the gut. "What in the hell are you doing?"

"Giving you your wish," Jesse gasped, nursing his stomach. His face was deathly grim, and his eyes were burning coals of anger. They stood in the creek staring at each other. "I think the wrong person died in that car crash."

Tears stung Jackson's eyes and he clenched his fists. He was more sober than he wanted to be. "The wrong person did die. It should have been me, not Amy and our unborn baby!"

His words exploded like an A-bomb with immediate fall out.

"Dear God, son." Jackson saw his father step into the creek. Pain and concern lay heavy in his father's gray eyes, and echoed in the weathered lines of his face.

Emotion choked Jackson. He had to turned away or cry. He turned away.

"Son of a bitch," James said.

"Shit. I'm sorry man," Jared muttered, parking his butt on the bank.

Jackson heard a choked sound from Jesse and saw that his brother was crying. "It could have been me. I could have lost Alexi and the baby. That's what you were trying to tell me last week. I had planned to make one more business trip to DC. I was going to leave Monday noon and return Tuesday morning. When she developed her headache Monday night, she just wanted to crawl into a dark room, which is exactly what she would have done if I had been gone. I insisted on taking her to the hospital and the doctor said we arrived there just in time."

Then Jesse hauled off and planted his fist in Jackson's face. Jackson's head snapped back and he staggered in the water. "What in the hell was that for?"

"For not telling us what has been eating you alive for the past four years. Part of loving is sharing both the good and the bad. We should have kicked your ass years ago and then maybe you wouldn't be in such sorry shape now."

"Your brother is right, son. You should have told us."

"What good would it have done?" Jackson yelled, clenching his hands.

His father's strong hand fell on Jackson's shoulder. Rather than adding to the burdens there as Jackson expected, the crushing emotions eased as his father spoke. "We could have talked, could have understood. You'd be surprised what a difference that can make. If you keep something closed up where it can fester, all it does is spread poison throughout your body. You boys have done enough, now. I think Jackson and I need to have a little time."

Jesse stomped out of the water. "I hope to God that you're man enough to decide to join the living, Jack. I have a son who wants to meet his uncle and I don't think a broken down drunk will be a good influence."

Jared stood up. "He's a cute little whipper-snapper. As often as he demands for Alexi to feed him, I think he's already figured out one of the best things about women."

Jesse went to smack Jared and Jared ducked, running up the hill. Memories of their fun times as brothers tugged on Jackson's heart.

"You want me to get the scratches polished out?" James picked up a boot from the bank. Boots were sacred to Weldons.

"No. I think I'm going to leave the scratches a while." A remembrance of Shakespeare was a remembrance of Nan. Shit, his gut hurt over her.

James shrugged and dropped the boot. "I feel like we should do something, but I don't know what. Me, Jesse, and Jared are here for you. God forbid, but if I ever have to deal with what you've had to deal with, I hope you'll be around to kick my ass and pick me up off the ground." He turned to go then looked back. "The guys at work have been asking about you. They told me to tell you to haul your ass back there. Joe has taking over the singing and they're dying as a result."

"Thanks," Jackson said, surprised to feel that he just might miss the guys at work. The mundane labor, like nailing boards, passed faster and the work progressed quicker if they sang things like "Car Wash," and railroad songs.

Jackson didn't guess he was going to get out of talking to his father. "You mind if I go put some clothes on?"

"Nope. Your mom's at the cabin waiting with coffee. We'll just mosey on up there and talk after you're dressed. You can tell us both about everything. Then we're going to have to evict you as a tenant. You can stay at the big house until you decide to start living life again. Shouldn't take long with your mom around."

"I think maybe I'll just stay at the cabin and fix it up."

"You're going to fix it up anyhow, but you've had too much time alone, son. You're coming home."

The minute he walked into the cabin in his underwear he knew his dogged dreary days of solitary depression were over. His mom sat at the dinette table folding a dishtowel. You knew Emma Weldon was praying when she had a dishtowel in her hands. He'd heard her often growing up. She looked at him. Her graying hair had more pepper than salt in it, and her eyes were grim, reminding him of the rare times she was angry enough to cut a switch to his hide. In the center of the table were about a dozen condom wrappers he'd discarded when making love to Nan and hadn't bothered to pick up and put into the trash yet.

Damn, he was thirty-five years old, not sixteen. This couldn't be happening. He scrubbed his hands over his face.

Jared stuck his head in the door. "Ma. You forgot one. I found this out in the driveway." He held up a condom wrapper.

Jackson snatched it away, literally ready to pound something and his brother's grinning face looked like a good place to start. Disgusted, Jackson stomped to the bathroom. He showered and dressed. His mother and father were waiting for him when he got out.

"Sit," his mother ordered, shoving a hot mug of coffee into his hands. "We had this discussion twenty years ago, so I'm not going to go over it all again. I've only two things to say. I hope that you used those condoms on just one woman and not a slew of women. And that you care a great deal about that woman."

Jackson started to speak and his mother held up her hand. "I don't want to know because technically it is none of my business. The second thing I have to say is that we taught you to be a responsible adult and that means not having sex until you're ready to take on the responsibilities and consequences that go along with the fun. From the way you live here, and the shape you were in this morning, you are no more ready for children than you were at fifteen." Tears gathered in her blue eyes and Jackson saw her unwavering strength falter. "Where have we failed you, Jack?"

God. He thought he couldn't feel any more and all he'd been able to do was feel. Everything cut so deep. "You haven't. I'm the one who screwed up. The choices I made killed Amy." He told his parents everything. It hurt them that he hadn't told them about the guilt that he felt. Their response seemed to mirror Nan's.

"Was Amy a bad driver? Anything not maintained on the car she drove?" his father demanded, eyes narrowed.

"No, and no. The other driver had a heart attack and crossed the centerline. Amy tried, but couldn't avoid his car."

Dishtowel in hand, his mom spoke up. "How was Amy not feeling well that night? Was she ill? Did she have a fever?"

"No. Just heartburn from a meatball sub she'd eaten while out buying a maternity dress for the party." Jackson's heart warmed a minute. Amy had been so ticked off that what she craved to eat hadn't set well.

His mom smiled. "Did she have on her new dress when you got home, or did you have to force her to put it on?"

Jackson rolled his eyes. "She had it on, of course.

"Doesn't sound like you forced her to go. Sounds like she wanted to go."

"She did, but—"

"Did she work all night with you?" his father asked.

"That's a stupid question. She was at home asleep."

"So son, seems to me that if you'd been irresponsible and had been driving after being up for twenty-four hours and had an accident that killed Amy, you'd have every right to blame yourself."

"We just shouldn't have gone."

"Good solution," his mom said. "All of us should just stop living and close ourselves up in a closet. Can't go buy food, because we might have an accident on the way to the store. Can't get on a plane for a vacation or a business trip, it might crash. Can't go to the beach, we might get skin cancer."

"Now you're really being ridiculous."

"No, you are."

"Don't you understand what happened? They died and I couldn't save them?"

"Is there any way that anybody could have saved them?"

"Maybe. If we'd been closer to the hospital, if I'd had the right equipment." But even as he said the words, he realized that it had been a big maybe. Amy had died even before the paramedics had made it to the scene.

His mother squeezed his hand. "Caring is different than feeling guilty. You can care and not destroy your own life. I grieve for Amy; she was my first daughter-in-law. I call her mother twice a month and we talk; we've moved past the pain to the memories. You need to, too."

"Your mother and I gave the best years of our lives making sure you had a chance at a good life. We aren't going to lose you. Not to a bottle of whiskey and not to guilt over something you couldn't control." His father stood. "Think about it, son. Pack up some of your clothes. We'll be expecting you for supper."

His mother leaned over and kissed his cheek. "I watered your African violet. If you aren't careful it will die."

"Thanks," Jackson said. They left. Jackson looked at the plant Nan had given him, now wilted and brown tinged, nowhere near resembling the lush little plant she'd given him.

Just before the door shut, his father stuck his head back in. "Were you in or on the pickup truck?"

It took a few seconds for Jackson to figure out what his father was talking about. "On," he said without thinking.

"It's in your blood. That's where your mother and I conceived you."

"John!" Jackson heard his mother wail.

His father grinned then nodded at the pile of condom wrappers on the table. "Looks like you found someone worth living for."

Jackson shook his head in wonder. He couldn't quite picture his mother and father on a pickup truck. Not like he and Nan had been. Parents didn't do those things.

CHAPTER FOURTEEN

It took Nan until Thursday to be able to draw a deep breath. No, he hadn't promised more than just sex, but she had felt so much more. More than she had ever felt with any one before. And part of her carried the heavy burden of his anguish.

He hadn't left her with any other choice but to leave him in the dark void he'd chosen. After tossing and turning all Tuesday night and not seeing Jackson at the construction site when she arrived at work on Wednesday, she'd decided to call Jesse and ask him to go see Jackson.

Her nights were restless, but not because of any fantasies. She still yearned for him, ached for his touch, but the ache was a bitter draught laced with sadness. She had nightmares now. During the night she saw Jackson trying to save people in the emergency room and couldn't help them. She worked right beside him and every failure left bloodstains on her hands.

After two nights she was ready to scream. Every woman who came into her care at work, she double-checked her assessment, their vital signs, and those of the unborn baby. She was a nervous wreck that something might go wrong, could go wrong at any minute.

By Thursday noon she was exhausted and still had three more hours left to her shift. She turned into the nurse's station to log in her notes on her patient's charts. Jackson wasn't at work, so no one gawked out the window. Still, Nan ran her gaze over the construction site. They'd made a lot of progress in two weeks. It wouldn't be long until all of the outside work would be completed. She told herself that this was a good thing.

"Nan."

Nan looked up to see Brad enter the nursing station. Dr. Dennison was at his side.

"Nancy, you remember Steve Dennison, right?"

Nan stood to shake his hand. "Of course."

"Nice to see you again, Nancy." He cupped her hand and once again she found his smile warm and friendly.

Brad touched her arm and she turned to him. "I'm glad I caught you. I only have a minute. The hospital board has asked me to attend their meeting tonight so I'm afraid I won't get to see you until tomorrow. What time are we supposed to be there, Steve?"

"Around seven. Don't worry about dinner, a buffet is being catered."

"I still don't know about the whole weekend. I'm trying to work out my on-call situation, but Nancy and I will be there for the party Friday. Is it okay if I pick you up about six-thirty?"

"Uh, well, I was going to talk to you about that tonight," Nan managed to say. Telling Brad she wasn't going to go with him in front of his colleague seemed pretty tacky; she couldn't do it.

"Oh, I'd forgotten. You prefer to drive when I'm on call. Why don't you meet me at the Sandpiper at six-thirty? It's a little pub on the dock. We can have a few minutes to talk beforehand."

"Fine." At least driving herself made it seem less like a real date and if she met Brad before the party, she'd be able to tell him then. Brad left in a whirlwind hurry, and Nan turned back to the charts, but couldn't focus on the words. She decided to take her lunch break first.

Since she had no appetite, she went to see Alexi.

Nan heard Jake's wail all the way from the end of the hallway. She knocked and stuck her head in Alexi's door. "It's me."

"Be warned. You enter at your own risk." Alexi was trying to get her gown opened enough to feed Jake who squirmed and kicked his little legs like a champion swimmer. He'd broken free of his blanket.

"What happened here?" Alexi's hospital room was a wreck.

"Jesse and Jake that's what."

"Uh. Oh. This doesn't sound good."

Just as Alexi opened her gown and snuggled Jake up to her breast, he gave one final kick. He hit a plastic vase made to look like a diaper pail that was sitting on Alexi's lap table. The blue carnations and white roses went flying all over the floor. The water poured into Alexi's bed.

Alexi's eyes boggled. "This morning it was my ice water jug." She pushed the nurse call button. Jake's wail was replaced by the gentle suckling sound of a baby nursing and Alexi tucked him closer to her body. While waiting for the nurse to respond, she pointed to two chairs stacked full of newspapers and magazines jumbled together with miniature sports balls and baby toys. "That's Jesse's." Then she pointed to a big pile of baby paraphernalia all over her bed. "That's Jake's. My stuff is in the suitcase in the closet."

Nan shook her head smiling. "I have to hand it to you, I'm not sure I would be as calm as you are right now."

Alexi brushed the cap of little black curls on Jake's head with her fingers. "I wouldn't have it any other way."

The nurse stuck her head in the door.

"Jake scored another one. He nailed the vase of flowers you just delivered. I need my bed changed."

"I should have known better than to set those there. That boy is destined to some sort of kicking greatness."

"Don't tell Jesse, he'll have him playing soccer in the crib before the week is out."

"I'll be back in a minute. It would be good for you to take your walk in the hall then, too."

Alexi groaned. "I thought once you had the baby the worst part was over with."

"Honey, it's just started," the nurse said grinning as she left.

"They cut you open then they don't let you sit a minute," Alexi grumbled.

"If you sat then you would be in worse shape and it would be harder to move," Nan advised.

Alexi narrowed her eyes. "I already have a nurse. I need my best friend right now."

Nan didn't miss a beat. "Well, isn't that just awful. What do they think they are doing to you, making you get up and walk? You didn't sign up for ROTC. I need to go whip them with my stethoscope."

Alexi grinned. "Better. Much better." She wrapped a blanket around Jake and he broke his suction from her breast. "Why don't you burp him while I lumber out of this bed and we'll wheel him down to the nursery so I can take a nap?"

"Let me wash my hands and you have a deal." Nan hurried. Before taking the baby she placed a large cotton diaper over her shoulder to protect the baby from any germs. The soft scents of baby lotion and the feel of his warm little body snuggled up next to her were indescribable. At thirty, she was more than ready to have and love a child, but she wanted it all the old fashioned way. She wanted a loving husband, a successful marriage, and all the earmarks of a happy family that she'd missed as a child. The prospects of that happening were dwindling every year.

Alexi rolled out of the bed moaning and groaning. Nan kept her mouth shut rather than tell Alexi that the more she moved the easier it would be.

As Nan patted Jake's little back she was rewarded with a soft burp and a big sigh. When it came time to put Jake in the rolling baby crib, Nan was reluctant to let him go. "I get first dibs on babysitting."

"Too late. Jesse's mom has already staked them out."

"Then she'll just have to share. If he starts wailing again, it might take two of us to settle him."

"You have a point."

They took the baby to the nursery, and as they headed back Nan glanced at her watch. "I've ten minutes left."

"Good. Just enough time to tell me why you've got dark circles under your eyes and you're about as tense as a bride marrying the wrong groom. I should know. Are you still going with Brad tomorrow night? Did you and Jackson go out Friday after Jesse's birthday?"

Nan blinked. Her whole life had changed in the space of a few days and she hadn't even been able to tell Alexi about it. What was there to say now? Nan sighed. "To make a short story even shorter, Jackson and I lit up the world in seventy-two hours, and then we crashed and burned. Brad still thinks I'm going with him tomorrow night, but I'm not. I'm going to meet him at six-thirty at the Sandpiper to tell him that I won't be seeing him any more either. I'm solo again."

"Whoa, whoa, whoa. You mean you and Jackson meshed?"

"We more than meshed. We mushed, mashed, and mated like there was no tomorrow, which as it turns out, there wasn't."

"Why?"

"He made a mistake. We both did."

"But he made "the mistake" first? He said that to you?"

"Yes, but—"

There was outraged fire in Alexi's eyes. "He told you that after the hours he's pumped me for information about you?"

"He did?"

"Hours. I'm going to string him up by his *mistaker*."

"Listen. It wasn't like that, but it's too complicated to explain right now. I'll have to tell you later."

"I don't care what it was like. You do me a favor. You go to the yacht party and you have a great time, because you're a great person and you deserve it. Forget Jackson and forget Brad. Find yourself some other man who isn't on that edge we talked about."

"Maybe next time."

"No, remember what you told me when my world fell apart? Today is the first day of the rest of your life. Don't do it next time, Nan. You deserve today."

Alexi's words stuck in Nan's head. They inspired her. What she needed was a new plan for her life. She did deserve a "today."

~~*

*J*ackson stood outside the cabin he'd lived in for the past four years and took a sobering look at it. Derelict and trashy were two words that came to mind. The rest of the words he'd just as soon not examine, because of what they might say about him. He could see some of the holes in the roof from where he stood.

No wonder Nan had split when she'd awakened to the rain last Sunday. Hell, had that been just four days ago?

Yeah. That his life had seesawed drastically in that time didn't surprise him. He of all people knew how quick one of fate's tornadoes could up and devastate a man's world, and then disappear into the sky, leaving only traces of a life behind.

Nothing had changed since his family had tossed him in the creek to knock the edge off his two-day drunk yesterday, except for the fact that he was now sober. He didn't buy into their view, his parents', his brothers', and Nan's. He'd never stop believing that if he'd been driving that night, life might be different. Amy and his child might have lived. The possibility would always haunt him.

That and the truth Jesse had slammed into him. By having his head held underwater until he'd thought he'd die, Jackson realized without a doubt he didn't want to die. Since then, the harsh wire brush of reality had scrubbed him raw.

Wanting to live was a whole damn step above merely existing, and it pissed him off to have that muddy mask ripped away. Leaving his thoughts and his scrutiny of the cabin's sorry-assed condition, Jackson headed up the steps. He'd left his guitar behind when he'd left yesterday. His Mom had him staying in the room he'd shared with Jesse while growing up, and the memories that kept cropping up from the memorabilia scattered about the room was too disruptive. Jackson figured he'd drown the memories with music. If he was singing, even to just himself, he didn't have to listen.

He grabbed his guitar from the messed up bed and Nan's image, naked, with her wild hair spilling onto his pillows played in his mind. A half-full bottle of whiskey sat on the floor next to the bed and he snatched it up, looking at how the sunlight made the amber fluid glisten like honey, like Nan. Determined, he marched to the sink and poured the whiskey, honey lights and all down the drain.

It was done. Over. He and Nan had their sex now they'd both go back to their lives. Walking out of the cabin, he saw the plant Nan had given him sitting on the dinette table where his mother had put it after watering it. Soon it would wither and die and he'd have nothing but memories of sex to remind him of Nan. Good, he thought, slamming the cabin door behind him. An action that had little effect because the damn door popped back open, reminding Jackson that the doorknob had fallen off and rolled to Nan's feet the last time he'd slammed the door. The lock itself had to be stuck now.

Memories of his weekend with Nan chased him all the way back to the family's farmhouse. He drove up and had to park his truck down the drive. His brothers, Jesse, James, and Jared were going one on two at the basketball net.

Damn, he didn't want to have to deal with anybody. He just wanted to be left alone. Just as he knew it would, the minute he stepped out of the truck the basketball came zinging his way. Jackson caught the ball and thought hard about just dropping the damn thing and walking on into the house, or hopping onto his crotch rocket and taking off down the road. But then he remembered the "ride" Nan had given him on his bike and he cursed. He hadn't ridden the damn bike since.

Jackson threw the ball to Jesse and stripped off his shirt. What he needed was a mean game. The time to whip his younger brothers' asses had come.

He came at them hard, leaving no doubt in the stubborn blue gazes glaring at him, that he had something to prove. "Every man for himself."

He didn't want their pity, and he didn't want their sympathy, but if they were going to offer him a hell of a fight, he'd take that gladly.

Nobody said a word. The next three hours were a grueling, muscle-straining marathon of grunts and sweat. Jackson was ahead by one over Jesse. Jared and James were tied at two below that.

Their mother had called them to eat more than an hour or two ago. They didn't even stop to answer her. Now it was dark, and the basket was about as visible as a gnat's ass. They were still playing.

Jesse knocked the ball from Jared and swung around to snag a basket. "*Damn*," Jackson thought, seeing his lead about to disintegrate. He jumped, straining over James head to block the shot but missed. Just as the ball was about to kiss the rim in one honey of a shot, a blast of water knocked it from its intended purpose.

Jackson's jaw dropped. His quick glance showed his brother's had the same reaction. Jesse's was the worst. In practically slow motion they all turned toward the house. Emma Weldon, a mother with a bone to pick, stood with the garden hose in her hand.

"You all sure enough had to hear me call you to supper. I'll put up with a lot, but when I make a meal for you, and your father and I haven't had all four of you to the dinner table at the same time in a while, I expect to be heard."

Before any of them could speak, she aimed the hose at them and let them have it. When they were soaked, she turned off the hose. "Dry up and get to the table. Dinner won't keep a minute longer."

All of Jackson's intense, sweaty effort fizzled at his feet. The looks on his brothers' faces rivaled Jackson's sentiments. Well, hell.

"I won." Jackson swiped water from his eyes.

"Bullshit," said Jesse, marching toward him.

"I hear anybody arguing and they get KP duty. There are towels at the back door. If you all aren't here in five minutes, nobody gets a piece of cherry pie."

James and Jared started laughing.

"Makes you feel like a yard ape again," Jesse said.

"Yeah, for a minute there I had to look down and make sure I wasn't wearing a diaper." James slapped the seat of his wet jeans.

"You need to," Jackson said. "Hell, you've gone and pissed your pants."

Jesse sniffed the air. "Smells like a skunk tangled with a pair of stink bugs."

For a second Jackson exchanged glances with his brothers. That last snippet of conversation had been a running joke between them from a time when James and Jared had been in diapers and they'd trapped a skunk under a laundry basket. Curious brats that they were they'd put their faces right up to the lattice holes of the basket and had gotten a hefty dose of skunk perfume.

Jesse started to laugh and it spread like hot butter on biscuit. Jackson was the last to join, but he laughed until tears fell.

"Three minutes left." His mother called out the door. Still laughing, Jackson ran for his shirt. "I get the pie," he said racing for the door.

Jesse, James, and Jared tried to butt their way in before him. Jackson ended up rolling in the door with all three of his brothers on his back.

"One minute left," Emma Weldon said, swatting at them with her dishrag.

Jackson parked his butt in his old chair and it wasn't until his father said grace, that Jackson remembered that he was thirty-five and not fifteen. For a few minutes, he'd felt like the boy he'd used to be, and as the intervening years came crashing back down on him, he wished he'd never had those few minutes of fun. It made what was left of him hurt so much more for what he'd lost of himself.

He forced himself to eat, to smile, to answer a question that strayed his way, but he didn't belong. He wasn't the man his family remembered and never would be again.

"My company has an interesting job tomorrow night," Jesse said.

Having first established his security company in Washington DC, where the world's leaders and cherished darlings were known to tread, Jesse had gained worldwide respect. Occasionally, he himself still presided over really important events.

"A VIP coming into town?" John Weldon asked, sliding his empty pie plate toward the nearly gone cherry pie. He gave Emma a sweet smile. She cut him a tiny sliver and he looked as if she'd stolen his last dollar. She pointed at her stomach, indicating he was on the heavy side of plump.

"Nope." Jesse stuck his plate up and received a bigger piece of pie than his father.

Jackson couldn't help but grin as his father glared at Jesse's slice of pie.

"Then what? James Bond moving in?" Jared asked.

Jesse rolled his eyes, and when he did, Jackson saw his dad switch pie plates with Jesse. Jackson had to hand it to his father. He was the fastest pie plate switcher in the world.

"Nope," Jesse said, picking up his fork.

"Cameron Diaz?" James asked.

Jesse didn't answer. He was glaring at his miniscule piece of pie.

"John Weldon, we're walking two miles in the morning instead of one."

John groaned. Apparently satisfied by Emma's punishment, Jesse lit into his sliver of cherry and crust.

"Well," Jackson muttered, compelled to get the lead out of the conversation. "What are you doing?"

"Providing security and transpo for a big yacht party in the bay. Then a team will trail the yacht for the weekend as it sails toward St. Simon's Island. It's a doctor at the hospital who's putting on this big shindig, and wants to make sure no one bothers the yacht."

Jackson tensed. Any mention of the hospital brought Nan immediately to mind.

"What's so special about that?" Jared frowned.

Jesse shrugged. "Not much, just a different sort of security detail for around here. Funny thing, when I was at the hospital with Alexi and Jake earlier, Alexi mentioned that Nan was going."

Hospital bigwigs, Jackson thought. Swanson. Nan was going yachting with Swanson and his buddies for the weekend. Well it didn't take her long to put their "just sex" weekend behind her. Jackson had clenched his fist before he realized it. He forced himself to shrug. "Hope it doesn't rain," was all he said.

When he saw his brothers pitching in for KP duty, Jackson left. He drove his truck out into the middle of an empty cornfield, right out in the open where he could see the stars. Grabbing his guitar, he climbed into the bed of the truck and started strumming. Yeah, as long as he was singing he didn't have to listen to the voice in his head calling him a fool.

But after awhile, even the music began calling him names. He didn't know what time it was when he hopped into his truck and headed for town.

~~*

A pounding on Nan's front door woke her up from her dreamless sleep. She rolled off the couch, stepped on Shakespeare's tail, and stubbed her toe on the way to the door. She'd left every light in the house on trying to chase the shadows from her heart. And she hadn't been able to sleep in her bed all week. Memories of Jackson were just too damn strong. She could handle the couch. They hadn't made love on the couch. A glance through the peep told her two things. It was very dark outside and a disheveled Jackson stood on her doorstep.

She considered ignoring him, but the memory of his anguish over the death of his wife and unborn child was too fresh, too sharp in her mind to turn her back on him even though seeing him stabbed her own heart.

She cracked the door. "What do you want, Jack?"

"Is it true?"

"Is what true?"

"Are you yachting with Brad for the weekend?"

"This isn't happening. We are not having this conversation. You are not here. Do you understand? You have no right to be here, Jack." Nan shut the door in his face, sure that she must be having another nightmare. She didn't have fantasies or dreams these days. Her "just sex" weekend had cured her of that, but had left her with a more incurable and twice as devastating—broken heart.

CHAPTER FIFTEEN

She never went back to sleep after Jackson left last night. So if today, Friday, was the first day of the rest of her life—she was in big trouble. It rained hard all morning and when she headed to meet Brad, the roadsides were lakes.

She had a flat tire on the way to the restaurant. She had to pull into one of those lakes to change her tire while dressed in all her finery. The hem of her dress got wet and she had to take off her shoes to keep them from being ruined. It occurred to her that she wasn't too far from the ragtag, barefoot little girl after all.

She arrived late for her meeting with Brad, but that wasn't a problem. Brad wasn't there yet either. He drove up behind her car in the valet line and suggested that they go on to the yacht.

So they sat in a private corner at the lavish party and Nan tried to tell Brad that she wouldn't be seeing him anymore. He kept talking about his convention speech.

"Brad. I don't see that there is any point in continuing to date. We don't seem to be connecting."

He frowned and replied in all seriousness. "What does connection have to do with anything? To have a future all you have to do is to make a plan. Emotions and feelings really don't matter. They fall in line eventually."

Did he think emotions were army recruits?

His cell phone rang. He glanced at the number. "It's the hospital. "I've got to go, but I'll put us at the top of my list, and we'll get this worked out."

"No. No lists Brad."

"Nan. We'll have to discuss this later."

"Sorry, Brad. There isn't a later."

"Why? What happened?"

"I don't know. Maybe when you set your mind on what an ideal partner would be, you miss seeing the real person in front of you." Even as she said it, Nan wondered just how guilty she was of the same thing. Brad stared at her and she met his gaze. But they were so distant from each other that not even the truth drew them closer together.

Brad looked as if he meant to say something more, but then focused his gaze on his phone. "I really have to go."

"I know." Nan smiled, relieved. "I'll see you around," she said then turned away and wandered through the party. Steve Dennison came up to her, looking like a blond Tom Selleck dressed in Italian leisure clothes.

He handed her a glass. "I brought you some champagne."

"Thanks." She was glad she'd worn a conservative black sheath with touches of gold at her ears and neck. Anything more casual and she would have been out of place. Many of the women wore jewels and finery.

"I overheard your discussion with Brad. He works too much. Do you need a date for the evening?" he asked with a twinkle to his eyes.

Nan smiled. "Thanks, but I think I'm going to take a break from dating, maybe sign up for gourmet cooking classes."

"You sure?"

"Positive."

He handed her a business card. "Why don't you give me a call when your classes are over. I love gourmet food."

Nan took the card. "We'll see." Across the room, someone called Steve's name and he left.

~~*

*J*ackson *stared at the big ass* fancy yacht from the lowly depths of his family's old rowboat that may have been in its prime before WWII. That was a big maybe. Any second he expected it to spring a leak and sink.

What in the hell was he doing out here? Nan was right when she'd slammed the door in his face last night. He'd had no business being there. Just like he had no damn business being here tonight. What was the purpose? All day long, as he rambled around the broken down cabin, making a list of everything that needed fixing, he hadn't been able to get her out of his mind. Hell, she'd been in his mind since Jesse married Alexi and he'd been Best Man when Nan had been the Maid of Honor.

Was he going off the deep end and crossing rational lines? Being out here staring at a damn boat because Nan was on it with another man was edging pretty damn close to irrational. It'd make sense if he had a bullhorn and had decided to ask her to forgive him. Selfish sense, but at least he'd have a purpose and a reason for being here.

Was he going to overtake the yacht like the pirate Black Jack had in Nan's fantasy and capture her? The memory of Nan Monday night as he played Black Jack to her captured heroine seared its way through his mind. Her breasts filling his hands as she arched her back with pleasure and squirmed against the light binding of his shirt. The leopard underwear. The mortified blush when she'd thought he'd read her secrets—hell, yes a part of him said. He'd love to capture Nan, put her in his bunk, and sail off as if the world didn't exist, as if he didn't have a care in the world— not even his own.

But you had her in your bunk and you kicked her out. You had her and you rejected her because you're a self-absorb, selfish bastard. Maybe a man exactly like her father had been? A man who'd make a wife and kid pay for something nobody had any control over? And there it was, plain as day, wavering on the sun sparkling water in front of him. The truth. All excuses aside, he'd deliberately gone after Nan, seduced her past her sensibilities, and the first bump in the road he hit, he walked out on her. He'd gone running, looking for that hellhole of a pit he'd existed in to swallow him back up. But he hadn't found it, because sometime over the past six months the pit had disappeared. Jackson slid the oars back into the water and gave them a hard pull. Nope, he had no business interfering in Nan's life. Not now. Maybe never.

~~*

*N*an sighed. *Maybe she wasn't* cultured enough, but she just couldn't get into the swing of the party. Nursing her champagne, she tried to look busy and found herself remembering how much more fun she'd had on a blanket by the creek, counting out strawberries and chunks of cheese to trade Jackson for some champagne. Then came the motorcycle. Damn it. Nan mentally smacked herself. Her eyes stung with the threat of tears, and the yearning ache for Jackson that was never far from the surface erupted again.

A band started playing in the stateroom, its volume way too loud, and the lead singer's voice was nowhere as smooth as Jackson's. Nan left for the cool peace of the upper deck, but couldn't escape the memory of Jackson.

A man grabbed her arm as she walked by the steering room. "I see Swanson deserted you again. I wouldn't be so quick to answer if I were out with you."

It was X-ray Eyes, the odious radiologist who had bothered her at the hospital party. Nan stepped back, tugging on her arm. "Let go."

"Hold on. No reason to get upset. Just want to get to know you a little."

He didn't let go of her arm and Nan could smell a good deal more alcohol on the man's breath than was in his aftershave.

"Let go of my arm, now."

"In just a minute. Why don't you come on in here with me and let me fix you a fresher drink. We'll get to know each other a lot better." He leered at her as he tried to pull her into the empty room.

That was it. Nan didn't care if she was overreacting or not. She swung around and planted her entire weight against the man. He stumbled forward, fell against railing, and amazingly went overboard.

He tried to save himself by grabbing onto her and she went over too, trying to help. As soon as she surfaced she heard all the commotion on the yacht. People tossed life preservers out into the water and Nan wanted to just drown herself. It seemed that between the hospital benefit and tonight, the only impression the hospital's upper crust would have of her is of a drowned rat. Nan grabbed the flotation device and promptly untied the rope from around it. The boat lay anchored in the harbor, not too far from the shore and Nan just couldn't face the people on it. She told the people at the rail that she would swim to the dock and go home.

A few yards from the yacht, a rowboat moved her way.

Jackson sat with a smug smile on his face. "Need a ride, sugar?"

Could her life sink any lower? She should have expected a fool stunt like this from him after he'd shown up banging on her door the other night. Nan pushed off towards the dock. "No, I don't."

"Why not? Where's Swanson?"

She pushed her wet hair from her eyes. "Brad's on call, permanently. And I don't want a ride because I can swim and you're obviously stalking me."

"I'm what!"

"You heard me."

"I was concerned. Brad Swanson isn't the right man for you. He's an ass."

"Sounds familiar."

"What's that supposed to mean?"

"You heard me."

"I'm not anything like him."

"If you say so."

"Nan, just get in the damn boat."

"No."

"Fine. I won't tell you they sighted sharks in the harbor last week."

"You're lying."

"Maybe. Maybe not." Jackson then went into a perfect rendition of the theme from *Jaws*.

Nan's heart sped up and she started looking around in the murky water. The sun was about to set. She screeched in frustration and swam over to the rowboat. "I'm going to shoot you for this, damn it. Why can't you just stay out of my life?"

Jackson leaned over and pulled her into the boat. She was a briny mess.

"I don't know, Nan. I just don't know." He kissed her and tears sprang to her eyes. She pushed him away.

"We want different things in life, Jack. Sex isn't going to change that. Go get a life. Go find someone who wants what you do, and is willing to leave your past alone. I'm not that someone. I want more than a good time when you're in the mood." Just hold on Nan told herself. She could keep it together until she made it to her car, made it home.

"I deserved that," Jackson said, his voice quiet, tight, completely unlike his smooth talking self.

Nan blinked away more tears. "No. You deserve more than that. You just aren't willing to let yourself have it. Take me to the dock. I want to go home."

Jackson looked as if he was going to say something else, but he didn't. He just rowed the boat to shore, his strong muscles straining under his shirt, reminding her of how good they felt against her, over her, beneath her. Everywhere. His jeans clung to his long lean legs and a breeze ferried in from the ocean, making him look as if she'd just ran her fingers through his silky hair. She clenched her fist and stared at the dark water, refusing to look at him again.

Once at the dock, he helped her get out of the boat. His touch was as unwelcome and as painful as her stabbing memories of him. Everything was too fresh, too raw. She couldn't deal with this.

"Where's your car, Nan?"

"I'll find it myself." She patted the tiny satin purse slung securely over her neck and under her arm. "Go! Go, row your boat!" She just wanted to be away from him. Away from all of the reminders of how good his loving was.

Another minute and she'd start crying.

"Forget it. When you're safely in your car then I'll disappear for good but not before."

"Fine," Nan said marching up the dock, stabbing at the tears that now fell. *Disappear for good.*

Jackson stayed with her, a quiet shadow just behind her, until she reached her car. She dug out her key and stuck it into the lock. Jackson placed his hand over hers.

Oh God. Nan shut her eyes, remembering him doing the same thing the night of the banquet as she opened her apartment door. She remembered the kiss that followed. She'd never forget any of his kisses. She'd never forget him. His memory would never disappear. More tears fell. She couldn't stop them.

"Nan. I'm sorry. So damn sorry."

She looked up at Jackson. His blue eyes were stark and bloodshot, his mouth grim. All of his smooth bad-boy self was gone at that moment.

"I'm sorry, too. Sorry I ever let you into my life. Good-bye, Jack." She twisted the key in the lock and pulled her hand from his.

Nan ignored the tears she saw spring into his eyes. She had too many of her own to worry about. Jackson opened her car door and she climbed inside, pulled the door shut, and cranked the engine.

He stood back. She blindly backed out of the parking space and drove away.

She spent the rest of the night crying. Crying because Jackson had been there in the rowboat, like some romantic fool coming after her. Crying because what she wanted from him would forever remain in her dreams and fantasies. Crying because she loved him, and because he had so much to give her and the world, but would never do it because he didn't think himself worthy. Crying for everything between them that was lost before it ever really had a chance to live.

~~*

*A*t *dawn on Saturday morning* Jackson rolled out of bed, grabbed his work boots, and quietly left the house before his parents were up. He thought he knew what hell was all about from the inside out. He was wrong. Nan was adding a new dimension to his torture. Her tears and her anger had been one thing, but the dead, resigned, hopeless look haunting her eyes when she'd said, *I'm sorry, too. Sorry I ever let you into my life. Good-bye, Jack,* reached deep inside him, and twisted him up. His sorry hadn't been good enough and never would be.

Even as he headed out to the old cabin, planning to put the place back into shape, he realized he was running again. But this time he was running from Nan and burying himself in work instead of isolation.

The supplies he purchased to fix the cabin filled the porch. It was going to take a hell of a lot of hard work. His family's assessment that the place needed to be bulldozed down wasn't far from wrong. Stripping off his shirt, he headed for the roof.

Several hours later, Jackson saw his father coming up the drive. He got out of the car and held up a pitcher of iced tea and what looked like a big bag of his mother's to-die-for biscuits.

Jackson set down his hammer and jumped off the roof. "Don't tell me, Mom threatened to tan my hide for skipping out on breakfast."

His dad grinned. "She did." Wouldn't even let me eat mine until I brought you yours. So I just had her pack us both a meal." He set the bags of biscuits on the truck hood, pulled out plastic cups and a tub of milk gravy.

"Oh man," Jackson said. He grabbed a biscuit, tore off a piece, and dipped it into the creamy white gravy.

"She made your favorite, thinking you'd be around this morning."

"Dad, this isn't going to work if—"

His father held up his hand. "You come and go as you please, just kinda let your mom know when you might be around and she'll settle into that just fine. She's worried. We both are and have reason to be."

Jackson broke off more biscuit and swabbed it with gravy. The second bite wasn't as good as the first. "I'm working on it."

His dad lit into his own bag of biscuits, which Jackson noted was half the size of his. "That's all anybody can expect of any man. You know over the years, working in the shipyard, and caring for this old farm, I've come to realize that most of life is fixing things. Seeing what's wrong, what's not working, and tackling those, one day at a time, one step at a time."

Jackson grunted and grabbed his tea.

Nothing much else was said as they worked on the biscuits and gravy. John patted his stomach after grabbing the last crumb. "It's been a while since I've done any roof fixing. Mind if I help?"

Jackson shrugged. "Suppose it wouldn't hurt."

"Good." His dad followed him up to the roof and as they ripped up old shingles and checked for rot, Jackson noticed that is dad wasn't as quick on his feet as he used to be. Time, years of working hard, and sacrificing had taken a toll. Just like he was working hard and sacrificing right now. His father didn't need to be up on this roof, he needed to be sitting at the fishing pond, catching catfish for fun.

John Weldon was a simple man, never claimed to be more than that, and had never wanted more than the simple life, a job that paid enough to feed his family, and a quiet farm to raise them on.

Jackson sat back and ran his gaze over the fields and woods of the Weldon farm, realizing something for the first time. His father was just as important of a man in the backbone of life as a world leader, a physicist, or even a doctor. And part of Jackson's obsessed climb for success, to be the best trauma specialist practicing, to be above his humble roots had been a misguided bid for importance. If he ever became half the man his father was, he'd be lucky.

Another truck approached, spinning a cloud of dust from its tail. Jesse, Jared, and James piled out.

"What in hell are you fools doing?" Jesse asked, glaring up at the roof.

"Fixing a roof," John Weldon yelled back, swiping the sweat of his brow. "Did your mama call you boys?"

"Yep," James said. Jared just nodded. Jesse kept glaring.

"And you all came running?"

"You've been married to her for nearly forty years. What do you think?" Jesse asked.

"That you didn't run fast enough. Get your butts on up here."

Jackson laughed.

James and Jared headed for the ladder. Jesse didn't move.

"It'd be easier to bulldoze this place and start over." The look in Jesse's eyes walked over Jackson like a man forced to wade through manure.

"Maybe," John Weldon said. "But then sometimes doing what's easy isn't what's best. This is one of those times."

Jackson wanted to tell them all to get lost. This was his mess after all.

"If this is one of those times, Dad," Jesse said. "Then you're going to have to climb off that roof and do the supervising. There isn't room for more than four men up there."

John Weldon looked as if he'd planned to argue.

"Don't tell me you're going to pass up the opportunity to whip our lazy asses back into shape?" Jackson challenged, thankful to have a good excuse to get his father out of the worst of the sun. "Besides, we're at the point where somebody's going to have to hand up the supplies."

"Hey, my ass is the best it's ever been," James said.

"That's not saying much," Jared said.

"Women aren't complaining."

"You boys stop assing off and get to work," John grumbled and climbed off the roof.

Jesse came up a few minutes later. "You know what, bro?"

"What?" Jackson glanced up from the rusty nail he was working loose.

"I'm damn glad to be here. And I'm even more damned glad that you're here."

"Well aren't we just happy," Jackson muttered.

"Yeah, I guess I am." Jesse reached over and held back the shingle so that Jackson could get to the nail easier.

Jackson looked up and met Jesse's gaze. "I'm glad. You deserve it." Their gazes held, saying everything they didn't need to have words to express. Warmth that had been needling around inside of Jackson all week wrapped around his gut. He went back to working on the nail, but a new breath of energy fueled his movements.

"So, how's the little tiger?"

Jesse grinned. "Wreaking havoc like a true Weldon."

Jackson laughed. "I'm going to have to go see him."

"That'd be a good thing, since you're his godparent."

"I've been meaning to talk to you. I don't think that—"

"I'm not taking no for an answer, bro."

"You don't understand. I'm not good enough to—"

Jesse gripped Jackson's shoulder and Jackson looked up.

"You don't understand. If something happens to me, there isn't a better man for my son than you."

Tears welled up in Jackson's eyes and he looked up at the damn clouds. "Shit."

Jesse squeezed Jackson's shoulder and then let go. "Welcome home, bro."

Jackson couldn't say anything. He just went back to work.

Later, while they were all sitting on the porch enjoying a cool drink after devouring the sandwiches Emma shuttled over, James turned to their dad. "I want to get your opinion of a project Jared and I are thinking about getting into after we finish the children's wing at the hospital."

"What's that?" John stretched as if his back was bothering him a bit.

"I'll get the blueprints out of the truck, while you tell him." Jared jumped off the porch.

"We're thinking about starting a subdivision. With the profits from the hospital job and, if we can pre-sell the homes before construction, we think we can swing it financially."

"Sounds reasonable. Why are you asking me?"

Jared returned with the plans. "Well, James and I thought we'd name the place Weldon Estates. It'll be near the Intercoastal with all of those highbrow estates."

Jesse laughed. "You mean the Weldon's are making a name on the right side of the tracks after all these years."

Everyone laughed with Jesse.

James spread out the plans.

Jackson leaned over and gave them a cursory glance. One minute he was just mildly interested and the next minute one of the plans jumped out at him. It featured a big sunroom with a spa. Whoever had drawn it had penciled in a nice sized garden in the back. To him it had Nan written all over it. He could just see her plants filling the sunroom. He picked up the blueprint. "Mind if I look at this one for a while?"

His question was met with a bunch of raised eyebrows, but no objections. He rolled up the plan and stuck it in his truck. Then he remembered the plant she'd given him. It had probably died after a week of neglect. He went into the cabin to look. It still sat on the dinette table, but instead of brown and shriveled, the little plant was green and lush. Little blue buds had sprouted.

He walked over and stared at it. The table was wet, too. Rain, like tears from heaven had fallen and watered the little plant, kept it alive, despite his neglect. Jackson picked it up to carry to his truck. Maybe…

He shut his eyes and an image of Nan flashed through his mind. *She was there. Naked. Lying on the bed waiting for him. He walked up to her, nudging her knees apart and stood between her legs, looking down at her ripe breasts, and warm sex. Everything of hers right at his fingertips. His erection swelled against the fly of his jeans and she reached out to cup him, rubbing him to rock hard.*

He knelt down, spread her sex open and pulled her bottom to the edge of the bed. He looked his fill of her, caressing her folds, sliding his finger into her warmth, caressing her until she was wet with need, ready for him to taste of her honey. She rose to her elbows watching him touch her, breaths gasping, nipples begging, and her pulse pounding.

Keeping his gaze locked on hers, he leaned down and kissed the excited, nub of her sex. She moaned and her eyes grew misty. He kept kissing, kept tasting, kept licking and loving until she cried for release, until her eyes turned desperate, and she arched her back, begging for more. Reaching up, he rolled her nipples between his fingers, playing a sweet melody in tune to the stroking of his tongue until she came apart for him. When she settled into the hazy aftermath of his loving, he started all over again. Demanding more as he unzipped his fly, he grabbed her hips, and buried himself deep inside of her. Then they were making love everywhere his gaze settle around him. In the barn down the road, on his bike, on the truck, in the truck. Anywhere and everywhere. He couldn't get her out of his mind. Her fantasy obsession had now taken him over.

He had such a hard on that he had to go take a dip in the creek before he could climb back to the roof.

CHAPTER SIXTEEN

The alarm went off and Nan groaned, forcing herself to roll out of bed. Shakespeare had a cold and Nan thought one was trying to catch a hold of her, too.

She'd dreamed about Jackson last night. Not the hot sexy dreams she used to have. This dream was different and recurring. Jackson was ahead of her on a long road leading directly into a black void, and she was running after him. Running as hard as she could, but she never reached him before he disappeared into the black void. All she could see of him was his back and as much as she cried for him, he never turned towards her.

Jackson had returned to the construction site. And every day she was at work, she saw him outside the window. He never looked her way. The windows were mirrored so he couldn't see that she watched, but didn't he wonder?

It'd been two weeks and thirty-six hours since she'd left him standing at the dock and had told him that she was sorry she'd ever let him into her life.

Part of her shouted no, that she didn't regret knowing Jackson's touch and the fire of his passion even if she never saw him again. But another part of her that still hurt so bad, cried, wishing she'd never known him.

Climbing into the shower, Nan turned her face to the water's sting, shocking herself to stop the tears. She had to put her mind towards the meeting today. It was D-day with the hospital board and the Nurses Trouble Shooting Committee and Nan hoped she'd written her opening speech in such a way as to express the nurses' concerns as well as garner the board's support.

She dressed, managed to get down a bagel and a glass of juice as she misted her plants. Then she saw the offensive gray hairs. Her beautiful gloxinia had Botrytis! How could she have let gray mold invade her plant? It'd grow like a cancer unless she weeded it out today. A dozen things preyed on her mind and nausea churned all morning long.

She walked into the meeting-room with all of her worries, nerves, and heartache sitting like a heavy rock in the pit of her stomach.

"You must be excited," Candy said, nursing a cup of coffee.

"I've had better moments." Nan smoothed her chignon and straightened her collar. "How do I look?"

"Like a professional. Relax. Believe me, there's more nurses awed by your reputation with the Lois Emerson Merit Award than you can imagine. Most that I know are coming this morning just to see you."

"Candy, if you think you're helping. You're not. I'm just a regular person, and a messed up one at that."

"You'll do fine. Here's Head Nurse Litton."

Nan turned. "Good, I want to run a few questions by her, before the meeting."

Time crept up and bit Nan on the seat of her nurse's whites before she realized. The meeting began. Her nerves jittered and her legs wobbled, but soon she slid into a rhythm and held her own. The welcome speech went well. She had competent answers to the board's questions. And by the end of the meeting, the board had decided to appoint a small committee to review the hospital's policies in regards to the nurses' grievances. For the first time it looked like real change in the hospital's policies was possible. It was more than the Trouble Shooting Committee had hoped for and afterward, rather than running to escape as usual, many of the board members stayed to talk a bit.

Mr. Townsend, having remembered her from the banquet, spoke of her as if she were his long lost daughter. "Nan, I want you to meet Wylan Merit. His wife was Lois Emerson Merit, for whom the award is named.

"Mr. Merit, it's a pleasure to meet you."

"No, Ms. Miller the pleasure is mine. Thank you for making my wife's memory an ongoing honor. It makes losing her to cancer a little more bearable."

Sadness laced Mr. Merit's voice, and edged into his gray eyes, but it was the sadness of a soft bittersweet memory and not the destroying regret that ate at Jackson. Tears pricked Nan's eyes and she forced a smile to her lips even as her heart wanted to know why? Why couldn't Jackson take Amy's memory and cherish it rather than punish himself with it?

Mr. Townsend dropped his cane and Nan leaned over to pick it up. When she stood, the world around her swam, grew dark, and disappeared.

She woke to find herself on a stretcher.

"What happened?" She tried to sit up.

Candy pushed her back down. "You fainted dead away and we're taking you to the ER."

"No. There's no need."

"Relax. There isn't anything you can do about it. It's hospital policy. Besides, Townsend has already called down there and ordered them to make his star nurse well."

"Oh, hell," Nan muttered. "Who came up with such an idiotic policy idea?"

Candy laughed. "I believe nurses did some years back, when working conditions were even more grueling than they are now."

Nan groaned. The ER would put her through the ringer.

Four hours later, she was more than ready to go home. The doctor finally returned. Nan felt as if she'd been through a week's worth of lab test since the ER doctor's admitting assessment.

The doctor walked into the room and Nan didn't like his grim expression. "We've received the results of your blood work and there are a few things we need to talk about. Why don't you sit down," he said, opening her chart.

"I've been lying for hours. I'm okay."

"No. I insist. I have to write you several prescriptions and we need to discuss your condition."

Nan sat. "What condition?"

"There isn't any easy way to say this. You're a nurse, so I'm just going to spell it out. You're pregnant and you're anemic."

Nan blinked. Then shut her eyes completely and leaned back against her chair. "Did you just say what I thought you said?"

"Yes. I'm going to write you a prescription for iron and prenatal vitamins. You'll get a list of foods high in iron along with your discharge papers. I want you to see an obstetrician immediately. Your hemoglobin is much lower than it should be and you're going to need close monitoring with this pregnancy. I also want you to see your physician and get a thorough check-up done. Based on my findings, I suspect that this anemia is a result of poor dietary habits and not anything more serious, but it wouldn't hurt to have everything checked out."

How could she be pregnant? She and Jackson had been responsible. They'd used protection. A little refrain that taunted the words "nothing is a hundred percent" ran circles in her mind. Just why in the world did she have to fall into the percentage that didn't work?

Her life was snowballing to disaster. How was she going to work and raise a child? Her mom had been a working mom and Nan had sworn she would be there for her child. She'd have to come up with a plan. There wasn't any other option.

A baby. She was going to have a baby, a soft cuddly, wailing bundle of lovable trouble. Both joy and fear filled her heart. She wasn't even sure what she said to the ER doctor. She took her prescriptions and papers and stumbled out of the hospital.

She headed to her car, but stopped halfway through the parking lot, blinking in disbelief.

Jackson, all work-boot-grubby-gorgeous sat on her car hood.

Tears sprang to her eyes. Tears for all the things she had dreamed she wanted for her family. Tears for the fact that she loved a man who could never be the husband she needed. She started to cry and couldn't seem to stop.

He saw her then. Got off the hood and walked her way. Nan started to run right at him. He quickened his pace, opened his arms. Just as Nan got to him, she ducked under his arm and dashed for her car. Hands trembling, she fumbled with her keys, trying to see through the tears.

"Nan, what wrong?" Jackson came up behind her.

"Nothing." She got the door opened.

"Nan, damn it. Tell me what has happened?"

Swiping her tears, she looked at him. Oh, God. How could he still look so good? "What do you want, Jack?"

He held up a little plastic bag. In it was a tiny blue flower. "The plant you gave me. It bloomed."

Nan could barely speak from the emotion clogging her throat. "I lied," she said. "I lied about African Violets bringing happiness to those who keep them. I made it up when I was a little girl because I wanted it to be true." He voice caught on a sob and she got into the car, shutting and locking the doors.

Jackson knocked on the window. Nan shook her head and started the car, taking off and nearly knocking Jackson over.

~~*

Jackson picked up the little bag with the flower. He'd dropped it in trying to get Nan to open the door and she'd run over it as she left.

What in the hell was wrong with her?

He got into his truck and followed her.

At her apartment, he knocked twice, didn't get an answer so he pounded on the door. "Damn it, Nan. Open up and tell me what is wrong or I'm going to call an ambulance."

He heard her sobs on the other side of the door and his heart wrenched painfully. In that moment, he knew he loved her. Whether he wanted to or not, whether he was able to or not. He loved her.

"Go away, Jack. You can't help me."

"Nan, for God's sake. What is wrong?" The pain in her voice ripped at him.

She opened the door. Her eyes and nose were reddened from tears and he could see the depth of emotional pain etched upon her face. "I saw a doctor today. I'm pregnant and to make matters worse my gloxinia has botrytis."

Jackson stumbled and nearly fainted on Nan's doorstep as shock drained the blood from his head. Why couldn't he help? Dawning pain hit him in the gut. She'd fainted at the hospital party. Her exhaustion and the other times she nearly fainted after then ran clearly through his mind. It all added up. "I'll be right back." Jackson shouted and headed for his truck. Brad Swanson had a lot to answer for.

On the way to Brad's office, Jackson recklessly pulled off the road three times wrestling with the overwhelming desire to go back to Nan and beg her to marry him. He didn't care if she carried another man's child. He loved her.

But then other things crept into his mind. His mother was right. Hell he'd been in better shape to handle a child at sixteen than he was now. How had his life ended up in such a sorry ass state?

It wasn't just Nan, there was a child involved and that child deserved a chance to be with its father. God, if there was any way he could have held his own baby... Jackson knew he would have fought heaven and earth to do it. God had chosen otherwise and Jackson didn't think he'd ever understand. Now that he found love again, he was losing that too. "It sucks, God. Do you hear me!"

Jackson found Swanson at his office. He grabbed the man by the collar of his Armani suit and dragged him out.

"Have you completely gone insane, Weldon? What are you doing? Call the police, Eleanor," Brad shouted as Jackson pulled him by the receptionist's desk.

"Your boss has a family emergency. Cancel the rest of his appointments. I'm taking you to see Nan and you damn well better do the right thing." He pushed Swanson into the truck.

"What's wrong with Nancy? Does she need a doctor?"

"No. She needs a man to be a man. Now shut up until we get to her apartment. If you talk, I might just change my mind and beat you up anyway."

"You've finally gone over the edge, Weldon. I'm going to prosecute you for this."

"I said shut up."

Brad said no more until they were at Nan's door. "Now what?"

"Do I have to spell this out? Knock on the damn door."

Brad knocked and to Jackson's amazement Nan opened the door.

"Brad? What are you doing here?"

"I'm wondering the same thing myself."

Jackson poked Brad in the back. "He's here to do the honorable thing."

"*He* is?" Nan said.

"I am?" Brad questioned.

"Yes, damn it. You got her pregnant. Now ask her to marry you, or you're going to wish you were dead."

"Weldon. You need to go back to med school. A woman doesn't get pregnant from one kiss."

"You mean you and she didn't, uh…"

Nan frowned and pointed an irritated finger right at him. "He's not the father, you jackass. You are. Are you ready to be a father?"

Jackson's mouth opened and shut like a fish out of water. Nan was pregnant with his baby? Joy and a truckload of fear lodged in his throat.

"I didn't think so. Let me tell you something. I will never marry someone because they feel obligated." Nan slammed the door in their faces.

"Well, Weldon—"

"Shut up or die, Swanson."

Jackson knocked on the door. She didn't answer it.

"I have to get back to my office."

"Do you have a death wish or something? I've got a family emergency here. Take my truck if you have to, but don't bug me. The spare keys are under the driver's floor mat."

His child! Dear God, he was going to have a baby! Jackson knocked a little harder this time, sweating more than the heat of afternoon sun called for. His guts were a whirling storm of mixed feelings, and he only knew one thing for sure. He couldn't lose Nan, couldn't lose this second chance at life. "Nan, damn it. We have to talk."

"You might want to give her some time to cool down. I think you just stepped all over those emotions she thinks are so important."

"Aren't you gone yet?"

"I can't possibly drive that thing. It doesn't have precision steering or anti-lock brakes. I'd probably wreck and either cause myself or someone else harm."

"Tell you what, Swanson. Why don't you go and stand in front of it, then I'll get in and show you how it works."

"No need to be sarcastic, Weldon. I'm only here because you screwed up, twice in fact."

Jackson pounded on Nan's door again, this time picturing Brad's face in front of him.

"You're determined to screw up a third time, aren't you?"

"What the hell is that supposed to mean?"

"Logic points to the fact that she's never going to believe you aren't trying to *do* the honorable thing until you can prove differently."

"How?"

"You obviously got to know her a whole lot better than I did. Considering her mind set, I don't think a simple marriage proposal will do. You'll have to figure out something bigger than that. Meanwhile, take me back to my office."

Jackson stomped to his truck. He either had to take Swanson back now or face murder one. Considering Nan was pregnant, he'd best stay out of jail.

"Why'd you quit medicine back in Chicago, Weldon? Not that I believe them, but there were reports that you were the best ER doctor on the staff."

"Why in the hell do you want to know?"

Brad shrugged. "Just curious as to why a man would spend years achieving something and then walk away."

"I put my career first and that choice killed my pregnant wife. You might want to change your ways before you have to pay such a price."

"I didn't know. I'm sorry." Shock replaced Brad's usual supercilious frown, and he didn't say anything else all the way back to his office. A police cruiser sat out front.

"Why don't you drop me off in the back?"

Jackson wisely swung the truck around to the back of the building.

"How did you do it?"

"Do what?"

"Nan is such a sensible woman. How did you make her fall in love with you?"

Jackson thought back to the weekend he had spent with Nan, remembered their passion, and realized that in those moments she had become everything to him. "For just a short time, when I was thinking clearly, I made her my world, and nothing but her mattered."

Brad left, shaking his head, and Jackson doubted the man would ever understand. But thank God he did. A baby. His Nan was going to have a baby. Nope, not exactly his Nan yet. As Jackson drove back to his parent's house to take a shower, an idea began to form.

Chapter Seventeen

He was back at Nan's two hours later. This time when he knocked on the door, she answered.

"Thank God," he said, looking her over. Her eyes and nose were red, but she'd stopped crying. He took that as a good sign. He leaned over to kiss her, and she backed away.

"Don't touch me. You're only here to talk, to plan what part you are going to have in this baby's life."

A twitch began in his right eye. A plan. Had she already planned him out of her life? Planned every detail of their child's life?

Jackson drew a deep breath and roped back in his emotions. Who was he to complain? He really hadn't given her many options and what else could he expect her to do when faced with a crisis? She was a planner, and he'd known that long before he loved her. He would just have to learn to take it in stride. "I've got a plan for you to see."

Nan blinked. "What kind of plan?" she said suspiciously.

"This kind." He held up the blueprints he'd borrowed from Jared and James. "A house. It's really something." He walked into the kitchen and laid them out on the table. "See the sunroom for your plants and the huge kitchen?"

"I hate to pop your enthusiasm, but I think we need a reality check here. What does a house have to do with making plans for this baby I'm carrying?"

He noticed she didn't say our baby. She said this baby. "Nan. This is for the baby and us to live in. I can have it built by the time he's born."

"He or she," Nan corrected, placing her hand over her abdomen. "It won't work. You're only doing this because I'm pregnant. I refuse to be an obligation."

Jackson turned grabbed her shoulders. She had to understand. "It's not just because of the baby. I picked these plans out before all of this. I saw them and knew you'd love them."

Tears welled in her eyes and she shook her head. "I don't want a house with you. I don't want to tie myself to a man I can't count on to be there in a crisis. Have you forgiven yourself yet? Are you ready to make a commitment? And what happens the next time the past grabs you by the gut? Are you going to go off the deep end, or tell me to get lost?"

"No, I…" What could he say? How could he make her believe him? And did he even know himself the answers to her questions? "What if I said I don't know but I'm willing to try?"

"I'd say let's be friends and see. Only time will tell."

"Friends, sugar? Now who needs a reality check?" He covered her mouth with his in a searing kiss. Her response was hesitant at first then the dam burst. He couldn't touch her enough. He couldn't love her enough and she couldn't get enough of him. He threaded his hands through her glorious hair, ran his lips and tongue over her silky skin, and kissed his way to the buttons of her shirt. Several buttons went flying in his haste to tear away all barriers between them.

"I need you like I need air to breathe, lady. You're under my skin, in my blood, in my mind, and sunk deep into my heart."

"Jackson," Nan sighed, shaking her head as if she didn't believe him.

"Believe me." He filled his hands with her breasts, loving the luscious warmth of her and the pebbled excitement of her nipples. "I love loving you, sugar."

He cupped her, lifting her breasts to his lips, laving attention with his tongue. Her breath panted in his ear and she buried her hands in his hair, pulling him closer to her.

He suckled her, following each kiss on her nipple with languid caresses down her body, stripping away her clothes, bit by bit. Then he swung her up in his arms and carried her to the couch.

"No," she said gasping, and sat up to leave. "Not the couch. I won't have anywhere to sleep free of your memory when you go."

Jackson gently pushed her back and nudged her legs apart, looking down at her lush sex. Looking his fill, just as he'd imagined. Then he knelt in front of her. "I'm not going anywhere but right here, Nan." He slid her legs apart and pulled her bottom to the edge of the couch. Spreading the folds of her sex, he bent down and kissed her there as he kept his gaze locked with hers.

She moaned and her eyes grew misty with desire, but she didn't look away. She watched him love her. Her breath came faster, her back arched, begging him for more, and her gaze turned needy. He ran his hands up to her breasts and plucked at her nipples. She came apart for him, her body shuddering with her release.

Jackson zipped down his fly and buried himself deep inside her with no barriers between them. He felt the full effect of her smooth, hot, passage as her inner muscles stroked and squeezed him almost past the point of sanity. She lifted her hips, taking him deeper.

"Don't move. You feel just too damn good and I want you to come again, this time with me. You make heaven such a smooth ride, sugar."

Nan shook her head. "This isn't going to solve anything, Jack." But she didn't pull away from him. She pressed her hips closer.

"Lady, whatever it takes, we'll work it out." He pushed deeper into her and started moving in a rhythm of sweet music that only they could make together. She met his every move, claiming more, and he stroked deeper until her sweet cry of heaven sent them both over the edge. It wasn't just sex between them. Never had been and never would be.

Jackson carried her to bed, wrapped her in his arms, and placed his palm over her abdomen. His child grew there and the wonder of it touched him deep inside of his healing soul.

"You have to believe me." He spoke close to her ear, brushing a kiss there between his words. "I love you. I loved you before my child began to grow inside of you."

Nan placed her hand over his. "I just don't know, Jack. I know I want and cherish this life inside of me. Beyond that, I just don't know."

He pulled her tighter, shut his eyes, and concentrated on breathing. One breath at a time. God, don't let it be too late. After a few minutes, Nan turned in his arms and wrapped her arms around him, holding him tight.

Some of the pain inside him eased. "My father said something a couple of weeks ago that's sort of stuck in my mind. Said that life is mostly fixing things. Seeing what was wrong, what wasn't working and fixing it, one day at a time, one thing at a time. Ever since, I've been fixing a few things about myself and now I'm ready to fix a few things about us, sugar."

"I want to believe, Jack. I just don't know if I can."

He felt her tears fall against his neck. And he leaned up on his elbow to see her and kiss her. "Take your time, I'll be right here. Right here with you. But I've one question that has been bugging me. I know I've been out of touch with the medical field, but hell, I can't be this much in the dark. What is your gloxinia and what in the hell is botrytis?"

Laughter lit Nan's eyes. "It's terminal, I'm afraid."

Jackson narrowed his eyes. "Nan, this isn't funny. What's going on?"

She laughed harder, gasping as she spoke. "It's one of my plants…it has gray mold…I had to amputate five of its leaves this afternoon."

Jackson's jaw went slack. "A freaking plant! You had me wondering all afternoon about a plant?" There's a price to pay for that." He started tickling her until the tickling turned sensual. Then he kissed her, tenderly, loving her more with every passing moment. "Seriously." He caught her gaze with his, rubbing his hand over her stomach. "Everything is okay? You went to see a doctor, right?"

"Yeah. I'm going to have to make an appointment with Dr. Schwartz ASAP, though. I'm a little anemic and I'm going to have to pay special attention to my diet."

Jackson frowned. "You haven't had dinner yet have you?"

"No, but I'm not—"

"Up and at 'em," he said smacking her bottom.

"Jeez." Nan rolled over. "Where are we going?"

"Out for liver and onions."

"YUCK."

"You're going to love them. I promise."

"You're promising a lot these days."

"That I am." He leaned over and kissed her. "I most certainly am."

~~*

*N*an's *alarm clock rang at* five in the morning and she rolled over with a groan. God help her but she didn't know what day it was and whether or not she had to work.

"Morning, Sugar." Jackson rolled over and snuggled up to her back. His morning erection pressed enticingly against her bottom.

"What day is it?" Her voice was still scratchy, and she felt as if tears still clogged her throat. But his arms about her were heaven.

He pressed himself against her and slid his hand to cup her breast. "Thursday."

"Jack, we can't. I've got to go to work." She stilled his hand by placing hers over his. She had a heavy weight in the center of her heart and she didn't know how to make him understand. "Last night. Everything. I can't seem to be able to take it all in yet. My head is spinning, but then I was still reeling from our weekend together, the hospital, and then you saying everything was a mistake."

He sighed. "Look at me, sugar."

Nan turned in his embrace so that she faced him. Unshaven, with his hair ruffled by making love and his eyes made bluer by an early morning haze, he looked rough and so damn sexy she wanted to cry.

Staring deeply into her eyes, he spoke. "I told you to leave, and you did. Only I couldn't forget you. I kept wanting to see your smile, kept aching to feel your touch, kept wanting to love you one more time. I picked up the house plans weeks ago because they reminded me of you. I didn't know it, but it all meant one thing. I love you, Nan. I didn't think there was enough left inside me to ever love, but I do. I want to marry you." He slid the heat of his hand to cover her stomach. "And I love this little one growing inside you, too."

Tears filled Nan's eyes and spilled down her cheeks. She loved him and her heart was breaking with both joy and pain. "I love you too, Jack. I've missed you so much, ached for you, worried about you. But you have to understand, I learned a long time ago that not even loving is enough. You couldn't answer me last night. Have you forgiven yourself? Forgiven God? Are you free from the past? Anger and guilt are deadly poisons to love. I can't do what my mother did. I just can't." Her tears turned to sobs.

He pulled her tighter in his arms, his muscles trembling as he held her. She could feel the rapid beat of his heart and the catch of deep emotion in his voice. "Nan, damn, sugar. Don't cry. It's going to be okay. We'll work it out. All I can promise is a step at a time. A day at a time."

She cried harder. "Don't you see? That isn't enough for me. I can't marry you until I know for sure. I have to know in my heart that you're free." She buried her face against him, hurting. She didn't want to be this honest with him. She wanted to take his love, marry him, and hope for a happily ever after, but she couldn't.

He cupped her head in his hands and turned her up to his kisses. The tears in his eyes ripped the bottom out of her world. "It's okay. You don't have to marry me now. Just let me love you, sugar. Give us a little time. We both have to be at work this morning. Let's take a shower, go to work, and tonight we'll sit down and make out a plan. We'll set some goals about our relationship, about the baby, about what kind of life you want to live and what kind of life I want to live. Doing that isn't going to fix everything, but I think it will make you feel better, be a little more sure about what we're doing. Won't it?"

"Yes." She sniffled, feeling like laughing and crying. Had Jackson really just suggested that they set goals and make a plan? Did he just say he had to be at work?

He exhaled and she could feel the relief escaping him. "Good." He rolled over, taking her with him so she ended on top. "Now about the sex. We're going to conserve water and time. Ever made love in the shower, Nan?" He played with her breasts as he spoke. "I'll be behind you, inside you. The warm water will spray your breasts, teasing them, and my finger will stroke your little hot spot until you melt with pleasure and I explode in you."

Jackson drove and Nan tried to collect herself. She had no doubt that as soon as she walked into work everybody would take one look at her and know what she'd been doing that morning. For the first time in her employment history, Nan was going to be late for work. Well, she might be right on time, but late for her. She'd always arrived ten to fifteen minutes early.

She glanced at her watch then at Jackson and had to smile. He wasn't the same man she'd left in Salty's Bar on New Year's Eve. Then she wasn't the same woman either.

He reached over and turned the radio up. "Did you hear that?"

She blinked. She'd been back in the shower. She had a feeling they were going to be taking many showers. When Jackson discovered her showerhead was moveable…hell, she shivered again just remembering how he'd made her come.

"Nan?"

She shook her head. "What?"

"Did you hear the radio announcement?"

"No. What was it?"

"They're predicting storms today. Heavy thunderstorms."

Nan glanced out at the sky. Now that Jackson called her attention to it, the air felt hot and thick, as if a weight pressed upon them from the heavens and compressed everything around them. "It's unusually hot for this time of year."

"I don't like it." Jackson studied the horizon. "There's a greenish cast to the sky."

"But not a cloud around. Don't worry. We survived the gale the night of the banquet. It can't be any worse. Before you found me, I thought I was a goner on my way to Oz."

Jackson laughed. "I enjoyed whatever ill wind blew your skirt up and planted you face down on my truck."

She leaned over and smacked his arm. "I'm trying to thank you for saving me and all you can think about is sex."

He pulled up in front of the hospital and stopped the truck. "Nope sugar, it's not just sex. But keep that in mind if you're thinking about thanking me for something."

"I'll keep it in mind."

"And while you're at it, think about letting me read that little black book under your pillow. I want to make all of your fantasies come true."

Nan just smiled. She had a few things she was going to add to her book before she let him read it. She opened her door to get out.

"Nan." Jackson leaned over and kissed her. "I meant what I said. I'll be right by your side. Take all the time you need."

She hugged him and got out. Maybe things were going to be all right. Still as she walked to the hospital entrance and glanced up again at the oddly green-gray sky, she felt a heaviness in her heart. How many times had she heard her mother hope that maybe this time things were going to be okay and they never were?

CHAPTER EIGHTEEN

Jackson slid the steel bar into position and drilled a hole through it. Then he popped the screw gun into place and anchored the bar. Everything that had happened between him and Nan over the past twenty-four hours chased around in his mind. He had a chance, a chance to change his life and he couldn't mess it up.

He might make other mistakes in life, but he wouldn't make the same ones. Nan and the baby would come first, no matter what. With her at the center of his life, he couldn't lose. And their child, he added. He still felt shocked, but a good feeling.

The only dark cloud hanging was that he couldn't tell her he was free of the past, because he didn't think he'd ever really be free from it. A part of him would always wish he'd made different decisions. And that same part of him would always feel some responsibility in Amy's death.

Only time and his future decisions would prove to Nan that she could trust him. More and more his father's words gave him a stronger foothold on life. Fixing things one day at a time. He could handle that job.

"Hey, Weldon. You better come look at this."

"What's up, Bo?" Jackson walked out from the covered area and immediately sensed the change in the air around him. Heavy black clouds churned in an angry mass directly above and the green edge to the sky had sharpened, deepened.

The air had heated, like a desert beneath a noon sun, but instead of feeling dry, moisture hung like a thick and ominous beast surrounding him. Even as he and Bo stood watching, the wind whipped viciously toward them, picking up little pieces of plastic and debris as it spun.

Luckily, most of the men had gone to lunch. He could see one heavy equipment operator already securing the job site. A quick glance showed him that the thirty-foot high scaffolds were empty.

"Where's Jared?" Jackson was sure that his brother would want to give the order for the few men still around to secure the job site.

"He and the foreman went back to the office to iron out a problem with the electricians."

"Tell whoever is left on site to double tie everything they can and if it starts lightning to get to shelter in the hospital." Bo nodded and moved off to spread the word. In the short time they'd spoken, the storm had doubled its intensity.

The fury unleashing from the sky seemed to come straight from hell itself. Lightning fractured the heavens like a broken strobe light, and golf-ball-sized hail thundered down. Jackson slid beneath the open steel beams of the building's structure to protect himself as he struggled to dump cement bags on a pile of loose boards that were beginning to dangerously blow.

A loud roar filled the air and Jackson looked up with his heart in his throat. A wide black funnel cloud plundered right toward the hospital and the construction site. He blinked, swearing he saw cars, telephone poles, and rooftops spewing about as the tornado whipped and twisted in an ugly dance of death. Nan was inside! He had to warn the hospital!

Snatching up a board to shield himself from the hail, he ran toward the nearest hospital door. He never made it. The force of the wind picked him up and slung him through the air as the tornado hit.

~~*

*W*hen the effects of her shower with Jackson wore off, which turned out to be about lunch time, Nan ran down to the pharmacy to fill the prescriptions the doctor had given her. Then, she immediately went to the cafeteria, skipped over the salads and sandwiches and went directly to the meat and vegetable selections. It wasn't gourmet fare, but the nutritional value more than made up for the lack.

As she ate, she considered what her hesitations were about a relationship with Jackson. Her problem centered on trust. Trust that he wouldn't desert her and their child when they needed him most. But the more she thought, the harsher the light she saw herself in.

How much reassurance did any person have what the future brought? Or how any one person would deal with the problems of life?

She swallowed the naked truth like a bitter pill. It wasn't Jackson who had a problem with commitment now. It was herself. It wasn't only his past harming their life at this point. It was hers, too. Her own insecurities were demanding that Jackson be flawless. He'd offered her his heart and she'd left it hanging in the air, demanding more.

She had to see him. She had to tell him that she'd marry him, now this minute, tomorrow, whenever. *She loved him* and that love swelled inside her, filling her needs.

Rushing from the cafeteria, she heard a thundering roar. The windows along the hallway she was in shattered into tiny pieces. Wind splattered chunks of ice through the openings. The building around her groaned, and she saw it physically shake. The lights went out and then the hospital's emergency generator kicked in. A

hushed silence fell for a brief second before people started to
scream and run.

~~*

Jackson felt himself flying and spinning. Oddly, he still held the
board, and hurled end over end with it until he slammed into a pile
of sand. Dirt filled his mouth, his nose, stung his eyes. And then
suddenly, everything stopped.

The roar moved into the distance and a horrific quiet settled
like a silent dirge. Rubbing the sand from his face, he struggled to
his feet and opened his blurry eyes to utter devastation. The new
wing they were building had been leveled and everything from the
heavy equipment to the port-a-potties looked as if they had been
dumped in a blender and minced. He limped across the field
toward the hospital, aware that his leg and shoulder throbbed, but
were curiously numb, too. As he neared the hospital, he saw the
damage and staggered beneath the fear bulleting through him. The
roof was mangled on part of the building, the windows were
blown, and cars were piled up against the walls like debris caught
in a dam.

"Nan!" he yelled, starting to run.

"Help me! Help me! Oh my baby!"

Jackson stumbled sure that Amy's cries rang in his head. Then
he thought it was Nan calling to him. He had to find her. Turning
to look, he saw a woman, trapped beneath several boards. She was
heavily pregnant. He turned to her and lifted the board off of her
legs to see her right leg rotated too far to the left. "I'm here. Just
hold on."

"The baby! Oh God, the baby is coming!"

"It's okay." Jackson checked her pulse as he kneeled down to help her. Her pulse was too rapid and weak, as was her respirations. His hands shook. She was in serious trouble. Failure seemed to loom over his shoulder and he shook it away. "What's your name?"

"Angela." She grabbed his hand, her dark eyes imploring him. "I'm going to die. Please don't let me die."

"You're not going to die, Angela, but you've got to help me. I need you to breathe deep for me, like they taught you in Lamaze. Slow and steady. Can you do that?"

She nodded, her face deathly pale against the dark cloud of her hair.

"Now I need for you to lay back. We have to put your head lower than your feet; and I have to look at your leg. Okay?"

Jackson's heart twisted. God, she didn't look like Amy, but their cries were the same. Jackson called out for someone to help him, but the area seemed eerily silent. The wind whirled about them and he noticed for the first time that a light rain was falling. The sound of sirens wailed from far away. He forced himself to shut out everything and focus on the woman.

She breathed as he asked, and he ran a quick assessment of her condition. Her uterine contractions were less than one minute apart, but her vital signs were screaming shock.

Just then he felt a hand on his shoulder. He looked up to see Nan next to him.

"Are you all right?" he asked, taking in her ragged appearance. Surface cuts lined her right cheek and her forehead was bruised.

"I'm fine. What can I do to help?"

Relief flooded Jackson. Relief that Nan was unharmed and relief that he had the help he would need to save this woman. He silently thanked God as he turned to Angela. "She's about to have the baby. Get her to breathe, but don't let her push yet. I need to examine her leg."

Nan immediately spoke to Angela and Jackson lifted the woman's dress to examine her. Her leg lay with her knee rotated almost forty-five degrees to the inside. A large hematoma covered her upper thigh and grew by the second. The pulses lower on her leg were almost non- existent. He didn't hesitate to act as his instincts kicked in. Ripping off his belt, he threaded it under the woman's thigh forming a tourniquet that he tightened immediately. Then he took three pieces of wood from the ground and splinted the woman's leg straight, using strips from his shirt to tie her leg in place. If what he suspected had happened, she could die if her leg moved the wrong way.

He looked up to see Nan helping Angela. Now he had to see about the baby.

"Scissors?" he asked Nan.

She slipped them from her pocket. As she leaned his way, she whispered. "How is she?"

Not good, he silently mouthed the words, where only Nan could see. "We need a stretcher, IV of D5W, and an OR set up with a damn good surgeon. I think bone fragments have nicked her femoral artery."

"I'll go get help."

Jackson cut away Angela's underwear. The baby had almost completely crowned.

"Don't leave yet, Nan. The baby is coming. Put pressure on her femoral artery above the tourniquet."

Nan did as instructed, and Jackson turned his attention to the woman. "Angela, this is very important. Whatever you do, whatever you feel, do not bear down. Your little angel is coming and she's doing just fine. You need to unbutton your shirt so that you can hold her next to your body when she gets here. She's going to need your warmth."

Jackson prayed. If the woman pushed to deliver the baby, depending on how badly her femoral artery was leaking, there might not be any way he could save her.

He looked at Nan. "Do you have anything sterile?"

"Several packages of gauze in my left pocket."

Reaching in, he found the gauze, a couple of packets of alcohol wipes. Quickly using one wipe on his hands, Jackson wrapped his fingers with some of the gauze and slid his fingers alongside the baby's head. He was able to help work the baby's shoulder out and the baby popped like a cork, rewarding Jackson's efforts with a robust cry.

"She's an angel, just as I thought." He laid the baby on Angela's chest and quickly clamped the chord by squeezing it between the scissors' handles and tying them closed with gauze.

"My baby. Thank God. You saved her." Angela wrapped the baby in her shirt, hugging her squirming little girl very close.

Jackson knew the woman had to be in excruciating pain, yet the simple joy that lay in her eyes curled around his soul. He took over applying the pressure on the woman's artery from Nan. "Get help fast."

Nan dashed to the hospital. Only then did Jackson see other people about. Some were hurt, and others were helping, everyone worked together. Nan came back in record time with a team of emergency specialists, and Jackson stood back to let them take over. They didn't question his diagnosis, but went with it and immediately began treating Angela for blood loss and shock. Within moments they were rushing her and her newborn baby into the hospital.

Nan turned to Jackson, her heart so full of love she thought she'd explode. He looked like hell and he'd never looked better. Sand had blasted him. He had tiny bleeding cuts everywhere. Seeing him alive was all she cared about. But seeing him with Angela had shown her a lot about the man she loved. He could hammer nails, strum a guitar, or pick up trash for a living; she didn't care. Because in the past twenty-four hours, she'd seen the depths of his heart and knew without a doubt, he was the man for her.

Now that they'd done their best to save Angela, she needed to tend to him.

She gently laid her arm on his shoulder. "You're hurt, Jack. You're in shock."

He winced and looked dazed. "Huh?"

"I said you're hurt. You're limping and your left shoulder is drooping. Let me look," she demanded, pulling back the collar of his shirt. His left clavicle was an angry black and blue and grossly swollen. She wrapped her arm around him. "Come on. I'm taking you to the ER."

"I can't, have to look for the injured."

"That's my job. The hospital has every available staff person out searching and the emergency squads are here now." She pointed to the slew of fire trucks, police cars, and ambulances. "It's a miracle, but so far there are only minor injuries. Angela was the worst I've seen. And you're next on the list. If you argue, I'm just going to have to get a med team from the hospital to come and cart you in, too."

"But—"

"No buts." Nan led him into the hospital. He didn't put up too much of a fight. She suspected it was because he was a little disoriented. She hated that she had to leave him in the ER, but she had her job to do.

Hours later, the search for injured ended and she came back to the ER to track Jackson down. He'd been admitted to the hospital with a broken clavicle and a fractured tibia. She found him strung up like a mummy and sound asleep. She called his family to let them know where he was then sat with him, and listened to the news. They were reporting today as a miracle. The tornado had caused extensive damage, but no lives were lost. Thank, God. When her eyes drooped, she decided to go home and take a shower, telling the nursing staff to call her when Jackson woke.

She hurried through her shower, grabbed a quick drive-through sandwich, and then made one stop before heading back to the hospital. Her worries that he'd be all alone and in pain were misplaced. She heard the laughter of men's voices all the way down the hall and saw the flustered face of a pretty young nurse as she escaped Jackson's room.

She knew why the minute she quietly ducked in the open door. Not only were the Weldon brothers in Jackson's room, but the whole construction crew had parked their hard bodies everywhere. Jackson lay strung up with orthopedic pulleys and ropes supporting the casts on his leg and arm.

In the middle of the room, a sandy haired giant stood telling a story. His weathered hands and crinkled green eyes were as big as Texas as he embellished his words with movement. "I swear to you. I've never seen the like in all my life. Everybody who had any sense was dropping into a ditch, but not Wild Jack. Man, he decides to pussyfoot it to the hospital."

"I wasn't pussyfooting. Somebody had to warn them about the damn tornado."

"Looked like pussyfooting to me. Anyways, one minute he was on the ground and the next he was in the air riding that damn tornado like old Pecos Bill. Only instead of a horse, he had this damn piece of plywood in his hands, and he was windsurfing upside down. Looked like a clip from a James Bond flick. I thought he was a goner for sure. I came looking for him at the ER so I could pay my last respects."

"Thanks for the sentiment," Jackson muttered.

Nan gasped and thought she was going to faint. How close had she come to permanently losing him?

"Nan, is that you?"

The men in the room parted, leaving her a direct path to him. She didn't hesitate to go to his side.

"The man's personal TLC technician has arrived, boys," James said. The men laughed and Nan blushed.

Jared shook his head. "Some men have all the luck. He gets to ride a tornado and then he gets to kiss the prettiest girl east of Kansas. All of us want to know how he managed this little miracle. So tell us, Nan, what was it about my sorry looking brother that captured you?"

All the men watched her as if she had the answer to Jeopardy's final question and their futures rested on being right.

"Smooth," she said, and they all frowned. All except Jesse. Jesse laughed.

"So he's a smooth talker." Jesse said.

"Ah," James said. "*That* kind of smooth."

"He's a Weldon that means he's smooth in be—" Jared's last word ended in a whoosh of air as Jesse poked him hard, and Jackson tossed a pillow in his face.

"Ignore him guys. He jumped into the gene pool when the lifeguard wasn't looking." James punched his twin brother on the shoulder. "I was supposed to be the only one born."

The men laughed. Nan's cheeks heated, but she had to laugh, too.

Alexi walked in, carrying a wrapped up bundle and Jesse leaped to his feet to help her. Nan caught her breath, a tiny corner of her heart unsure how Jackson would react.

"Time's up fellows. I've got somebody I want to see, my Godson."

If a face could launch a thousand ships then the look Jackson centered on the bundle Jesse handed him could oust a thousand men. Nan wasn't exactly sure how, but in seconds the room cleared, except for family.

Baby Jake in the crook of Jackson's good arm had his rapt attention and vice-versa. "Hey, little fellow. Sorry it's taken me so long to see you. I'll make up for it. Just as soon as you're ready, we'll skim rocks across the creek and I'll teach you how to ride. There's nothing like a ride on a good motorcy—"

"Ahem, bicycle," Alexi interjected.

"Bicycle then." Jackson rolled his eyes then winked at Alexi. "Dirt bike maybe?"

"We'll see. In about thirty years."

Baby Jake let loose a wail as if that verdict displeased him. "He's a Weldon all right," Jackson said. "You did a good job, Alexi."

"Amen to that," James said. "Uh, bro. I hate to barge in but I'm waiting to hold my little nephew."

"Me, too," Jared added.

"Me first," Jesse said, reaching over and lifting Jake away from Jackson. "There's a football in the gift shop I want him to see." Jesse stood and carried Jake to the door. "You boys coming to see him kick? Alexi says he's a star player."

James and Jared jumped up and headed out the door. Alexi laughed. "I'd better keep an eye on that crew. That boy is going to be spoiled so bad that—"

"Don't worry. He'll soon have to have a cousin to absorb some of that attention." Nan rubbed her stomach.

Alexi's eyes boggled. "You mean…that—"

"We're pregnant," Jackson said. "But don't tell anybody until we can make it official."

"Oh, oh, oh," Alexi said. "This is great. I love you both." She hugged Nan, laughing. Hugged Jackson and dashed out the door.

"Our secret is out," Nan said. "Do you mind?"

"Not at all." Jackson patted the bed. "Come here, sugar."

"I brought you something," she said handing him a box.

He smiled, reaching for her with his good arm. "All I want is you."

Her heart fluttered as she put the huge box in his lap. "Then open the box." She kissed him and stepped back.

He opened it slowly, taking out her little black book. "Is this what I think it is?"

"Yeah, figured you'd need something to read while you're out of commission."

He groaned. "I'm strung up like a turkey and you give me your fantasies to read? Hell, sugar, are you trying to kill me?"

"Only with pleasure. Now finish opening your present."

He pulled out the house plans next. She'd taken a minute to label the rooms, for the baby, for them, and filled in the names of different plants she wanted to have in her garden. Tears filled his eyes, then he sat up, shocked. "You're giving Shakespeare a bedroom? Nan honey, uh, I don't think that—"

She laughed. "That's just until we fill it with someone else. Like a brother or sister for this little one." She patted her stomach. "Now finish your present."

"I don't think I can take anymore present." He reached for her instead and pulled her half into his bed for a blistering kiss.

"Let's figure out how we're going to conceive junior's sibling," he mumbled against her mouth, reaching for the buttons to her shirt. Jackson might be one handed, but he was very adept anyway.

"You already know how," she said swatting at his hand.

"There are so many delicious ways to get there that it's going to take years to decide." She groaned and he managed to undo her top two buttons.

She tried to scoot back off the bed. "If you aren't careful, I'm going to tie you up with your support ropes."

"Promise?" he asked with an interested gleam in his eyes, leaving no doubt what he wanted her to do after she tied him up."

"Ahem. I hate to interrupt, but I've only have a minute."

Surprised to see Brad at the door, Nan jumped up. The top of her shirt flopped open and she snatched it closed.

Brad raised his brows about ten notches. "I see you're in good hands, Weldon."

"The best," Jackson said and Nan swatted his good arm.

"Uh, Brad, uh, did you need to see me about something?" Nan asked. Red-hot embarrassment burned through her.

Brad shook his head. "I came to see Weldon. I received a woman into the OR earlier, by the name of Angela Simmons. I think this belongs to you." Brad held up Jackson's belt then laid it in a chair by the door. "I had to go in and repair her femoral artery. The vascular surgeon was held up by the tornado and she couldn't wait. I took care of her artery problem then the orthopedic surgeon fixed her femur. Maybe the rumors in Chicago about your skills weren't too far off the mark."

"I didn't do anything more than what another trained professional would have done."

"Maybe. But then, maybe someone else wouldn't have been as quick to diagnose the problem and she didn't have much time, especially in the middle of having a baby. I think your decision to walk away from medicine was a bad one."

"Maybe it was," Jackson said.

Brad turned to go, then stuck his head back in. "Made her your world, huh?"

"You got it," Jackson replied. Brad left and Jackson shook his head. "Maybe there is hope for him yet."

Nan narrowed her eyes. "What's this about world?"

Jackson latched his good arm around her bottom and kneaded her closer. "Nothing. Now where were we before he interrupted?"

"You were opening my present, which you had better finish or else."

"I think I like the sound of your "or else," he said, but reached into the box and pulled out a black velvet box.

"What's this?" He opened it revealing the simple gold bands she'd bought. It was a set of wedding rings.

She took his hand and leaned down to look into his stunned blue eyes. "Jack, will you marry me, for better or worse, for richer or poorer, in sickness and in health?"

She heard his answer loud and clear in the kiss he leveled on her. The tornado had nothing on him.

EPILOGUE

Jackson laid his stethoscope against his patient's back and listened to her lungs. Then he straightened with a smile. "Well, Mrs. Cooper, I pronounce you well. You sound as clear as a bell."

"Humph. Don't feel that spry. These seventy year old bones are protesting every move I make."

"You taking that calcium I prescribed?"

"Every day, as regular as the sun rises."

"Have you been down to the new senior's center yet?"

"What do I want to fool around with those folks for? Probably don't do much else but gossip and complain about their aches. I've got enough of my own thank you very much."

"I hear they've opened up their heated pool. It has a special section set up for water aerobics. I'll bet you lunch that if you took a twenty-minute class twice a week, within a month your bones would ache less. Bones need to move some not to hurt and sitting at home alone doesn't help them. Did I tell you that they've a gourmet cook in on Wednesdays that teaches you how to prepare simple, tasty meals?"

Mrs. Cooper narrowed her weathered eyes. "What's his name?"

"Hers," Jackson said, grinning. "It's Weldon. Nan Weldon. She's my wife and the best cook around, excepting for my Dad's BBQ and my Mom's biscuits."

"Your wife? I might have a few minutes to wander over that way."

"She'd like to meet you. I'll have the nurse set your next appointment up three months from now, but if you get to feeling under the weather, you get in here to see me. You almost waited too late with that cold. Pneumonia isn't fun."

"I hear ya."

"Good." Jackson helped Mrs. Cooper off the examining table and walked with her out to the reception desk.

"Mrs. Cooper was your last patient today, Dr. Weldon," said the new receptionist they'd recently hired for the Midtown Clinic. She was organized and cheerful, a good plus for the office.

"How are Dr. Sanchez and Dr. Thornton holding out?"

"They're all caught up."

"Any walk-ins?"

"No, sir."

"Then I'll head home. Dr. Sanchez is on call this evening. Did you fax the new schedule to the answering service?"

"Already done. And I've put the charts for tomorrow's patients on your desk."

"Great. I'll see you in the morning," Jackson said and went to ditch his stethoscope and collect his briefcase. He left the clinic with an eager sense of anticipation heating his blood. He had a surprise for Nan. He'd picked the package up at the Travel Agency during his lunch break and couldn't wait to deliver it. He'd get home, take a shower and then figure out just how he would clue her into the fantasy he had planned.

~~*

"*N*an! *We've rats in our new* house. I can't believe it!"
Jackson came into the room holding three shredded rolls of toilet
paper in his hands. He'd just showered and had Nan's surprise in
his back pocket, but rats took precedent.

"Shh." Nan pressed her finger to her lips then pointed at little
Jason Weldon curled up asleep in his crib.

"He's already asleep?" Jackson whispered disappointed.

"For an hour or two. You're going to be busy anyway."

"Yeah, like finding an exterminator to get rid of the rats."

"We don't have rats. The cabinet door must have been left
open."

"And?

"Shakespeare. He loves to sharpen his claws that way."

"That cat," Jackson muttered turning around.

"Where are you going?"

"I'm going to the pet store to buy some mice. It's about time
somebody taught Shakespeare how to be a real man-cat."

Nan had pictures of Jackson on all fours trying to teach
Shakespeare how to chase a mouse. "I have a better idea. Come
look." Jackson had been gone all day and she couldn't wait to get
her hands on him. She led him to the room she'd picked for her
office. "Sit here," she ordered, pointing to an office chair.

He sat, puzzlement furrowing his brow. "What is it?"

"Shut your eyes and relax a minute while I get things ready to
show you."

"What?"

"Trust me. Just do it and don't move."

Jackson shut his eyes. Anticipation spiking her excitement, Nan took out a silk tie. She tied on wrist then pulled his arm behind him and tied his other wrist, effectively handcuffing him. "Nan?"

"Don't peek."

His eyes popped open. "Nan? What are you up to?"

"This." She clicked the CD player on. The slow sensual music she'd chosen filled the room. She dropped the terry cloth robe, revealing the silk teddy she'd bought.

"Uh, sugar, before we get into this there's something in my pocket you need to see."

Nan smiled. "I bet there is." She shimmied her breasts, his gaze lowered and his eyes gleamed.

Then he shook his head. "Really. It's in my back pocket. Can you get it out? I'm sort of tied up at the moment."

"Back pocket?" She moved closer to him, straddled his long legs and reached around him, making sure her breasts rubbed his chest. She pulled out the packet. "What's this?"

Her heart sped up a beat at the surprise. Out of all the things on her personal list of fun things to do, travel was the only one she hadn't made happen yet. She'd never been anywhere but South Georgia.

"A trip," he said grinning.

She jiggled up and down, kissing the packet of papers. "Really? Where to?" She opened the brochure.

"Maui, sugar."

"Hawaii! Oh, Jack!" She thumbed through the papers, more than thrilled. Then she noticed something wrong. "There's only one plane ticket."

"That's right, sugar."

"But...I can't...I couldn't go without you." Tears sprang to her eyes and she closed the brochure. "I'll wait until we can both go."

"No, sugar. You need to go. You have to go. The beach is perfect. Hot. Very Hot. And deserted. It's a private residence and beach."

Nan shook her head, swallowing the lump of disappointment in her throat. "It sounds perfect, but it won't be any fun without you."

"You won't need me, sugar. Rumor has it that there's this ultra sexy guy who lives in the beach house next store."

"Jack, this isn't funny. Now stop kidding around." Nan tossed the brochure on her desk and glared at him. She was fast losing her mood to get her hands on him in any sexual way.

"No really. This guy, he likes watching women sunbathe in the nude, uh, a particular woman that is. He likes to see the sun glistening off her oiled body. In fact, I'm pretty sure he sits there and fantasizes about tasting the woman. She'd smell a little like coconuts. Her flesh would be hot from the sun, hot and moist. He'd sit there, watching her, until he couldn't stand it for another minute. Then he'd walk down to the beach. She'd look up at him and say—"

"You want me, baby, don't you?" Nan said, understanding dawning. Her fantasy. He'd set up her fantasy and she had no doubt he'd be the man next door watching her naked on the beach.

Jackson lifted a brow. "Depends on what you're offering, sugar?" He ran his gaze over her, examining the teddy she wore with interest.

She began to move her body in gentle erotic ways, giving him a little hint of what she had to offer. Moving over to him, she slid her breasts against his arm, kissed his ear with her tongue, and ran her finger over the emerging bulge in his pants.

"I think you like this."

He shrugged. "Maybe."

Nan only smiled. He was so smooth, but she could see the gleam in his devilish blue eyes. He had the look of a man intent on having her. She wondered just how long he'd hold out on that maybe. She also wondered just how long he'd hold out watching her sunbathe in the nude. She gave him five minutes before he'd be on the beach, picking her up. It was going to be an interesting trip.

Grinning, she slid the straps of her teddy off her shoulders and cupped her breasts as she stood in front of him. His shoulders jerked as he fought against the bindings and he grabbed his bottom lip between his teeth.

"Come, here, sugar." His voice was husky with need.

Nan pouted. "Not yet. I'm still having fun." She slid a finger down her stomach, under the satin crotch of her teddy, and edged the satin aside, giving him a tiny glimpse. "Remember Black Jack the pirate? Remember his poor captured bride to be that he didn't think he wanted? You offered your body up for research."

He groaned and she smiled. She planned to test him to his limits and beyond.

Excerpt From WILD IRISH RIDE
WELDON BROTHERS SERIES - BOOK ONE

He should have stayed away, he thought, stepping deeper into the shadows as she drew nearer. He saw she was wearing the damn pearls. Of course she would, it was her day to wear the cursed things. He'd never forget what she and those pearls had cost him. Reporters, like sharks in a feeding frenzy, snapped pictures and yelled questions. Alexi ignored them all. He had to admire that, he thought, his jaw clenching in protest.

Where she was going?

He knew what it was like to be shark bait and Alexi was sailing through the water with her head held high, but even through the light rain he could see she was bleeding inside as she drew abreast of him. Tears streamed down her face and her full lips trembled. She stumbled and reached for something to break her fall, but only grasped air.

Shit. He rushed forward and caught her arm before she hit the ground, his instinct towards her stronger than his will.

"Oh!" She turned and surprise washed over her face. She breathed his name, as if he were an answer to a prayer. "Jesse."

Hell, she still looked too damn innocent and vulnerable for his good. Twelve years and she still had the power to get under his skin even though he knew how deadly she could be. Maybe it was time to turn the tables, collect on what he missed and wipe her from his mind. She couldn't be as good as he remembered her being.

Alexi blinked as heat invaded the chill that had stolen through her since she'd seen the pictures of Roger. She tingled as she looked at the rugged face and chiseled chest of the man who'd just saved her from falling. Half a day's dark stubble covered his rough jaw; and his deep sea-blue eyes, crinkled at the corners from the sun, warily assessed her then stared at her mouth. Tension oozed from him. She had no trouble connecting the man to the wild devil who'd led her astray years ago then broke her heart.

Small towns had their good side and bad side of the tracks, and the wild Weldon boys had been known a time or two to paint their side a bit blacker. Jesse's reputation had been the worst. She hadn't believed that until he'd used her to steal from her family. Over the years, she'd heard from Jesse's mother Emma, who worked at the hospital, about Jesse's stellar military career and security business in Washington D.C. Knowing he'd turned his life around made her glad, but didn't ease the hurt he'd left behind.

"Still a virgin on the run after all these years, Lexi?" he drawled. His voice, as steamy and seductive as Southern summer day, challenged her on an elemental level, a sensual one.

"Almost," Alexi said, letting the last illicit picture she had of Roger fall from her grasp to the ground. She'd only ever been with Roger and *he* didn't count. Not anymore. She sucked in air, latching onto Jesse's appeal. The reporters encircled them. Jesse lifted his hot gaze to her eyes and smiled.

"Almost?" Slow and sexual, his grin spread awareness through her. "Sounds frustrating. Interested in changing that?" He ran his finger under her chin and she caught her breath.

Yes, some part deep inside her shouted. Yes, she wanted to change that. Here was one situation her grandmother couldn't smooth over with a lie. With the cameras rolling, Roger and her grandmother would get a clear picture that Alexi meant it when she said she wasn't marrying Roger ever.

"Yes," Alexi said to Jesse, stepping closer to him. Waves of his sex appeal washed over her. Waves she had no trouble remembering, though she'd only been seventeen when she'd last dipped into them. His nearness and touch sparked something inside of her that wanted to rebel against everything that had just happened to her. "Kiss me," she demanded, loudly.

Jesse arched his brow and asked softly, "What's your game Lexi?" He slid an arm around her and pulled her flush to his bare chest, her breasts to his smooth, hard muscle. Then his mouth covered hers. She gasped at the desire shooting through her as his demanding tongue entered her mouth and his gaze dared her to respond.

She wound her arms around his neck, pressed closer to him, and met his tongue with hers. Surprise that she'd taken him up on his challenge filled his eyes and he hesitated, but only for a moment before he delivered a four-alarm kiss. He bent her back over his arm, inserted his leg between hers and had one hand cupping her bottom, no doubt knocking the socks off the gossip hounds surrounding them. In one kiss Jesse thoroughly ravished her from the inside out and she burned for more. By trying to deliver a message to her grandmother, Alexi wondered what message had she delivered to herself instead.

Jesse ended the kiss, but kept her captive in his embrace as he stared into her eyes. She ran her fingers into the silk of his hair and then surprised herself by kissing him again. His heat chased away the chill Roger had left inside her and she couldn't seem to get enough of it. He groaned then and deepened the kiss. Her hands clung to his broad shoulders, feeling the heat of his bare skin and the strength of his muscled torso. The cameras continued to flash and the world swirled crazily around her as her heart pounded hard at the line she crossed by embracing a half-naked Jesse so intimately in public.

He smelled faintly of aftershave and some indefinable, but intriguing scent. His body, strong and sure, eased around hers, a balm to her chaffed emotions. Yet before she could lose herself in him completely, he eased back and stared hard at her. Emotion and desire collided in her heart, springing tears to her eyes. "Get me out of here, please," she whispered.

Cool cynicism descended into the heat of his gaze. "So that's your angle. You need a hero, even if it's a Weldon." Glancing up at the reporters around them, he cursed. "Well, your highness, these days I charge for services rendered, and I expect to get paid." He scooped her into his arms and rammed through the reporters. "I'll be your hero for a price."

"What do you mean by that?" she asked, struggling in his arms as he headed to the parking lot. Reporters followed.

Jesse stopped a moment to meet her gaze. A sensual promise curved his lips. "We'll take care of the details later. The choice is yours, Lexi. Me or the sharks following us?"

"You," she said, wondering if she'd just made a deal with the devil in Georgia.

Excerpt from HARD IRISH
WELDON BROTHERS SERIES - BOOK THREE

The world wouldn't end if he kissed her again. Tonight. All she had to do was walk down the stairs... Rocky didn't give herself time to question. She put her feet in motion and tip-toed downstairs, though marching would have fit her mood better. She was still sane enough to consider that he might have taken pain medication and might be asleep.

Rounding the corner into the living room, she found the couch empty and searched the shadows for Jared, then gasped.

He stood at the French doors, looking at the backyard. He wore only a pair of form fitting boxer briefs and the hard-shelled boot strapped to his leg. His crutches were back at the couch, so he'd already gone against his brother's advice to keep weight off of his injury. Somehow that didn't surprise her.

What did take her breath away was the sight of him. Every lean inch of him was honed and tanned to perfection. He dropped the curtain and turned to face her. His broad shoulders and rippled abs made her weak in the knees, but it was the want in his gaze that did her in. It was as raw and edgy as her need, only sharper. The hungry predator had found his juicy prey.

Had she actually thought she could share another roll-on-the-floor rock-her-world kiss and escape unscathed? Rethink time.

"I came to see if you're all right." She moved over to the couch and picked up his crutches, planning to take them to him. "You should be using these."

He didn't wait, but moved her way—faster than she thought possible.

He reached her. "They'd only be in the way of this."

She didn't have a chance to breathe before he caught her in his arms and planted his mouth on hers, instantly hot and demanding. She opened to him, meeting the thrust of his tongue with hers, groaning deep from within as her starving senses found succor for her every want. His tongue tangled with hers, leading her in a seductive dance unlike any other.

He wrapped his arms around her, pulling her tight against his supple heat and burning erection. She pressed her palms to his chest, half thinking to stem the flooding tide, but then went crazy in a quest to feel and know his every contour. His muscles rippled as he shuddered at her touch.

Excerpt from COCKTAIL COVE
FRANKLY, MY DEAR SERIES - BOOK ONE

CHAPTER ONE

*F*or *her thirty-ninth birthday* present, Nikita's husband, Tom, came out of the closet swinging both ways on the sexual pendulum. That was three months ago, just after her nose had detected both a strange woman's perfume and an unfamiliar men's cologne clinging to his clothes.

Her nose never led her wrong and she'd nailed him for his perfidy right in the middle of their 400 square foot custom made his and hers closet. He confessed, dumped the blame at her feet, and took off as free as a bird. She had sat stunned between her Gucci and Louboutins.

Like most women clinging to the slippery side of their thirties, she'd been so busy dodging fat and wrinkle bullets that Tom's betrayal smacked her right between the eyes.

She was still in therapy. She might be perfectly coifed and dressed to the nines in Versace on the outside. But inside, on this doomed day in July when summer blooms lost their virginity to Atlanta's fickle weather, she floundered for a sweaty palmed grip on the conference table's polished edge. The law firm of Cross, Gibbons, and Biddle was nothing but a glorified shark tank. Like most attorneys' offices the illusion of comfort surrounded her, gleaming mahogany, plush carpeting, expensive art—all the little extras to put you at ease before feeding time.

Thankfully, her divorce attorney, Sandra Price wore powerhouse red and looked as calm as James Bond under fire because Tom's smug you're-about-to-be-chum smile had Nik clenching her teeth.

"There won't be any papers signed today," said Bob Cross, Tom's attorney. His sharp teeth flashed making her feel like a surfer on Styrofoam watching Jaws attack.

Nik had never liked Bob Cross and now she knew why. He'd been best man at her wedding and he was as human as a Great White. Cross continued speaking, "My client is petitioning the court for a two week delay in finalizing the divorce settlement."

"For what reason?" Sandra asked, laying her pen down with a snap. "Your client has delayed twice already."

"My client has changed his mind concerning the dispersion of their assets."

Blood drained with dizzying speed from Nik's head. Tom, golden-boy extraordinaire, broadened his smile and Nik bit her lip. Somehow her therapist's advice to forgive and forget wasn't holding up against Tom's tactics.

"Your client violated his marriage vows. He isn't in a position to disagree."

"My client was forced from his home to seek out comfort due to the emotional and physical alienation he experienced from his wife."

"That's a lie," Nik said, half popping from her seat. How could Tom even begin to say something like that? If anything she'd been a golf widow. The man spent more time on the fairway than he spent in their bedroom and that included fore-play as well.

"Relax, let me handle this," Sandra said under her breath, patting Nik's arm. Nik sat and forced her mouth shut as twinges of hurt nipped at her. Tom's smile grew.

When would she ever learn? She'd let the sharks see that she was bleeding.

"Your theatrics are tiring, Mr. Cross. We both know the truth and so will the court. What about the settlement does your client dispute?"

"He'll be left with no viable residence. The house is being sold and your client is receiving the condominium. My client is asking the court for the deed to the lake house, since it has little emotional value to your client and has been a place of refuge for my client over the years of their unsatisfactory marriage."

Icy shock slammed into Nik. She opened her mouth to say something, refute, deny, or scream, but could only choke on the emotion clogging her throat.

Sandra remained the epitome of cool disdain. "Impossible. My client purchased that property in conjunction with her brother prior to the marriage. Your client has no legitimate claim on her share of that asset."

"We'll let the court decide that. Now, in the matter of dissolving their investment properties, my client was the creative force behind these projects. Therefore a fifty-fifty split does not reflect his share of the work involved. My client has a multitude of witnesses and receipts to prove that your client has squandered money on an extravagant lifestyle..."

It was *her* money that had been the capital for those investments. And what right did he have to criticize how she lived? Nik couldn't take anymore. She jumped up and rushed to the bathroom barely making it to the privacy of a stall.

Her heart raced at a dizzying speed, and she gasped for air, fighting off the anxiety that hit her like a truck. From the time she was little, with only English boarding schools and a string of nannies as substitutes for jet-setting parents, Nik had always had a problem with nightmares and anxiety. But instead of diminishing as she grew older, it had worsened during her five-year marriage and now skyrocketed with her divorce.

About the Author

USA Today Bestselling Author Jennifer St. Giles/ J.L. Saint/ Jennifer Saints might have a split personality. Or as a nurse and mother of three, she knows how to multi-task. She writes in a number of genres from gothic historicals, paranormal thrillers, romantic suspense, and sexy contemporary romance. She has won a number of awards for writing excellence including, two National Reader's Choice Awards, two-time Maggie Award Winner, Daphne du Maurier Award winner, Romance Writers of America's Golden Heart Award, along with RT Book Club's Reviewer's Choice Award for Best Gothic/Mystery. She loves hearing from her readers via her website jenniferstgiles.com or you can find her on facebook.com/pages/Jennifer-St-Giles and Twitter @jenniferstgiles

From the Author's Mouth

What can I tell you about me?

I don't play video games or watch horror because I can't take the heat, but give me a kickass thriller every minute of every day and I am there. Be prepared for a Hoover Dam meltdown if you're with me and the movie is sad. So, to avoid disaster, I love romantic comedies.

Never coffee. Always tea. Never beer. Always champagne. There's more, but hey, gotta save some secrets until after the first date, right?

I grew up in Miami. Went to nursing school in Georgia, where I now reside. I raised and home schooled three great kids. I wrote for nine years before I sold a book, which made me a firm believer that a person should NEVER, NEVER, NEVER GIVE UP ON THEIR DREAMS.

I remember my father's remark after a particularly scandalous story about one of my ancestors, a story that involves a conspiracy, treason, betrayal, murder, and execution, a story that after a drink or two in the bar, I might be enticed to share. Anyway, what my father said was, "You can't keep a good man down." And I kind of see that in myself. Not that I am necessarily good, because the definitions of moral words are often relative, but I do persevere, and I am resilient. Nothing in life has ever worked out the way I planned for it too. In many areas of my life, I have yet to reach the level I thought I would, of where I envisioned I would be, but I haven't given up. I won't give up. I continue to work hard and do everything I can to help who I can and to make my dreams come true.

Besides great kids, family, and friends, that perseverance has so far garnered me a USA Today Bestselling tag and twelve plus books on the shelf in a number of genres (contemporary romantic suspense, historical suspense, paranormal suspense, and contemporary romance). I've won a number of writing awards, two National Choice Awards, three Maggie Awards, a RT Book Club Reviewer's Choice Award, the Daphne du Maurier Award, the Marlene Award, and the Golden Heart Award to name most of them. I work with several amazing women in a charity to raise money for a shelter that helps abused and homeless women and children. I've revived my nursing career after a long hiatus, have renewed my license, and' have found the right job for now.

I know there are many more great things ahead.

I write romance because I believe that when you boil all of life down to its essence, if you take a human being to the very core of his existence, then you will find that what matters more than anything else is to be loved and to give love.

Life is all about choices and to pull from one of Erich Fromm's quote, *I choose to create and to love rather than destroy and to hate.*

I hope you enjoy my stories.

Go forth, dream, believe, create, inspire, and love,

Jenni (J.L. Saint, Jennifer St. Giles, Jennifer Saints)